STAR WARS
CRIMSON CLIMB

WRITTEN BY
E. K. JOHNSTON

Disney
LUCASFILM
PRESS

LOS ANGELES • NEW YORK

To the CSIS agent who
monitors my internet history.
We had fun with this one, eh?

*F*or ten giddy seconds, she lets herself think about the life she might have had, if only things had gone a little bit differently.

Money. A ship. Han. Whatever work they could find. A real smile when she thinks about him, not the mask she's built up to survive.

But she'd always be looking over her shoulder, because Han never would. The best way to protect him is to go.

The best way to protect herself is to stay.

The chime of the elevator ends her contemplations, but her decision is already made. She doesn't know who else is alive on this ship, but no matter who those doors open to, Qi'ra has chosen her next steps.

The figure who steps out of the elevator is only a moderate surprise. Qi'ra hadn't even known she was on board. Vos kept his secrets, and Qi'ra hadn't exactly had the time to ferret them out when she and Han arrived with the coaxium. Maybe he didn't think it was important. Dryden Vos's underestimations were rare, but they did happen. She is living—and he was dying—proof of that.

Neither of them are exactly dressed for combat, but both are ready for it. The newcomer's gown is long and lined with a silver fabric that glimmers, even with the windows shaded. Qi'ra recognizes the fabric. There is more than one way to don armor. She steps delicately through the mess Qi'ra has made of their former boss's receiving room.

"Well," Qi'ra says with all the casual dignity Dryden Vos could ever muster, "I suppose this makes you my second-in-command."

Her visitor smiles, mouth spread wide over so much teeth. Neither of them are fools. Fools don't last in Crimson Dawn, and they, they have lasted.

"You can trust me as much as Vos trusted you," she says.

Qi'ra looks down at the crumpled body on the floor, surrounded by the ruin of all the things he'd hoarded in life. Any handful would buy Qi'ra a life somewhere else, but she'd never be free of him, not really. Crimson Dawn is tattooed on her skin, but the marks run even deeper, and there are darker things in the underworld than Dryden Vos. In the end, this has always been her only choice, made for her by a clear glass door and a hopeless promise. She thinks of the familiar face, and smiles.

"I suppose you can only try to kill me so many times," Qi'ra says. She sits down in her chair and places her hands on her desk. She sends the departure command to whoever is at the helm. She'll make a ship-wide announcement when they're clear of the planet. "Let's get started, shall we?"

◖

On a beach not too far away, a boy she knew once starts his next life, too.

CHAPTER ONE

I t took less than four hours after Moloch dragged her back from the Corellian spaceport for Lady Proxima to decide what to do with her. Qi'ra wasn't sure how much of that time was taken up by punishing the guards who had let Han escape. She tried not to think too much about it, either the punishment or Han being gone. Both were painful for different reasons, and Qi'ra always tried to avoid that sort of thing.

She couldn't avoid it this time.

Left alone in a cell in the scummiest part of the White Worm headquarters, Qi'ra had too much time to think. She couldn't stop making plans, looking for angles, trying to find a way out. There wasn't one. She knew it as soon as Moloch's pincerlike hands clamped around her arm and pulled her away from the spaceport barrier. But she couldn't make herself stop.

She had gotten by by telling herself that she was a survivor, and to some degree, it had been true. Even this cell wasn't the worst place she had ever lived. Qi'ra had come up from worse than nothing, something Proxima was all too fond of reminding her, and she had thought it made her stronger. She was always hungry, always plotting, always searching for the next score. And all of it had come back, full circle, to worse than nothing.

It was Han's fault. She had let her guard down, but it was Han's fault she had done so. Ever since he'd come to her attention in the competition for Head, she'd under-estimated him. No. Not him. She'd underestimated his effect on *her*. His easy charm and persistent optimism were a siren song, lulling her into a false sense of security. It had happened during the droid incident, when he had almost pulled the position of Head scrumrat right out from under her, but Qi'ra had still managed to come out on top, so she hadn't pushed him away. He was useful. He was loyal. He would help her.

He had left her behind. Yes, she had told him to. And yes, she had meant it. But that had been in the heat of the moment, when she could afford to care about someone other than herself. Now the grim reality had set in. At least she had the small victory of having ensured Han's freedom. He got away, and despite everything they had learned about the harshness of reality growing up in the sewers of Coronet City, he had told her he would come back for her someday.

The worst part was she absolutely believed his promise to come back for her. He would, someday, if he didn't get turned into so much paste by some trigger-happy lowlife with more blasters than sense. What neither of them had been able to take into consideration in the horrible anxiety of the spaceport was the time between now and then, and how she would spend it. There would be a lot of it. And Qi'ra was not in a position to make any good choices.

She could cling to the idea of him, a triumphant return and a rescue from what was sure to be an absolutely terrible future. She could hold on to that hope no matter what Proxima did to her. She could find the silver lining. She could wait for him, getting through the pain and torment by imagining the life they'd have. That was what Han would have done, if their positions were reversed. Qi'ra was sure of that, too.

She wouldn't wait. Hope was for fools, and she couldn't waste her imagination on pretty futures that might never come. She would die here, at Proxima's command, or she would live for the exact same reason. There was no choice. There was only the inevitability that her cell door would open and she would be forced to accept whatever waited for her on the other side.

Han's dice were still in her hand. They were all she had left, and they were next to useless. They weren't worth enough for a bribe, and they certainly weren't worth enough to pay off the stolen coaxium. Just two hard cubes on a little chain, a thing that Han had from his father and thought lucky. Qi'ra knew better, yet she couldn't bring herself to throw them away. They would be taken from her, sure enough, and that thought filled her with rage.

There it was, the one thing that might get her through this. If she could harness that anger into determination, she might keep her head, literally and metaphorically. Proxima was vindictive, but she was no fool. Qi'ra still had value, even if she was no longer a trusted member of the White Worms. Throwing her away would be a wasted investment. Surely Proxima would see that. And if she didn't, Qi'ra would remind her. Not because she was waiting for Han, but because she was damn well going to survive without him.

When the cell door creaked open, a stream of light making her wince in spite of herself, Qi'ra was as ready as she could be. She heard the hounds coming, so she wasn't caught off guard. She stood up straight, brushed off her coat and skirt as much as she could, and ran her fingers through the mess of her hair. She would not be stripped of her dignity on top of everything else. She had earned her place here, once, and the Worms were going to remember it. At the last moment, on impulse, she tucked Han's dice into her mouth. It was awkward, and she almost spit them back out, but the door was opening, and she had to pay attention.

The Corellian hounds were scratching the ground as

they waited, long claws scoring the floor as they pulled at their chains and whined. Moloch did not lead one. Instead, he leaned on his staff, but Qi'ra could clearly see the stun baton he carried at his waist. Qi'ra flinched without meaning to when she saw it. She knew she wasn't the only Worm who had nightmares about that weapon, but she was definitely the only one who was about to live them. If he could have smiled cruelly, he would have. Instead, he stood aside and the hounds came into the cell.

Rebolt and Syke could hold their hounds back if they wished. Qi'ra knew they were strong enough. Both boys were approximately the same age as Qi'ra and were taller and broader across the shoulders, for whatever that was worth to a scrumrat who'd spent their whole life scrambling after scraps. Rebolt's cruel sneer cut sharply across his pale face. Syke at least looked like he was trying to control the hound. He wouldn't meet Qi'ra's look, keeping his dark eyes on the floor, and he had both hands on the chain. Rebolt had no such mercy, face flushed with a victory that wasn't even his, and let the hound come close enough to bite her, if it wanted to.

"Enough," Moloch said. Both boys instinctively translated his command into Basic and mastered their hounds. "We're here to bring her to Lady Proxima, not for fun."

Moloch grabbed her like he had at the spaceport. She had resisted then, just long enough to tell Han to run before it fully sank in that she was lost and there was no point in trying to fight, but she didn't resist now. She gave him no excuse for cruelty, but he took it anyway. At the spaceport, he had only squeezed her and knocked her to the ground before hauling her away. Now that he wasn't in public, he could be much more creative.

The stun baton touched her lightly, sending a painful current through her. She would have screamed, but with the dice in her mouth, only a high-pitched whine emerged from her throat. Moloch laughed, a gurgling sound that seemed more like a growl.

"That's the lowest setting, of course," he said. She focused on understanding his words, the translation an all too brief distraction. "You'll scream eventually."

Qi'ra didn't doubt him for a moment.

Moloch dragged her through the tunnels, walking too fast for her to match his stride. She stumbled, scraping her knee, and then he nearly jerked her shoulder out of its socket to pull her back onto her feet. The hounds nipped at her heels, just enough to make her skip forward and keep her off balance. Now that she was moving, she felt light-headed from fear and her resurgent adrenaline, but even that was nothing new. It would just take her a few moments to master it.

The window behind Proxima's pool had been fixed. There was no more daylight in the room. All of the Worms were gathered, from the youngest pickpocket all the way to Karsot, an older Grindalid who leaned on his electrostaff near the water. No one would get close to Proxima this time. The ground had even been cleared of debris, just in case.

Moloch dragged Qi'ra to the front of the room, and a torrent of whispers followed them. Qi'ra ignored everything. The only person in the room who mattered to her right now was Proxima, who was rising from the watery nest where she brooded with her young.

Proxima was covered in lesions, angry and red against the pallid gray of her skin, from her brief exposure to the sun. She had removed her elaborate jewelry, and Qi'ra could see the marks where her skin had burned around the metal. It was amazing that no one had ever taken advantage of the Grindalid weakness before, that long, sinuous body so ill suited for life on the surface of Corellia. In the sewers, Grindalids were all but untouchable. On the streets of Coronet City, they held on by grasping others and turning them to their use. Perhaps that was one of the reasons Proxima employed mostly children. They wouldn't think of such things, especially not once all the independence was drilled out of them. It was a miracle Han had, and it was clearly something that would not be repeated. Still, a weakness was a weakness, and Qi'ra would not forget.

"Qi'ra." Proxima's voice rang in every corner of the room, penetrating and grating and strangely melodious all at once. "You were given every chance. You were given every advantage. And yet you betrayed me."

Someone else might have pleaded for mercy, insisting that Han had dragged her to the spaceport against her will in the chaos surrounding the window break. Proxima might have fed that person to the hounds, and Qi'ra was not so foolish anyway. They had all been here to see what happened. They all knew what she had done.

The other Worms closed in around her, some with eager expressions on their faces and some pushed from behind by the lieutenants. Qi'ra saw Rebolt again, vicious even without his hound, and Syke and Jagleo. None of them were wearing the badge of Head, which Qi'ra found perplexing. Proxima had held a great contest for the position when Qi'ra became Head, but she'd had ulterior motives. Right now, the gang leader required order and a clear chain of command.

"Ema, come forward," Proxima demanded, and Qi'ra had her answer.

Proxima hadn't picked one of the older scrumrats. That didn't bode well for the ones still around. No one ever asked what became of the older kids. There simply weren't any, past a certain point, and that was answer enough.

"Shall it be hounds or staff?" Proxima asked the girl.

Qi'ra didn't so much as look at Ema, keeping her eyes locked on the creature rising out of the pool in front of her. They all hated the hounds, unless they were picked to be handlers, but Ema hated them even more. Qi'ra didn't know whether the girl's fear would make her more or less likely to pick them. The staff would be better in the long run. The staff wouldn't leave scars or acquire a special taste for Qi'ra's blood. It would hurt more, but the pain wouldn't linger as long as a mauling would. Ema didn't understand the threat of lasting punishment yet.

The stocky fourteen-year-old was relatively new to the Worms, having joined when her parents died. Unlike most of them, she'd had the benefit of a well-fed childhood. Nothing about her was undergrown or scrawny, even after two years of hard living in the sewers. She had scars from the hound who had caught her trying to break into a supply crate on the back of a White Worm speeder. She'd been recruited after that but always gave the hounds a wide berth, even though becoming a handler was the surest way to power within the gang.

"Staff," said Ema.

Qi'ra risked a look and saw the almost unholy glee on the girl's face. It was her first taste of power, and she liked it.

Moloch threw Qi'ra to the ground, rattling her teeth because he'd held her hands back long enough that she couldn't break her fall. It didn't matter. Karsot was on her with the shockstaff seconds later, and the world changed to a horrible, painful white.

Electricity coursed through her veins, enough to hurt

but not enough to stop her heart. Torture was no good if the victim died, and the Grindalids were all experts. The scrumrats tried to draw back from her as she writhed on the floor in agony, but they weren't permitted. The Grindalids kept them close to her, witness to her punishment so that they would never try to stage their own escape.

With the dice in her mouth, Qi'ra couldn't scream. She made plenty of noise, so the Worms got their show watching her suffer, but Moloch grew increasingly frustrated when she didn't give him what he wanted. He yelled at Karsot to increase the intensity, and Qi'ra felt her bones lock in unnatural positions, her joints and ligaments unable to handle the pain any other way than freezing in its grasp.

"Enough!" Proxima said.

The light faded back to gray, but the pain did not recede. Qi'ra panted on the floor. She would not get up until they made her. She wasn't entirely sure if she could.

"Let that be a lesson to you all," Proxima said. "This is what waits for you if you betray me. This is your fate."

She didn't mention Han, Qi'ra noticed. No one would mention him because he had been successful. He had actually gotten away. Proxima wouldn't remind anyone of that.

Proxima sank back into the pool, and the other Grindalids pushed their way out of the room. Qi'ra was still on the ground. No orders had been given, but the message was clear. She was at the mercy of those she had very recently been in charge of. She had been a good Head. It was almost a relief.

Almost. Han's plan had almost worked. He had bartered coaxium for freedom, and if it only bought one ticket, well, that was life. His plan had also almost gotten her killed. And now she would pay the price for his delinquency because he never imagined his plan would fail. She had wanted it so badly, had believed in him and trusted their combined skills to get the job done. They had come up together, survived the trial for Head scrumrat together. But they hadn't been enough. She'd wanted to be that girl, the one who looked to others for help and thought that escape was in her grasp. The floor beneath her was as cold as the truth: she was on her own, and survival was the only goal. There would be no more reckless plans, no more trust. She would learn another way to get by, and she would learn it as fast as she could.

As the scrumrats closed in around her, Qi'ra decided she would never settle for *almost* again.

CHAPTER TWO

Being Head had meant receiving the first portion of food at meals. It had also meant deciding who else ate, and in what order. Qi'ra had tried to be fair. The scrumrats had enough things to fear. If she was the one person in the world they thought looked out for their interests, then they would be loyal to her. It was a good plan, and had served her well. But it only lasted as long as she was Head.

Any good will she had accrued was gone, and as the mob closed in around her, Qi'ra's only thought was to protect her face. Scrumrats were afraid of many things, and when presented with something they didn't have to fear, they could be vicious. She knew this, because she was one of them.

Hands pulled her in every direction, catching in her hair and on her clothes. Little fingers pulled at the laces on her boots while bigger ones rolled her over to get to her jacket. She kicked instinctively—too many years spent guarding what she'd got—and the fingers dug in harder, nails pressing through skin.

The older kids succeeded in getting her coat off, and an immediate fight broke out over it. Rebolt, showing more intelligence than she thought he possessed, cleared a path for Ema. He didn't fight *for* her, exactly. If he handed the coat to her, it wouldn't be a prize; it would be a danger, a sign of too much owed and an alliance that didn't quite exist. But he could make sure that Ema ended up with the coat. It would be her victory, and she would know he'd helped. As far as Qi'ra could tell, the girl barely needed assistance. She tore through the other children, fists flying as she grappled for the object that everyone desired.

Distracted by the coat, Qi'ra didn't know the exact moment the smaller kids succeeded in stealing her boots. They didn't fight amongst themselves, and turned immediately to the skirt she wore over her leggings. It was waterproof and had a number of pockets—empty, thanks to Moloch's search when Qi'ra was brought in—and even if it was too big for the kid who ended up with it, it would still keep them warm.

Ema had mostly dispersed the main melee around the coat. She headbutted a few of the smaller scrumrats off the pile, and then the others began to recognize her. Qi'ra's coat was nice, but it wasn't worth angering the person who controlled when and how much you ate. Resistance melted before her, and by the time Ema picked the coat up off the ground, only slightly torn and a little bit dusty, everyone was keeping a respectful distance. She pulled it around her shoulders, running her hands down the soft fur that lined the collar, and then put two fingers in her mouth, issuing a piercing whistle. All the fighting stopped instantly.

"It's time for dinner," Ema announced. She might have been commenting on the weather, like nothing was out of the ordinary.

The little kids balled up Qi'ra's skirt and added it to their haul with the boots. They would trade the bundle to someone the right size, or sell it, perhaps. They were lost to Qi'ra in any case. She lay on the ground, mercifully untouched for the moment, the aurodium plate of Han's dice bitter on her tongue. Cold was already seeping through her unprotected leggings.

The scrumrats filed out of the room in as orderly a fashion as they could, with Rebolt and Ema in the lead. Syke and Jagleo were near the end, but it didn't matter. Their place in the hierarchy had always been assured. As she passed Qi'ra on the floor, Ema looked down scornfully.

"Don't bother showing up," she said. "There won't be any for you, even if you do."

Qi'ra had no intention of going to the dining hall. Once she was free, she had only one destination in mind. With the Worms diverted by food, Qi'ra hauled herself to her feet.

Her head was pounding, but her legs seemed solid enough. The floor beneath her stockings felt disgusting, but there was nothing else for it. Leaning on the wall, she made her way down the corridors until she came to her sleeping hole.

She didn't keep much here. None of them did. Anything left behind in a bedroll was a prime target for stealing, and ownership was always a matter of muscle. It was clear that Ema had already moved in. The scummy pillow and thin blanket had been moved, and the bunk itself was oriented toward the other door—the one the hounds came out of, if they ever came to this part of the hideout. Qi'ra spat the dice out into her hand, then tucked them into the paltry pocket in her leggings and moved to the bunk where Han had slept.

If there was anyone cocky enough to keep something of value in his bunk, it was Han. Like Qi'ra's, it was clear that someone else was already in residence, but there had been less shifting. Qi'ra patted down the pillow, looking for any strange lumps, and then pulled the blanket off the pitiful excuse for a mattress. She pried up the corners, checking underneath, but there was nothing there. Maybe Han was smarter than she had given him credit for.

"It was socks." Qi'ra spun around and saw Rebolt standing there, that sneer still on his face. "He kept socks under the mattress. But they're mine now."

He looked down at her feet, and the grin on his face became even wider.

"Too bad," he said. "Socks aren't much, but they're better than what you've got now."

He turned and went off toward the kennels. Qi'ra flipped the fourth corner of the mattress up and found the little divot she'd been looking for. Rebolt had found the socks and stopped looking, but that wasn't all Han had hidden under his bed. The dog biscuits were old and flaky, but they were food. Han had kept them in case he ever needed to bribe one of the hounds, but that wasn't what Qi'ra had planned for them. There was no telling when Ema would allot her a portion at mealtime.

Qi'ra tucked the biscuits into the pocket with the dice and finally stopped to take stock of the damage. The good news was that she wasn't locked up, and Proxima seemed to be finished with her official punishment for now. The bad news was that her unofficial punishment would be doled out whenever her fellow Worms thought she made a good target. Eventually, and Qi'ra could only hope it would be soon, Proxima would pass the final sentence. Qi'ra had no coat or boots, and her leggings weren't very warm. Anything she managed to get ahold of would probably just be stolen again, so she'd have to be careful.

For a moment, she was tempted to run. She could go to her safe house in the Silo while everyone was eating. She'd kept the little sanctuary intact for years, just in case, and now might be the time to use it. No one would guess she'd go back to the Silo voluntarily. The only two people who knew about it—Han and Tsuulo—were dead or gone, and there were no sewers there, so the Grindalids would have to follow her the hard way. She would be safe, but she'd still have nothing. And she'd be back in the Silo, the rotting heart of the Bottoms and the indisputable worst place on the entire planet. There was no future in the Silo.

Qi'ra found a bunk that was high up and drafty. No one wanted it because it was cold, and anyone who tried to get at her would have to climb. She lay down so that her feet were near the top of the ladder. If someone climbed up, she would kick them in the face. It wouldn't hurt them as much as it would if she still had her shoes, but it was better than nothing. It was too cold to sleep, but Qi'ra had no intention of being that vulnerable anyway. She listened as the scrumrats came back to their barracks, still scuffling amongst themselves because they didn't have anything better to do. The older ones were headed out for the night, but the younger ones curled up to snatch some sleep. Qi'ra watched them settle. They knew she was up there, but they dismissed her as no threat.

The ladder shook, and Qi'ra prepared herself, but she knew from the distinct lack of noise who it was. Only one scrumrat had been a dancer, smart enough to invent her own style of fighting based on the movements her body was already familiar with. When Jagleo's face appeared, Qi'ra let herself relax, but only a little bit.

"So you're demoted," Jagleo said. "Which I am sure you already noticed."

Qi'ra didn't say anything. If Jagleo wanted to talk, Qi'ra would certainly let her, but she was done volunteering information, possibly for the rest of her life.

"Ema's a tyrant, so she'll do fine," the thief continued. "The little kids are too scared of her to stage a coup, and the older ones don't take her seriously. Which is stupid, because there's a reason Proxima didn't pick one of them instead."

It didn't take a genius to notice that Proxima was interested only in children. They were small and easy to influence, which made recruitment simple. They didn't eat much and could be controlled with the promise of rewards, which made them easy to raise. They could go out in the sunlight, which was the chief reason Proxima needed non-Grindalid gang members in the first place, but their small size and nimbleness meant they could usually climb and hide well, which was handy.

"Syke thinks she's planning a purge of the older scrumrats. The four of us in particular," Jagleo said. Her dirty blonde hair fell into her face as she theorized, and she brushed it aside. "With you and Han out of the picture, Syke, Rebolt, and I would be easier to deal with. But I think he's wrong. She won't just kill us outright. Not while we're still useful."

Qi'ra still said nothing. Anyone else might have gotten frustrated with her, but Jagleo was used to silence, even under normal circumstances.

"There will be a big raid," Jagleo theorized. "She'll talk it up, have us practice, get us all organized, the whole deal. But after, when the smoke clears, the scrumrats left over will have something in common. They'll all be young."

Jagleo reached into the pocket of her coat and withdrew a gauzy-looking black piece of cloth. She shook it, and Qi'ra realized it was a thin jacket. Not good for much, but better than it looked and much better than nothing.

"Rebolt thinks the hounds will save him," Jagleo said. "And Syke thinks if he ever trains up Taomat to attack Rebolt, Moloch will promote him. They're always going to need someone to take the hounds outside. But you and I have never played that game."

She passed the jacket over to Qi'ra, who sat up slowly and pulled it around her shoulders. It was scratchy, compared to her fur, and there was no place to hide anything in it, but it was still a jacket.

"I can't do much for you now," Jagleo said. "And I'm no good to you if they start treating me the same way. But when it goes down, I'll have your back. We'll survive and then we'll see what's next. I know you'll have a plan because you always do, and I'll keep you alive long enough to do it."

Jagleo set down a small ration packet. She'd already opened it and eaten most of what was inside, but Qi'ra could see that about a quarter of it was left. Not a meal, but also not dog biscuits.

"You have a deal," said Qi'ra. She reached out and picked up the packet, then poured the crumbs into her mouth and shook the foil to make sure she'd gotten every single one.

Jagleo was an unexpected ally, even if the little thief wouldn't be able to do much. Qi'ra would take all the help she could get. The only part that was up in the air, as far as she was concerned, was how much help she would extend in return. Qi'ra had been on the receiving end of a plan gone sideways, and she had no intention of ever being in that position again. If she had even a flash of doubt, she'd abandon Jagleo in a heartbeat.

Qi'ra nestled herself into the bunk, her new jacket around her shoulders and the gaping hole in her belly slightly filled. She could work with this.

CHAPTER THREE

Things got significantly worse.

The morning after her failed escape attempt, Qi'ra learned her final fate. Proxima had found a buyer for her, a Corellian trafficker named Sarkin Enneb, who was in the market and didn't mind a bit of defiance in the merchandise. Sooner was what she'd hoped for, but it was still uncomfortably fast for a decision that would probably have a deeply unpleasant outcome.

"You did not fetch a good price; disobedience is considered a very bad quality for a slave," Proxima said as Qi'ra stood shivering before her. "But your other attributes were enough to interest him. I have full confidence that he will scour the fight right out of you."

Sarkin wasted no time and put a tracking chip in her wrist as soon as the contract was signed. The high-tech chips had been made mostly obsolete by advancements in scanner technology, so they didn't bother trying to keep the location of them hidden from whoever they were implanted into anymore. It would kill her if she tried to escape or remove it, and that was enough. She met Sarkin's bright green eyes while he was implanting it, wondering what sort of man he was. The best she could hope for was disinterestedly negligent, but she could already see the brutishness in his angular face. Disinterested people didn't buy defiant girls.

"I don't like the look of you," Sarkin said. He was much too close to her; she could almost feel the bristly hair that grew on his face and head, but she knew better than to resist. "Oh, you're pretty enough, but there's too much spirit in your eyes. I'm going to take it. You'll be worth more when you're biddable."

His fingers, each one tipped with a sharp nail that could clearly pierce and rend her skin if he chose to hurt her, were tight on her arm. She knew she'd have bruises later. She could tell he wanted her to fight him, wanted an excuse to bloody her mouth or tear out her hair. Qi'ra would let him have only the bruises for now. He already knew she was defiant. His sneer turned vicious when she didn't give him what he wanted, and one of his nails cut into her arm where the fresh wound from the chip already throbbed.

Proxima shifted in her pool, annoyed that she couldn't hear everything that was being said, even if she could guess at most of it.

"We still have an arrangement, Sarkin Enneb," she groused. "You don't get to break her just yet."

"I did read the contract," Sarkin said, not taking his eyes off of Qi'ra. His pointed ears twitched, betraying a bit of his frustration with Proxima. Qi'ra knew she would pay for all of it later. "She'll stay here for now, and you'll make sure the job gets done. After that, though, she's all mine."

The cut on her wrist was jagged and bleeding lightly. It would certainly scar. Qi'ra stood still as the blood ran down to the tips of her fingers and started to drip on the floor. She would take care of herself only when there was no one around to watch her.

Sarkin turned toward Proxima and didn't so much as bat an eyelash as she loomed over him. Qi'ra knew why she'd been sold, but it was strange that Sarkin wasn't going to take her yet. She wondered what the terms of her contract were. She didn't think she'd have any additional protection or accommodation, but it would have been nice to know the details.

"I'll return when the job is finished," Sarkin said. "Or send a representative. If you get her killed, I will expect my credits back."

Proxima didn't give an answer, and Sarkin clearly hadn't expected one anyway. He simply turned on his heel and marched out of the room.

"Get out, Qi'ra," Proxima said. "Go and enjoy what limited freedom you have while you still can."

It was uncomfortable to think that living as Head had made her soft. Qi'ra had fought for the position and, once she had it, had fought to keep it. Much of her time had been spent enforcing discipline, mostly in the form of food rations, but she'd also spent a lot of time as a trusted courier for Lady Proxima herself. Some of those people had been scared of her, too, adding tips to their payments to the White Worms in the hopes that she would put in a good word for them. The additional credits hadn't been much, but they'd been hers. Between them and the perks of having first access to meals, Qi'ra had never been stronger.

All of that was gone, now. She'd forgotten what it was like to be last in the food line, at the mercy of whoever was in charge. Ema delighted in making her life miserable in a thousand different ways, from taunting her about portions to parading around in Qi'ra's coat, preening like she'd grown the fur herself while Qi'ra shivered in the damp of the Coronet City sewer system. Qi'ra grew thin and listless, her skin papery and dry and her hair brittle. Even Jagleo couldn't help her enough to stave off the slow fade of gradual starvation. The dice in her pocket stuck out obviously now, a protuberance at her hip where no extra flesh remained.

The dog biscuits were long gone, and Qi'ra was at the mercy of the food line when Proxima started sending her out again at Sarkin's behest. For a few weeks, she'd hidden in the corridors of the White Worm hideout, trying to gather information. Proxima was definitely planning something, and even though Qi'ra was technically no longer Proxima's problem, she still ran with the scrumrats. She didn't want to be caught flatfooted when everything came to a head. For a while, no one had cared what she did. It was like she was a ghost, beneath the notice of everyone.

The scrumrats stopped picking on her, moving on to more entertaining prey. Qi'ra gave them very little in the way of sport. She never fought back and didn't even ask them to stop, let alone beg for it. It was almost boring. It hurt her pride more than anything else, but she saved a lot of energy by not fighting battles she couldn't win, and having her aggressors give up completely was an unexpected bonus. She walked around vaguely for several days until the general consensus was that her spirit was totally broken and she would be nothing other than obedient.

Lady Proxima was not fooled.

The Grindalid was old, older than most of the scrumrats realized, and she had seen many humans grow up in the coils of her gang. She knew when they were truly defeated, and Qi'ra knew there was little chance of tricking her. Thus when Proxima declared that she should join a scavenging team, Qi'ra didn't argue. She couldn't have anyway; Sarkin had demanded that she earn him a cut while she waited for whatever his endgame was. The others grumbled, afraid that she would slow them down, but a few growls out of Moloch's favorite hound shut them up.

The streets of Coronet City were busy as ever. Industry seethed in the shipyards, and more and more Imperial orders came in every day. If you could afford to build ships, or if you had the connections to sell them, you were set. If you couldn't, well, that was trickle-down economics for you. The scrumrats fell back on their usual tricks of petty theft and pickpocketing. The older ones had more complicated scams, but Qi'ra's had been so intrinsically tied up with Han that she didn't have anything left. Another mistake. She had relied on him too much when the only person she could fully trust was herself.

For the first few days, Qi'ra pretended to be a beggar, lulling what few charitable souls existed in the Golden City into a calm sort of pity while her assigned partner for the day picked their pockets. She was good at it, and even Ema couldn't deny her food when she started bringing in results. After a week, Qi'ra was strong enough that her hands stopped shaking from hunger, and she could pickpocket on her own. Jagleo became her partner then, the girls splitting up marks on the streets and playing people off each other if they noticed their credits had gone missing.

"Hey!" The angry grunt from a stocky Pantoran drew the attention of every shift worker in hearing range.

"I'm so sorry, sir," Qi'ra said, her voice pitched higher than usual after stumbling into him. She waited half a breath and then burst into tears. "It's so far from the market back to my house, and my mother needs my help to make dinner for my family. I have to hurry or I'll be late."

Through her tears, Qi'ra watched as Jagleo moved through the crowd. Her grace was unmistakable, but no one was watching her because every eye was fixed on Qi'ra. She mustered up a fresh wave of tears and the Pantoran fully recoiled from her.

"It's all right, girl," he said gruffly, patting her on the shoulder a bit reluctantly. "No harm done."

He went on his way before she'd stopped crying, hustling through the crowd to avoid the attention. Qi'ra hurried away in the opposite direction, turning three corners before she dropped the persona and slipped into an alley, where Jagleo met her, a grin on her face.

"We should go on tour," the thief said. She pulled several wallets out of various pockets and began emptying them, throwing them casually behind her when they were stripped and pocketing the contents.

"I think we might need a bit more material," Qi'ra said. She had only one wallet, the Pantoran's, but it was payday, so she wasn't disappointed.

It wasn't much, but it kept Qi'ra occupied enough that she didn't spend too much time wondering if Han was flying yet, or thinking about how she wished she'd starved Ema when she had the chance. Sometimes Jagleo was called off for bigger jobs, and on those days, Qi'ra faced the streets alone with the sort of grim determination that had gotten her out of the Silo in the first place. She couldn't depend on anyone, but she could use whatever they gave her.

When Proxima held court, Qi'ra stood off to the side and near the back. The younger scrumrats would crowd forward, eager to show Proxima what they'd stolen in her name. They still loved her, a little bit, for saving them from whatever loneliness they had come from before they joined the White Worms. They still thought they were more to her than a pair of hands and skin that could withstand the sun. They didn't realize that the violence done to them by Moloch and the other lieutenants was done on Proxima's word.

As much as she wanted to fade, Qi'ra wouldn't disappear, and thus she inevitably came to Proxima's attention from time to time. It was always the same. Ema would be giving a report and artfully leave out the part that Qi'ra had played. Some younger kids would grumble, and when Proxima asked for clarification, Qi'ra's name would come up. Qi'ra couldn't make them stop, and Ema didn't seem to realize that she was setting herself up for even more embarrassment, so Qi'ra had no choice but to play along.

"Qi'ra, my dear, I can't see you, come closer," Proxima said, even though her eyes saw more clearly in the gray light of her meeting room than any human's did.

Qi'ra pushed her way through the others until she stood just behind Ema. She could tell the younger girl was furious and trying to keep it to herself. Ema might have mastered her facial expression, but her shoulders were still tight and her hands were still clenched at her sides when she got angry.

"Ah, there you are," Proxima said. "I am so pleased to hear that you are continuing to help your little brothers and sisters, even though you belong to someone else now. They benefit from your experience quite a bit, I imagine. Ema, tell me more about how Qi'ra helped."

Ema seethed but started talking. Proxima didn't take her eyes off Qi'ra the entire time. Qi'ra had always been good at keeping her face still, but now she could hold her whole body like that, neutral and passive. Moloch scoffed at her, clicking mouthparts inside his mask, and the other scrum-rats avoided her. But Proxima always knew better. The old Grindalid had seen broken humans before. She'd broken them. And Qi'ra knew that her facade wasn't quite good enough to fool the lady of the White Worms.

It was like a game between them, and Qi'ra could only guess the reason. Proxima knew she wasn't completely crushed and, for some reason, was in no hurry to finish the job. Qi'ra wondered if it was merely a game for the gang leader, something to keep her amused while she put together the details of the mysterious job with Sarkin. Perhaps it was more sinister, a part of the plan Jagleo feared, coming together in a way that none of them would be able to predict in time. Qi'ra didn't particularly care. She suspected that Proxima was just waiting until one of the scrumrats made a play against her. Or even waiting to see if Qi'ra would make a play against Ema. It would have been a foolish waste of energy. Anything Qi'ra might take from Ema, she would owe to Sarkin. She wasn't tempted to try her luck.

So she stared at Proxima, and Proxima stared at her, and both of them wondered what, if anything, the other was planning. By the time Ema was done talking, they were at yet another impasse. The ball was always in Proxima's court, though, and it was only a matter of time until she played it.

"Qi'ra, I want you to get a better coat," Proxima said. "It was good of you to give up your old one, but it's getting colder in the tunnels, and we cannot have you getting sick while we wait for Sarkin to return for you. Talk to Karsot about it, and he will make arrangements for you. All of you, go and enjoy your dinner."

At the back of the room, Karsot nodded briskly. The scrumrats filed out, chattering amongst themselves at Proxima's unexpected good mood. The look that Ema shot at Qi'ra could have melted beskar, but Qi'ra wasn't thinking about her. Proxima was up to something, stirring up a fight between Qi'ra and the girl who had replaced her and cloaking it in generosity that extended to all of the kids. If Qi'ra could be rewarded, surely any of them could. It was a reason to stay loyal, a reason to do their job without asking questions or showing too much independent thought.

Qi'ra didn't really care why Proxima had done it. It was a test or a feint or a deliberate baiting, but the only thing that mattered was that Qi'ra would get a coat out of it. Ema already hated her; adding a bit more fuel to the fire wouldn't make too large of a difference. And Qi'ra would be warm.

Karsot was waiting for her after dinner. Her portion had been noticeably smaller than usual, but she didn't care. She followed Karsot down a corridor that the Grindalids discouraged the humans from using. It was the place where Proxima kept what she had them steal. It was always locked up tight and guarded, but any scrumrat caught in this hallway without permission was punished severely. Karsot went to one of the doors, fumbled with the keypad, and then motioned for Qi'ra to go into the room.

On first glance, the room was full. Shelves were crammed, and overflowing crates littered the floor. Upon closer examination, though, the room was full of junk. Sure, there was a lot of stuff, but it wasn't worth very much. Unless Proxima had a large stash of credits somewhere else, the White Worms were not having a very profitable term. That explained why Proxima was so eager to sell Qi'ra to Sarkin Enneb. Credits were always better than goods.

Qi'ra went to a shelf that contained mostly clothing. She rifled through a few crates until she found something that she thought would suit her, and then she stood back to try it on. The coat was longer than her previous one, which was good because she still didn't have a skirt to wear over her leggings. It smelled terrible, but that was the least of her worries. Qi'ra found a few pockets immediately and noticed a few spots where more could be added. It wasn't fancy, and it definitely wasn't as flattering as the coat Ema had taken from her, but it would more than serve her.

"I don't have all day," Karsot hissed.

Qi'ra hurried to the door. She didn't wait around while he locked up. She didn't need an escort back to the barracks. If Proxima saw anyone else wearing this coat, she'd know that someone had interfered with her instructions directly, and that never ended well. Qi'ra could keep this one and not even spend too much time thinking about how to guard it. For the first time in weeks, she was almost comfortable.

The junk room nagged at her, though. So much stuff with so little value couldn't be good. Jagleo still had no more details to support her fears, but Qi'ra thought this might be another indication she was right. Proxima had a plan, and Qi'ra was going to find out what it was.

CHAPTER FOUR

T he price of the new coat became apparent the next morning after breakfast. When Qi'ra would have followed the other scrumrats out into the streets for their daily pilfering, Karsot blocked her way with his electrostaff. Qi'ra waited, watching as the last few stragglers left, and tried to keep her heart from racing.

"You've got a new job," Karsot announced.

Qi'ra let him push her toward one of the speeders. She hadn't been in a real vehicle since her return from Han's ill-fated escape attempt, and it hurt more than she expected to feel the wind in her hair again and not see that grin beside her. She pushed aside the memories of Han and focused as Karsot drove her through the industrial lots that sur-rounded Corellia's pride and profit: the shipyards.

The smell of hot metal and burning ozone filled her senses, a welcome change from the damp rot of the sewers. Karsot dropped her off with a group of workers who were almost as bedraggled as she was. There was no indication of how she was supposed to get home. The others didn't look at her, beyond a cursory glance or two as they pulled on gloves or adjusted their hats after the wind of traveling. They were all humanoid, which surprised her. There were many jobs in the shipyards that needed more than two arms.

A voice came from the front of the crowd: "Right, you lot, pay attention." A human man with a loudhailer was addressing the assembly. "You're here to work, not stand around. If you haven't been assigned to a work group already, make your way to the front."

Qi'ra joined the queue and watched as the people in front of her were sorted off into shifts for the day. When she reached the front, the man glared down at her.

"What in all the shiny hells am I supposed to do with you?" he asked, obviously not impressed by her diminutive size.

Qi'ra had no idea why Proxima had sent her here, so she didn't offer a suggestion. Before the man could throw her out of the shipyard, he scanned her identification—false, obviously—and his eyebrows shot up.

"It seems you have an assignment already," he said. His eyes assumed the familiar blank look all bureaucrats got when bribery was in play. He pointed to a tall woman flanked by a squad of stormtroopers. "Go on, then."

Qi'ra made her way over to her new boss. This was a surprise, but she was determined not to show it.

"Hands," said the woman, and seized both of Qi'ra's when she held them up. She looked at them carefully and hissed. "You'll do. Follow me."

Qi'ra set off after her, trying her best to keep up with the brisk pace set by the Imperial security squad. The others in her group did the same. Messing with Proxima or the other scrumrats was one thing, but there was no way Qi'ra would try any tricks with someone who had such obvious Imperial connections. She would do exactly what she was told, and hope to avoid any more attention than she was already receiving. They crossed an open square and then entered a squat gray building. The lighting was bad, but Qi'ra could see workstations, each with its own light source. This would be detail work, then.

"You may address me as Manager Veteri," the woman said. "I have very little patience and almost no sympathy, so if you cannot do the job I require, just disappear."

A few people shifted uncomfortably from foot to foot, but Qi'ra might as well have been made of stone.

"Your task is simple," Veteri said. "The navicomputers for each new Corellian-made ship have been programmed with the latest data and the most accurate course settings. You will secure the chips containing that data to the control boards meant for each vessel. Precision is key, speed is better. Get to work."

There was a small scramble as each person found their way to a workstation. Qi'ra got one in the back, where it was darker but much warmer. She blinked a few times to get her eyes to adjust. Years of sewer living and working with creatures who couldn't bear the sun had made her comfortable in low light. Then she began to work.

It was a tedious job. The welding irons smelled foul, and each piece had to be laid down carefully. Speed was next to impossible, since the stormtroopers stalked the aisles, making everyone nervous. In the back, Qi'ra was much less supervised, and she took the opportunity to study the people she was working with. The crew was made up of standard Corellian street hires. It was common for nonspecialized workers to crowd outside the shipyards each morning in the hope of getting a day's wage. Han had spoken of it more than once, a plan that invariably devolved into a dream of being noticed as a genius shipbuilder or stealing the ship he was working on and making a break for it. Qi'ra had no time for such fancies. Sarkin would take the wage anyway.

The manager was interesting. Now that they were inside, Qi'ra could see that she was quite young. She was tall, which would make it easy for people to misjudge her age, and the authority of her bearing also made her seem older. In truth, Qi'ra would guess that Manager Veteri was barely older than

Qi'ra was, and that opened up all sorts of questions. The Empire was at the height of its power. It didn't need young people overseeing factories. It had plenty of older, experienced ones. The girl certainly moved like an Imperial, and spoke like one, but now that she was looking closer, Qi'ra saw that her clothing didn't fit her quite as immaculately as most people of her status would insist upon.

A droid buzzed beside her, and Qi'ra realized she was falling behind while she daydreamed. There was no point in worrying about what people were wearing. All she had to do was her job, and then whatever it was Proxima and Sarkin had sent her here for. She turned her attention to the chips in front of her and concentrated on welding them into place until she had made up the difference in her work pace.

There was a break for lunch in which food was not rationed. Qi'ra knew better than to stuff herself—she knew from experience that she'd only be sick—but she did eat slowly and methodically through the entire break. When she returned to work, it was with her first full belly since the botched coaxium job. If nothing else, the day was a win for that.

The afternoon was just as tedious as the morning, with a couple of pauses while Manager Veteri fired people she didn't feel were working fast enough. After the fourth ejection, the room was almost completely silent except for the hiss of the welders as the hot metal hit the control boards.

Finally, after they had spent fourteen hours sitting hunched over, a chime sounded.

"All of you may return tomorrow," said Manager Veteri, like she was granting them a great gift. "You have been adequate."

Qi'ra didn't pocket her meager daily pay. She simply dropped it into Karsot's waiting palm as he hustled her back into the speeder. The lunch had been worth it, and tomorrow there would be another.

The next six days were the same. Karsot dropped her off, Manager Veteri looked at her like she was scum, and Qi'ra spent the whole day welding. Her stomach grew stronger, but she still didn't stuff herself too much. The food wouldn't last forever, and she didn't want to be used to it when it was cut off. On the sixth day, Veteri announced that their task was complete. They would no longer be required at the shipyard. The workers received the news with the sort of acceptance that only came from years of living hand to mouth.

"However, should you wish a small bonus, you may help us carry the finished boards to the warehouse," Veteri said, again like it was a gift.

A few of the workers turned their noses up and left, unwilling to take final scraps when they could go and look for another job, but most remained. Qi'ra helped carry the finished control boards to the clean room where they would be sterilized and then stored until their installation on whatever ship they were bound for. She made the trip from the workroom to the warehouse several times, committing each step to memory, though she didn't know what for. On her last trip, Veteri stopped her.

"You did better than I expected," she said. Qi'ra didn't know why she cared. "If I return to this slag heap of a planet, I might just seek you out."

The words were empty. No one would find her in the sewers, and even if they did, Sarkin wouldn't just turn her over. Qi'ra didn't even take comfort in the idea that she'd done her job well enough to be noticed. It was over, and now she would be back to wondering how she was going to earn her dinner each day. Veteri waved her on, and Qi'ra went to collect her credits.

Karsot was waiting for her, and for the first time, he wasn't holding his hand out. Whether he knew that there was more money or not, he'd been instructed to let her keep her wage. Qi'ra tucked the credits into several of the concealed pockets she'd managed to stitch into the coat during her few hours off over the past week. Ema might find some of them, if she decided to shake Qi'ra down, but she'd never get them all. The drive back to the White Worm headquarters was completely silent. Moloch was given to bluster and threats, filling the silence with whatever he could think of. Karsot was the quiet one, but that didn't make him less of a danger.

Moloch told you exactly what was going to happen to you before he did it. Karsot let you imagine it first.

When they returned to the compound, Karsot didn't turn her loose as he had done before. It was dinner, and if she was late she would miss it, but he marched her past the common room and straight into Lady Proxima's lair. The Grindalid was waiting for her, already emerged from the pool instead of remaining with her spawn until she was needed above. The scars from Han's sunlit strike were red and rampant on her face, but Qi'ra was smart enough not to stare at them.

"Qi'ra, my dear," Lady Proxima said. "I hear you have had a good week."

"She's kept her wage for today, like you asked," Karsot said. "The overseer said they were done, so she doesn't have to go back in tomorrow."

"Excellent," Lady Proxima said. "Sarkin and I are very pleased with your work, Qi'ra. I knew you were too valuable to let molder away in my tunnels, and too skilled to waste on pickpocketing."

Qi'ra was puzzled. She hadn't made that much money working at the shipyard, especially since Proxima let her keep today's credits. She could have stolen more in less time, even on a terrible street. She hadn't taken any chips, let alone any of the finished boards. They would have been impossible to smuggle out, no matter how big her coat was.

But she had seen where all of them were stored. She knew the path from the shipyard gate to the warehouse, because she had walked it so many times. She knew when the shift was over, and she knew which guards would be at the gate overnight.

Proxima needed something of worth, something better than the junk her scrumrats could steal. Something better than their scams could turn up. Qi'ra had been part of that once, a great scheme that ended with her being made Head. She doubted there would be such a reward this time, but the intention was clear.

"You want the control boards," Qi'ra said.

"Yes," hissed Sarkin Enneb, stepping out from the shadows. "Yes, I do."

CHAPTER FIVE

The plan came together very quickly, because no one was entirely sure when the control boards would be shipped off-world. As a smuggling operation, it wasn't particularly elegant: the navigation data was worth a great deal, and the chips were ready to go. None of the buyers would have to do any assembly. The control boards could simply be fit into the ship, and that was that.

It was the biggest scam the White Worms had attempted since the coaxium debacle, not that anyone so much as breathed the word. The little kids were sent out at all times of the day and night to spy on the guard rotations, the better to pick up the details that Qi'ra couldn't have noticed, since she had primarily been inside the shipyard. The older scrumrats, with Ema at the head, were tasked with preparing the bolt-holes and dead drops for use. Only Jagleo and Qi'ra were assigned to work with Moloch's team, and Qi'ra knew that galled Ema and Rebolt both.

For several days, they were too busy and given too many supervised tasks for Jagleo and Qi'ra to talk. Qi'ra could tell the thief was burning to, and she wasn't surprised. This was the big thing that Jagleo had been worrying about: Proxima's excuse to cull the herd. Not even Jagleo's current position in the gang or her knowledge that she was the best thief the White Worms had ever seen was enough to calm her down.

"I can't go back to dancing," Jagleo said, voice low, when they finally had a moment to talk. "Not alone. I either need guild support or gang support, and there's no way the guild would let me in now."

No one ever asked where the oldest White Worms went. Some of them did become outside contacts, carefully culti- vated by Lady Proxima to continue to serve her needs even though they were no longer under her protection. But more of them simply disappeared. Rebolt was currently the oldest, Qi'ra was pretty sure, but she, Jagleo, and Syke were close to him in age, and there was a whole crop of kids between them and Ema.

"Qi'ra, what do you know?" Jagleo demanded.

Qi'ra hadn't exactly promised to help her, and promises meant nothing even if she had, but right now, there was no harm in letting Jagleo in on some of the details. If the thief calmed down, she was less likely to get them all pinched, for starters. Also, she made Qi'ra anxious, too focused on all the things that could go wrong.

"There's four hours of downtime in the shipyard," Qi'ra said. "There's limited cleaning staff and inspection droids, and a few dozen guards on the perimeter. Proxima's plan is that Moloch and the other lieutenants will attack gate three and draw as much of the security over to them as they can. Then the scrumrats with him will disperse, giving them too many targets to chase. Meanwhile, you and I break into gate two, which is now exposed. From there, it's a short hop to the warehouse where the control boards are. Once we have everything opened and secure, we signal the transport team, and they come clear everything out."

"Everything or everyone?" Jagleo asked.

"Even if they don't let us on the transport, we can get out the way we came in," Qi'ra reassured her. "Both of us are good at evasion, and I know you've got hiding places you haven't told anyone about."

She didn't know that, actually, not for sure. But Jagleo flushed, and then she did. Now it was simply a matter of staying close to the thief so that they could hide together.

"Are there any chips left over?" Jagleo whispered, leaning in close. "Just a few loose ones? We wouldn't even have to sell them right away. We could wait until the heat died down. It would give us a way out if Proxima really does try to get rid of us."

Qi'ra had considered it, of course. When she was working at the shipyard, they were all checked every day when they left. The chips were small and could quite easily be pock-eted. Jagleo had a good point. Proxima wanted the boards. If the girls got their hands on even a few loose chips, they could make enough money to get off-world.

Of course, Qi'ra had been down this road before. An easy skim and a quick escape had seemed too good to be true the first time she tried it. There was no way she was trying it again. No matter how much Jagleo's help had made the last few weeks survivable.

"All the chips were attached," Qi'ra lied. "I have no idea if there were any extras left over, or where they might have ended up."

Jagleo trusted her and didn't ask again.

Qi'ra couldn't stop thinking about it. Not the chips or the potential to run, but the lie. The ease with which she told it and the ease with which it was accepted. Lady Proxima trusted her again, as much as she ever would, at least. Enough to let her have credits and dress warmly without fear of her things being stolen. The coat might be thanks to Sarkin's influence—if she got sick, she'd be worth even less than she already was—but a habit was a habit, and Proxima fell back on hers just as easily as anyone else. Qi'ra could lie to Proxima and sabotage the theft. She was their only inside source, and they relied on her completely for a great deal of information.

Betraying Proxima would cause a bloodbath. Not just the Grindalids, but any of the scrumrats who got caught in the cross fire. Rebolt and Syke for sure, and probably Ema, along with the group of little goons she was assembling as her cronies. Qi'ra didn't care about any of them enough to save them, but she wasn't quite sure she was ready to cause their deaths. There was no guarantee of her own safety, even if she managed to get Jagleo to one of the hiding spots, and Grindalids had several nasty traditions about what to do with people who caused the death of their family members. None of Qi'ra's plans ended with her being eaten.

No, the only way forward was to do everything she could to guarantee Proxima's success, and then deal with Sarkin when he became the next obstacle in front of her. Jagleo was right: there was no place for her on Corellia without the support of the White Worms, and there was no easy way for her to get off-planet. This raid had to go so well that Proxima would keep Jagleo on as an adult. Qi'ra had fewer options but slightly more security. Proxima hated giving people their money back. She just needed to survive and then keep surviving under Sarkin's thumb.

Jagleo went off to practice fighting, something she always did alone so no one could guess her moves, and Qi'ra drifted through the barracks, not really sure how to fill her time. Two human boys, Broon and Fixit, stumbled into the corridor behind her, breathing hard.

"What happened?" she asked. The boys had been on surveillance. If they had been seen, there would be trouble.

"Nobody saw us!" Fixit said. It was an instant defense, and it wouldn't have saved him from Moloch, but Qi'ra wasn't interested in causing pain.

"Just tell me," Qi'ra said. "Quickly."

"We were at our watching post," Broon said. "It was getting dark, so we were waiting for Oggro to come. He can see better in the dark, so he's been taking the night shifts."

Rodians could see infrared, so Oggro was a valuable scout. He would be on Qi'ra's team the night of the actual raid, assuming he survived that long.

"All of a sudden, about a thousand Imperial stormtroopers march out of one of the hangars," Fixit said. "They all had blasters and who knows what else. They were pointing scanners all over the place, and we didn't want to get pinched, so we ran back here. No one saw us, though. We left before they scanned where we were hiding."

"Did you tell Oggro?" Qi'ra asked.

"We didn't see him," Broon said. "We thought it was more important to get back and tell someone."

It was, but not every scrumrat would have made that call.

"Very well," Qi'ra said. She pulled the remnants of her authority around her like a cape. "You boys head for dinner, since your shift was over anyway. I'll pass along the news."

"Thanks, Qi'ra," Fixit said, still breathing a bit hard. "I'm really glad Lady Proxima didn't just kill you."

Qi'ra resisted the urge to roll her eyes as the boys

scampered off, and then made her way to Lady Proxima's chamber. It was there that her luck ran out, because Ema was on sentinel duty. It was a highly sought-after job, guarding the chamber, mostly because it was inside and it was dead easy. Qi'ra had handed it out as a reward. Ema, apparently, was awarding it to herself, even though she was supposed to be leading the teams preparing their smuggling routes.

"What do you want?" Ema asked. "I'm not changing your food ration again, no matter how much you beg."

Qi'ra had never begged. She hadn't even complained. She spoke to Ema as little as possible, though the girl seemed to remember every occasion.

"I need to speak to Lady Proxima," Qi'ra said.

"You can tell me, and then I'll tell her if she really needs to know," Ema said haughtily. "I don't want you wasting her time. She's got new babies in there, and she's tending to them."

That was information that Ema definitely wasn't supposed to share. Proxima never wanted anyone to know when her spawn were young and vulnerable. As far as the White Worms were concerned, anything in that pool could kill them at any time.

"Get out of the way, Ema," Qi'ra said. Her patience was running thin, but she would absolutely not let the brat know that she was getting under her skin.

"I never have to get out of anyone's way, ever again," Ema said.

Qi'ra hadn't punched a lot of people in her life because she wasn't exactly built for it, but she knew the theory very well. Han thought he'd taught her, along with a few less savory attack methods, but the truth was she always pretended she didn't know how, even though she'd been watching the Grindalids spar since she was a kid. They didn't exactly have shoulders or fists, but from what Han told her, the theory was the same. And also she learned how to not break her fingers.

Ema was completely unprepared for the hit and went down like a box of hammers. She was too surprised to grab at Qi'ra's ankles as she stepped over her. She did flail out, or try to, just before Qi'ra shut the door, but all that accomplished was getting her fingers caught. She howled. Qi'ra would in all likelihood pay for that later, but in the meantime, it felt very, very good.

"What is all that racket?" Lady Proxima demanded, rising from the water. "Qi'ra, what are you doing here?"

"I have an important update about the shipyard," Qi'ra said, ignoring the first question.

"What is it?" Proxima sounded cranky. The offspring must be very new indeed.

"Two of our scouts reported a heavy Imperial presence,"

Qi'ra said. "They must have come to pick up the control boards earlier than we expected."

"I've had no reports of a ship landing," Proxima said. "Not one that could support a sizable number of stormtroopers, in any case. Whatever they're here for, it's not the panels. They must have been here for a while already. It's probably just some training exercise or a flight school. There's no need for us to worry about it."

"I think there is," Qi'ra said. "It's a lot of blasters."

"I will not have you spreading rumors or second-guessing me, do you understand?" Proxima said. She reared over Qi'ra threateningly. "I say that nothing has changed, so nothing has changed."

Qi'ra didn't fight battles she couldn't win. "I understand," she said.

"Get out," Proxima said. "Tell whoever was guarding my door they get no dinner for failing me."

Qi'ra made sure she was fully turned away before she smirked, but the good feeling was short-lived. She was positive that the Imperials were going to be a problem, and now it looked like they were a problem she was going to have to solve by herself.

CHAPTER SIX

Qi'ra's mind raced as she stalked the halls of the White Worm hideout looking for Jagleo. She didn't want to go to the thief for help. She didn't want to go to anyone for help. But this problem was too big for her to handle herself, and she was running out of time. She needed to learn how to extract aid without giving away too much in return. Now was as good a time to practice as any. And she already knew all of Jagleo's tells.

There were now three operations running all at once: the scam Proxima would tell the Worms was happening, the scam that was actually happening, and whatever wild cards the Imperials threw into the mix. Qi'ra had always known that Proxima didn't really care about her child-thieves, no matter how much she talked about feeding them and keeping them safe, but she hadn't thought the old Grindalid would throw so many of them away. There was only one outcome in a fight between scrumrats and stormtroopers. Proxima was sending them to a slaughter, and so far only Qi'ra—the one she no longer had a full claim on—would know about it in advance. The White Worms must be in a worse position than Qi'ra had originally guessed.

The presence of the Imperials also opened another avenue of opportunity for Qi'ra herself. Manager Veteri had seemed genuinely impressed by her work. If Qi'ra went to her and told her about the raid, the manager might just think that was good enough to take Qi'ra under her protection, or at least get her a job and a new identity somewhere far away from Proxima's corner of Coronet City. It was tempting, a golden opportunity of timing and chance, and that was what made Qi'ra turn away from it. Betting on other people was too risky. There was just as much chance that Veteri would hear her story and then shoot her.

She was so deep in thought that she nearly crashed into Syke, who was running up the corridor like his own hounds were after him.

"What did you do?" he asked. He didn't sound angry. "Ema wasn't allowed to have dinner. She wouldn't say anything, but it has to have been you. She's furious and going on about the raid."

"I needed to talk to Proxima, and I had to go through Ema to do it," Qi'ra said shortly. She didn't have time for this. "I'm the main source for planning, but Ema was on a power trip and wouldn't let me by."

"I have a bad feeling about this one, Qi'ra," Syke said. He was rolling back and forth on the balls of his feet, like he had somewhere to be. "It's really big, and it doesn't feel like we have enough people to pull it off. Moloch's nervous."

"It'll be fine," Qi'ra lied to him. She wasn't even sure how much she was going to try to protect Jagleo. She certainly didn't have the capacity to protect Syke, as well. "It's a precision job, that's all. Moloch just hates it when we can't use the hounds, because it reminds him how much he needs the scrumrats."

The best lies were mostly true, and Syke bought this one completely. He stopped fidgeting, and his hands relaxed by his sides.

"You missed dinner, too," he said. "Are you okay?"

"Yes," Qi'ra said. He was clearly waiting for an explanation, but she gave him nothing more.

"Well, I gotta get back to the hounds," he said. "They're not coming with us, but they can tell something's up, so they're going to take a while to settle tonight."

If Syke's ambitions were real, he'd use the restless hounds to his advantage. They were already worked up, so conditions were primed for him to finally turn Taomat loose on Rebolt and see if his careful training had paid off. But Qi'ra knew he wouldn't. Syke didn't really want to be head of the hound keepers. He just knew that if Rebolt was promoted, he'd be out of luck. He was reactive, and that made him dangerous to ally with. Han's plans were routinely terrible, but at least he was smart enough to put himself first.

"Have you seen Jagleo?" she asked before he could run off.

"No," he said. "She wasn't at dinner, either. Nobody finds her bolt-holes."

Qi'ra stood aside to let him pass and then continued through the corridors. She was more careful now. She didn't want to run into anyone else, especially Ema. One punch had been cathartic, but she wasn't sure how many she had in her. When she passed by the room where her bunk was, she saw the black gauzy jacket that Jagleo had given her all those days ago hanging down like a flag. She hadn't left it like that. Someone was in her bunk.

"It's just me, Qi'ra," Jagleo said as Qi'ra entered the room. She'd picked that bunk for its vantage point, after all. "I wanted to be sure you found me."

"It's all right," Qi'ra said. "I was looking for you anyway."

She climbed up, and the two girls crammed into the bunk together. Jagleo had a ration pack, and she split it in half. Her hands were steady, but she looked nervous.

"Fixit said there's a lot of Imperials," she said.

"He told me there were thousands of them," Qi'ra told her. "I think he's exaggerating."

"Even one platoon is too much for us," Jagleo said. "One squad might be too much for us."

"They're not providing security," Qi'ra pointed out. "They're just near the shipyard for some reason. They make a lot of noise. We'll be able to avoid them."

Jagleo looked at her, and Qi'ra stared right back. Her face was calm and her body language was completely under control. Jagleo would get nothing from her that she didn't want to give. For a moment, Qi'ra considered telling her everything: about the junk room, the debt Proxima must owe someone, the risk she was planning to take. Jagleo had those hiding spots. She would be useful, if things went sideways. But Qi'ra had hiding spots, too. And if she was alone, no one else could get her caught.

"You and me," Jagleo confirmed.

"You and me," Qi'ra lied.

It got easier every time.

◠

The first part of the heist went off without a hitch. Moloch was excellent at causing a ruckus, and the noise that engulfed the area around gate three was impressive, even for him. There were several explosions, and then the sirens began. Qi'ra watched as the guard on gate two received the message and then dispatched almost all of his own watch to help. Only two guards remained.

Jagleo crept forward, as graceful and delicate as a ribbon in the dark. She had a blow-dart gun, and was able to hit both guards silently as smoke. They were on the ground before they realized what was happening. Qi'ra joined her, and they both scaled the wall. Once they were inside, Qi'ra opened the gate just a fraction, barely enough to be considered open but enough that it wasn't locked. The transport team wouldn't follow until she signaled, but this meant she wouldn't have to come back for them.

The girls made their way across the yard, Jagleo dropping the bioluminescent cones that would mark a path for the transport team to follow. They'd be faded by the time the sun came up, and they'd disintegrate shortly after. No one would notice them in the morning. It was still noisy over by gate three, and the girls didn't see so much as a cleaner droid as they crept through the shadows. When they reached the warehouse door, Qi'ra stepped forward again with the decoder that would open the lock. She set the device in place, and then froze.

The door wasn't latched. There was already someone inside.

Jagleo's eyes were wide in the dark, her breathing suddenly very loud. Qi'ra made a split-second decision. The only way she was going to get out of here was with maximum chaos.

Before Jagleo could ask what she was planning, Qi'ra shoved the warehouse door open and ran inside. She deliberately stepped into the security sensors, sounding alarms.

Jagleo was right behind her, still trusting that Qi'ra's plan was for both of them. Qi'ra pulled her under a table and then cautiously stuck her head out to see who else was in the room.

Several meters in front of her was a tall figure who had been loading a repulsor sled with the crates Qi'ra had helped pack and was now swearing loudly as the alarm sounded. Whoever it was, they could see the door was open but not who had come through. From her hiding place, Qi'ra saw the exact moment the figure decided to cut their losses and make off with what they had, perhaps a quarter of what the sled could carry.

The guards would arrive soon. Qi'ra slid out from under the table and ran to the crates. She picked up six control boards, as many as she could carry without the weight slowing her down. She shoved them into the bag around her waist.

"What are you doing?" Jagleo yelled, finally finding her voice.

"I'm not going back empty-handed," Qi'ra told her. "Not again."

She ran toward the emergency exit. She hadn't told Proxima about it because it wasn't important to the White Worm plan. But it had always been part of hers. Jagleo scrambled after her, a few boards in her arms, but Qi'ra knew she'd never keep up. She didn't have a bag, and this route required both hands.

"Stop!" shouted a partially mechanized voice as they exited the building to the side of where they'd gone in.

Qi'ra risked a glance over her shoulder and saw that the shipyard was flooding with stormtroopers. She didn't see the figure with the sled. Jagleo froze instinctively at the Imperial command, but the trooper wasn't actually talking to them. The transport team had come into the yard when the alarms sounded, even though that wasn't the signal. Rebolt was supposed to be in charge of them. He must have ordered them in. Qi'ra was pretty sure it was going to be the last thing he ever did.

"Qi'ra," Jagleo said, starting to run again.

Qi'ra didn't wait for her. The sound of blaster fire filled the air, along with screaming and the smell of burning flesh. Some of the scrumrats tried to run, and the troopers followed them. It led them away from Qi'ra. At gate three, massive floodlights were turned on. Whatever Moloch was doing, it was going to have to stop or he would be exposed.

This couldn't have been what Proxima intended, even if Sarkin was pushing her. Her scrumrat collection would be thinned out, but she wasn't making any profit. Maybe Moloch was after something else entirely and Qi'ra's heist was a diversion. It didn't matter anymore. Qi'ra had what she came for tied around her waist, and she was almost to her escape point.

The girls reached the wall near gate five. This part of

the wall was shorter, which was why Qi'ra had chosen it. It also faced the Bottoms—the neighborhood of Qi'ra's much-detested Silo—so most Corellians would avoid it out of habit. The wall was inclined, the better to stand up on the boggy ground, and the rocks that built it were rough enough for handholds, if you were quick at climbing. Qi'ra was up the wall in a flash. She heard Jagleo curse and drop her control boards before following. They hit the ground on the other side, winded but otherwise whole.

"Qi'ra," Jagleo said, but clearly she already knew the answer. They'd worked together long enough that Jagleo could tell when Qi'ra was done. Any potential future they'd had together—an aging-out scrumrat and a runaway—was over. Proxima had put her with Qi'ra knowing that Qi'ra was the most likely to survive, but after that Qi'ra would give Jagleo nothing. She was on her own. She didn't waste time looking disappointed, even if her voice betrayed her feelings.

Qi'ra turned and headed off into the Bottoms. No other Worm knew these streets like she did. Jagleo wouldn't follow. She'd make her own way home. Or she'd get caught by the authorities. It wasn't Qi'ra's problem.

The Bottoms were a familiar place, even though she hated them. Qi'ra made her way to her safe house, doubling back from time to time to make sure that no one was behind her. The noises from the shipyard faded after an hour or so, but the lights stayed on. The shooting was over, but the cleanup was still underway. Qi'ra slid into her safe house, trying not to think about the last time she'd been here, and hid the control boards in one of the gaps in the floor. Then she wrapped herself up in one of the nearly ruined blankets and took a seat in the corner of the room so that no one could sneak up behind her.

It seemed like forever until the dawn.

CHAPTER SEVEN

The White Worm tunnels were quiet as Qi'ra let herself in and made her way through the maze. She didn't know how many had survived, and she wasn't in any particular hurry to find out. She had half of the control boards with her, carried in the bag that hung heavy from her belt. The rest were still stashed away in her safe house. She'd bring them in eventually, but she wasn't going to put all her eggs in one basket.

When she got to Proxima's chamber, there was no sentinel. This would have been alarming on a regular day, but if numbers were down, the soft jobs might go undone for a while. Qi'ra opened the door and went in.

Proxima was already out of the water, both Moloch and Karsot flanking her. The assembled children were young. None of them looked older than fourteen. There was no sign of Ema. Karsot held Taomat on a leash. The hound was calm, at least. The scrumrats were all on edge.

"Sometimes we must make difficult choices," Proxima was saying, the attention of the kids fixed on her. "We knew that this was a risky plan, but your older brothers and sisters decided to keep you safe. They have made it possible for the White Worms to get stronger, even if we had to say good-bye to a few of them."

Qi'ra joined the back of the crowd. She wasn't tall enough to stand out, even though she was older. None of the kids even looked at her. They were hanging on Proxima's every word.

"There may be some difficult days ahead of us," Proxima continued. "You each have a job to do, and I know you will do it well. Everyone will get an increased breakfast this morning, because you have all shown why you are members of the White Worms."

Also, Qi'ra thought cynically, there were at least twelve fewer mouths to feed.

The scrumrats began to file out, eager to get to breakfast but still in a bit of shock from the events of the night before. Some of them had visible injuries, mostly pavement burn and other scrapes that would be acquired in a chase. None of them seemed to have been shot. Moloch's sleeve was a bit singed, but that could have been from any number of things.

"Qi'ra!" Lady Proxima called out, spotting her at last. "You have returned safely! When you didn't come back last night, we feared the worst."

"I didn't want to lead anyone to you, Lady Proxima," Qi'ra said. "I made sure I wasn't being followed before I came home."

"You see, children," Proxima said. "We take care of each other. Come here, Qi'ra."

Qi'ra made her way forward. Moloch leaned on his cane, but for the first time in a long time, the sight of him didn't chill her blood.

"What happened, Qi'ra?" Proxima asked. "Why did all the alarms go off?"

As a rule, Qi'ra didn't lie to people who could kill her. But the only other person who knew who had set off the alarms was gone. If Jagleo had intended to come back, she'd already be here. Qi'ra wished her the best of luck with the dancers' guild, if she was even still alive.

"There was someone else in the warehouse," Qi'ra said. "They were loading up a repulsor sled to steal their own take. When we opened the door, we startled them, and they set the alarms off."

Proxima made a sound of distaste, but she wasn't as angry as Qi'ra had seen her get in the past when someone else tried to steal what she considered her score.

"I suppose it was a good target," she said. "And the warehouse served its purpose. Moloch was able to steal a whole shipment of Imperial credits. That's why the stormtroopers were there. They were escorting a payment."

Credits were much better than control boards, especially Imperial credits. They didn't have to be fenced, and they were untraceable. Still, Proxima never turned down more money.

"I was able to carry a few control boards with me," Qi'ra said. "I didn't realize you had another objective, and I didn't want to come home empty-handed."

Possibly she was laying it on a bit thick, but Proxima was never one for subtlety. Qi'ra pulled the three control boards out of her bag and handed them over to Moloch.

"Wonderful, Qi'ra," Proxima said. "I feared the worst, of course. We lost so many."

Qi'ra didn't answer. She knew that Proxima would have been just as pleased if she'd been caught up in the cross fire, too.

"We will rebuild," Proxima continued. "We must recruit new scrumrats and train them. In the meantime, Qi'ra, I wish we had you back permanently, but Sarkin is expecting you. He'll be pleased that you survived. Don't waste his momentary favor."

Qi'ra inclined her head and took Proxima's words for the dismissal that they were. The Grindalids were talking amongst themselves in their own language, too quickly for her tired brain to process. She supposed it didn't matter. She wasn't a Worm anymore. Just what she and Han had wanted, except in the worst possible way.

Qi'ra shoved thoughts of Han aside even as her fingers closed around the dice in her pocket. He had no place in her memory. She had survived despite his foul-ups and lack of foresight, and she didn't need him anymore. She was furious that she ever had. As she left the chamber, she noted that there was a humanoid shape in the sentinel's position. She didn't give it much thought. Maybe one of the kids was trying to look good now that they were closer to the top of the pyramid.

A harsh snarl was her only warning. Qi'ra barely managed to get her hands up to protect her face before Ema came hurtling out of the sentinel's alcove, fingers extended like claws, almost howling in her fury. The younger girl didn't check her speed, and both she and Qi'ra crashed into the wall. Qi'ra pushed her away and managed to keep her feet while Ema stumbled. In the few precious seconds that bought her, Qi'ra came to several conclusions.

First, Ema was beyond reason. Short of a Grindalid lieutenant appearing to make her stop, she was going to keep attacking Qi'ra. Second, Ema was out for blood. She didn't just want Qi'ra hurt; she wanted Qi'ra dead. Third, Ema wanted to do it with her bare hands. Qi'ra had only one option, and that was to run.

She tore through the familiar tunnels, corridors she'd grown up in and memorized until she could have navigated them in her sleep. She knew every corner, every loose panel, every protruding bolt or screw. If the person chasing her weren't a Worm, Qi'ra would have lost them in a heartbeat, leading them toward dead ends or getting them disoriented in the maze. But Ema hadn't wasted her time as Head. She knew the tunnels, too. Qi'ra's only advantage was that she had a clear head and Ema was overcome with rage.

Most of the tunnels circled the main chamber, leading back on themselves again and again so that the hideout felt much bigger than it actually was. The corridors were mercifully empty, since everyone was either dead or eating breakfast, and so there was no one to slow Qi'ra down. She knew she'd get winded soon, though. She had to pick a destination, either someplace where Ema wouldn't follow her or a place she could use in her favor.

Her feet ached as she ran, her new boots not the same good fit as the ones that had been stolen. Her lungs burned. But she didn't slow down. In a flash, she knew where she was going. She ground her teeth together and ran on.

She could hear Ema panting behind her, the exertion doing nothing to cool her temper. If Qi'ra was lucky, Ema wouldn't realize where they were headed until it was too late. If she was very lucky, Ema would figure it out and refuse to follow her. It was the kind of solution Qi'ra liked. Both of them left her alive and unharmed.

"I am going to kill you," Ema said, grating out each word

around a harsh breath. "I should have killed you as soon as you came back from the spaceport."

She should have, but Qi'ra wasn't about to make it easier for Ema to identify her own mistakes.

"I am going to wring your pretty neck and feed you to Proxima's offspring," Ema shouted.

It was a common threat amongst the scrumrats. None of them really got to see Proxima's offspring, but the idea of worms living in the sewers was innately terrifying, and it didn't take much to make imaginations spin.

"You'll have to catch me first," Qi'ra taunted, risking more provocation to keep Ema off balance and unaware of her surroundings.

The younger girl howled and turned on a fresh burst of speed, but it was too late. Qi'ra had arrived at her destination, and Ema followed her in without so much as a thought.

Qi'ra climbed up on top of Taomat's cage, because it was still empty. The other cages each had a growling, angry hound inside. Ema realized where she was like she was slamming into a wall. Her fury faded immediately, and her fear became all pervasive. Still, she was Head of the White Worms, and that wasn't for nothing.

"You can't stay up there forever," Ema said, defying her own fear and taking a step closer to Qi'ra's perch.

"I can stay up here long enough," Qi'ra told her.

She opened her hand, revealing the cage control she had snagged on her way into the room. With one push of a button, she could open all the doors. Ema was a sweaty mess from her run through the compound, and she had opened up some injury from the night before, so now there was blood dripping down her side, as well. She would be an irresistible target for the hounds, especially since none of the handlers were there to stop them.

"Qi'ra," the younger girl begged, so terrified it was almost a squeak. "Qi'ra, please."

Qi'ra knew exactly what would happen if she showed mercy. Ema would be solicitous for a few days, maybe even a week. But even after Qi'ra left with Sarkin, Ema would always remember that she had made her vulnerable. That she had made her cry. That she had made her beg. It would fester in her until the hate was powerful enough to boil over, and then Qi'ra would be at risk of attack again. Han would have done it, put the controls down and said something with a laugh and smile that set Ema at ease and made her forget that she was angry in the first place.

But Han was gone, and his plans were always terrible anyway.

Qi'ra flipped the switch, and the cage doors snapped open. The hounds realized they were free and began to stalk toward their prey. For a moment, Qi'ra thought that Ema was so scared she would just stand there frozen until the hounds dragged her down, but then Moloch's favorite beast snapped at her. She broke and ran, all of them hot on her heels.

Qi'ra sat on top of the cage until the screaming faded. Then she set the control mechanism back where she'd found it and left the kennels. She even made it to the common room in time for breakfast.

CHAPTER EIGHT

Two days after the raid, Qi'ra woke to the crackling electricity of Moloch's stun baton in her face. She managed not to scream, but only just. Her heart raced in her chest instead. He couldn't haul her out of her bunk. She'd kept the top bunk because of the vantage point, even though it was drafty, and he couldn't reach her with his appendages wrapped up in his full-seal armor. The baton got the point across without any need for extra talking. Qi'ra got a move on.

The scrumrats all slept in whatever clothes they were lucky enough to possess. If any of the dead ones had left anything behind, it was pillaged by now. By some miracle, Qi'ra's skirt had turned up on the end of her bed the first morning after she'd loosed the hounds on Ema. Her boots had shown up the second. She pulled on her new coat and tried not to think about what had happened to the old one.

"Took hours to calm the hounds," Moloch grumbled as

he marched her through the corridors, but he didn't rebuke her any further. He didn't care how the Worms sorted out their politics. His position was pretty much locked, and he didn't waste time worrying about the brats.

Qi'ra didn't tell him that his hounds would be better off if Rebolt or Syke were still around to work with them, because she wasn't stupid. She didn't say anything at all, because she didn't know why he had woken her up so roughly, but she suspected that it couldn't be good.

Moloch shoved her through the door to Proxima's chamber and shut it behind her. He stayed outside, which pricked every nerve Qi'ra had. Unscheduled private meetings with Lady Proxima were rarely a good thing.

The chamber was gray as always, but instead of dull children or drab locals, the group that stood in front of Proxima's pool could only be described as *fancy*. Once upon a time, Qi'ra had dressed like that. When she and Han and Tsuulo had been vying for the Head position, their mission had involved infiltrating a well-to-do party, and Qi'ra didn't think she'd ever forget what it felt like to dress and eat and talk like she had credits to burn.

Sarkin stood beside Proxima, much closer to the pool than anyone ever got. The Grindalid towered over him, but there was no doubt in Qi'ra's mind as to who was in charge. She had spent two days wondering what Sarkin was waiting for, and now the wait was over. He had brought his own people, not as a show of force but simply because Lady Proxima couldn't object.

"Proxima was just telling us about the raid, Qi'ra," Sarkin said. He was resting both hands on the butt of a large blaster. "I asked to meet you here because it sounded like you somehow managed to foul up the whole thing on purpose."

Years of practice kept Qi'ra's flash of panic from rising to the surface. Sarkin was much smarter than she had given him credit for. Proxima had accepted her story, but Sarkin knew there was something more. She blinked twice, readying herself to speak.

"I did the primary scouting," she said. "Later, I was told that there was a large number of Imperials present that we hadn't accounted for in the plan, but when I brought the intel to Proxima, she told me it wasn't important."

"Liar!" Proxima screeched. Water surged over the lip of the pool as she flailed in Qi'ra's direction. Two of Sarkin's people took a step away from the water, but Qi'ra held her ground. Proxima couldn't actually get to her where she was standing.

"Since Proxima wasn't changing her plan, I made my own backup one, just in case," Qi'ra continued, like Proxima hadn't said anything. "I knew the wall that faced the Bottoms was shorter than the others, and easier to climb. That neighborhood is full of places to hide. When the Imperials started shooting, I knew where to run."

"You didn't know that you were the distraction, did you?" Sarkin asked. His bright green eyes gleamed in the murk of Proxima's audience chamber.

"I didn't know for certain," Qi'ra said. "I suspected that there was more at work than the theft we were planning, but I didn't know any of the details."

"The real theft was Imperial credits," Sarkin admitted. "A whole crate of them. Enough to buy quite a bit on this shit planet. But not enough to pay off all of Proxima's debts to me and to certain other parties."

Proxima seethed in the pool, the water churning as she thrashed beneath it.

"I managed to get a few of the control boards that I thought were the target," Qi'ra said, eyes as wide as she could make them. Credits were always better than goods, but goods were usually better than nothing. Let him believe that she didn't understand what they were worth in relation to what Proxima must owe. Let his people think she was foolish and unworldly so they wouldn't expect trouble later on. "I handed them in to be sold. Will that make up the difference?"

Sarkin laughed. Qi'ra fought the urge to relax. Despite everything, he seemed genuinely amused with her.

"We're leaving," he said. He looked her over with a distasteful expression. "I suppose that's all of your things? Or rather, all of my things, now."

Qi'ra nodded, not quite trusting herself to speak. Her bruises from their first meeting had faded, but she hadn't forgotten them, or what he had promised her when he made them. At least Proxima was familiar.

"You didn't think three control boards were going to make a difference, did you?" Sarkin asked.

"No," Qi'ra said. His wide mouth curled into a feral grin, and she let him think he had won something.

"Qi'ra," Proxima said, one last-ditch effort to recover some of her authority, but the power in the room had long since shifted.

"I'm supposed to deliver credits to Dryden Vos to clear your debts, not half-welded tech, and you know it," Sarkin said, turning back to the Grindalid. "You can't manufacture a failure to pin on this girl. She's already outplayed you."

"What?" Now Proxima was truly angry.

"You think she just happened to have a perfect escape route *and* a secure place to go to ground?" Sarkin demanded. "You think it's a coincidence that she's the only kid over the age of fourteen left alive in your silly little gang?"

Proxima drew herself up as tall as she could, water sluicing off her skin back into the pool. With as much dignity as she could muster, she turned back to Sarkin.

"She will be punished accordingly," Proxima said. "She has stepped out of line before, and she knows I don't allow anyone to disobey me twice."

"She's not yours," Sarkin said. He turned back to Qi'ra with a smile that was mostly teeth. "She's mine, and she's not half as biddable as you think. I heard they're still picking skin out of the hounds' teeth."

"Ema was afraid of the hounds," Qi'ra said, letting Sarkin's imagination do the rest of the work. Some of his people actually winced. So much for thinking she was harmless, but it was worth it. Proxima made a few stifled noises, but the conversation had moved on without her. It was between Sarkin and Qi'ra now.

"You will break," he said. His leonine features spoke of nothing but the promise of cruelty. "And I will enjoy it."

Qi'ra knew it was all over. She had played every card she had. There was no escape from a man who owned her. Even if she ran, he could kill her with the press of a button from parsecs away.

Once, in a crowded spaceport, she'd clung to Han and worried about being sold to traffickers. Even though that was what had happened, she didn't fear it now as much as she once had. She couldn't stay on Corellia. Even if she stuck to the parts of town without sewers, she'd be protected only for so long. If she survived long enough that Sarkin took her off-planet, she had a small chance. Not a good one, but something survivable. It wouldn't be easy, but nothing in her life ever had been.

"I'm ready," she said, even though she knew that didn't matter.

There was no one to say good-bye to, so Qi'ra just led the way out of the tunnels. Sarkin's second had the credits and carried them back to his private shuttle. As they took off, Qi'ra spared one last look out the viewport over the freighter boneyard, where so many of her small dreams had died until she'd stopped having any dreams at all. The shuttle was cool and dry, and the sewer smell was already fading. Sarkin watched her with a cold expression on his face. She didn't like the violence she saw smoldering in his eyes.

It's mostly called the Silo by people who don't live there. The children who call it home do so because they don't know any better. They don't know that a home should be dry and warm, not wet and rotting back into the swamp. They don't know that a home should be safe, not full of dangers, each more violent than the last. They don't know that a home should be a place you want to return to, not a place you grow up to fear. They don't know that home should be better than a slum even other slum dwellers avoid.

There are two kinds of kids in the Silo: the ones who will live and the ones who will die.

Qi'ra decides very early to live.

◉

It's an easy decision and a difficult process, living. Corellia is a world of production and profit now, and there's very little space for those who can't directly provide both. Little hands and little feet aren't good for much of anything, and everyone knows it. Children are a burden that most people can't afford. In the Silo, the worst part of the Bottoms, it's even more dire. Skeletons of factories that used to be places where a wage could be earned reach out of the swamp like grasping fingers, and that's what the Silo has become: a place for those who are ruined.

Qi'ra doesn't remember life without the smell. Brackish water and tepid slime. She never thinks about life outside the Silo, because even the Bottoms barely exist outside the muddy desperation of having nothing. There is always an ache in her belly and a chill that runs deeper than her bones.

But she will remember the day she picks the wrong pocket. She doesn't really know how yet, doesn't have the finesse of training or the skill of practice. All she has is desperation, along with eyes to see that someone else has something she wants. In this case it's food. A dog biscuit tucked casually back into a pocket because the beast hasn't earned it yet.

When Moloch grabs her arm, she doesn't fight him. She can't. She has the biscuit in her hand, though, and if she's going to die, she might as well earn it. She stretches out around his grip and bites down around the whole horrible thing. The taste is foul, and she absolutely doesn't care. Moloch is so surprised that he drops her, and she's too stunned to run away. He takes her back with him instead, throwing her at Proxima's feet and telling the story with only slightly exaggerated details.

Proxima doesn't think it's funny, but she does recognize hunger when she sees it. And that's how Qi'ra joins the White Worms.

CHAPTER NINE

Whatever grand plans Sarkin Enneb had for Qi'ra were scuttled almost immediately as a result of his own bravado. Sarkin liked to have his things on display, the better to watch any fractures he'd made widen into cracks. Qi'ra was unceremoniously dumped in a room in Sarkin's lavish Corellian estate after he removed her from the Worms, but she didn't stay in the room very long. A girl approximately her own age was waiting for her.

"My name is Salbee," the girl said. "I'll be showing you around. It's important you learn quickly. Sarkin does not have a patient temper."

Qi'ra looked the girl up and down. She was obviously well fed, though she was still on the small side. She was taller than Qi'ra, but almost everyone was. As far as Qi'ra could tell, she didn't have a mark on either of her wrists. This meant either she was free or Sarkin had chipped her somewhere else. It didn't particularly matter at the moment, so Qi'ra didn't ask.

"Qi'ra," she said instead.

"Come on then, Qi'ra," Salbee said. "We'll get you a uniform."

Salbee took her to a supply room and sent the requisition droid to get the clothes Qi'ra would need. Salbee wore a serviceable pair of brown trousers that tucked into the tops of her boots and a billowy gray shirt with a brown vest over it. There were pockets and hooks for her to store any tools she might need while she was working. Qi'ra didn't think it looked so bad. It was definitely better than anything she'd ever been issued as a Worm.

What the droid returned with for Qi'ra was an entirely different story. She couldn't quite keep the disgust from her face, and Salbee giggled. It wasn't fair to target her resentment at the other girl, but Qi'ra couldn't help it. She wanted to tear her eyes out for laughing.

"You can change over there," Salbee said. She pointed to a curtain in the corner of the room. Her expression was no longer amused; she'd clearly remembered what Qi'ra was in the household.

Behind the curtain, Qi'ra stripped off her old clothes. She wished she had time for a wash before she dressed again, but a spiteful part of her was glad that she'd get sewer filth on her new clothes. Sarkin's selection for her made it very clear what her purpose was going to be, and he probably knew how much she'd hate it, too.

First to go on was a black jumpsuit that covered her from ankles to wrists. Any sense of modesty was immediately negated by the sheer fabric and skintight fit. Qi'ra shimmied into the overdress—if something that small could be called a dress. It was bright green, belted at the waist, and shone with iridescent beading that had a bluish tint when she moved. It covered her from just below her collarbones to less than halfway down her thighs. As long as she didn't move, she was perfectly comfortable, but as soon as she took a step, she knew that she was going to be uncomfortably on display.

The worst part was that the dress was genuinely pretty, and Qi'ra liked the colors. If she had been wearing it by her own choice, she would have reveled in it, drawing eyes and attention with every movement. Instead, she wanted to shove every shimmering thread of it down Sarkin's throat. She slid Han's dice down the front of the dress, using the belt to hold them in place between the two layers of fabric. There was no room for a pocket in this outfit. Salbee wouldn't meet her eyes when she came back, only mumbled something about needing to hurry and led the way back out into the unfamiliar corridors of Qi'ra's new home.

After such an unsettling beginning, Qi'ra wasn't really surprised when the rest of her orientation at the Sarkin estate was rushed and mostly unhelpful. Salbee gave her advice, like to always do what she was told and to do what she was told as quickly as possible, but didn't have time to show her where anything was before bringing her back to Sarkin's audience room.

They went in through a side door fashioned to look like one of the wall panels. Qi'ra assumed there were several more hidden entrances for security purposes but didn't bother looking for them. Like Proxima's audience chamber, the room was designed to intimidate, but where Proxima used darkness and overt displays of power, Sarkin was more subtle. The walls were hull-metal gray, inset with blue stones arranged in geometric patterns. A soft glow emanated from the stones, but the main source of light in the room was the giant skylight cut into the ceiling. Sarkin himself sat in a plain-looking chair at one end of the room. Anyone who came to see him would have to enter and then walk several meters forward, passing at least six guards in the process.

Salbee handed her a tray with a jug and a cup on it and told her to go stand beside Sarkin's chair. She disappeared back into the wall, and Qi'ra felt an irrational surge of jealousy. Taking the smallest steps she could get away with, Qi'ra made her way over to where Sarkin sat idly twirling a stylus in his fingers while he awaited his next petitioner.

"Carry the tray in one hand, girl," he hissed at her.

"Don't lug it around like a rock in front of you. Use your shoulder for support if you're too weak."

Qi'ra adjusted her grip. It was much more unstable this way. She stood on Sarkin's right so that if he wanted a drink he could simply turn to her and pour. She didn't know what was in the jug, if it was alcoholic or just water, but it was heavy and getting heavier by the minute.

Proxima had not encouraged idleness of any kind, and standing still with a tray balanced on her flat hand was pretty close to being idle. That didn't make it easy, of course. Sarkin was clearly setting her up to fail. Her arm would give out and everything would crash down, and then he'd be able to punish her. By the time Sarkin's first meeting of the day was over, her arm was already shaking. She wondered if she should just get it over with, but if she was expected to continue standing here after her punishment, she'd be in even more trouble. Qi'ra ground her teeth together and tried to think of anything else besides the ever-heavier tray.

There was no doubt in her mind that the job would be better performed by a table. It was done by a person to show Sarkin's wealth and status. It was done by a girl like Qi'ra because Sarkin wanted her to know that she was too weak to outlast him.

By the time the third petitioner of the day came into the room where Sarkin held court, Qi'ra's fingers were numb.

She was rapidly approaching the end of her strength, and now her only worry was where she should spill when the tray inevitably fell. She managed to hold on until the petitioner had left, and then she turned slightly to her left and tipped the tray backward so that it landed behind Sarkin's chair, keeping the mess to a minimum.

Any relief she felt was short-lived. Sarkin was on his feet almost before the tray stopped clattering, roaring curses at her. He grabbed her arm, twisting it and pulling it up so that she had to go up on her toes to avoid a sprain or dislocation. She kept her eyes firmly on the floor.

"You stupid girl," Sarkin yelled. None of his other attendants so much as flinched. He dropped her arm and hit her across the face so hard that she staggered backward, tasting blood on the inside of her cheek. "I know you're basically a sewer worm, but I thought holding a tray would be simple enough for you."

He stepped close and hit her again, this time driving her to her knees. He kicked her in the stomach and then on the shoulder as she curled around the pain. From the doorway, Sarkin's secretary coughed lightly, and Sarkin stopped kicking her. She looked up to see him straightening his jacket and tucking a handkerchief back into a pocket.

"I have a schedule to keep," he said. "I'll deal with you later. Clean up this mess if you want any dinner."

The liquid she'd spilled was dark blue and stained the

tile floor. There was blood, too. Qi'ra had no idea where she would even start looking for cleaning equipment, but Salbee appeared out of nowhere with a bucket of soapy water and a rag for her. Neither of them said anything as Salbee picked up another tray with a new jug on it. She fit the tray against a brace she wore on her shoulder, which helped take the pressure off her arm. Qi'ra couldn't bring herself to be surprised that she hadn't been offered such a tool. Sarkin wanted to hit her, and so he would come up with reasons to do it.

Qi'ra washed the floor behind Sarkin's chair as thoroughly and slowly as she could get away with. There were only three more petitioners after her display, and then Salbee took her down to the kitchen, where she scrubbed dishes until the cook sent her to bed, hours later. Her hands were a wreck from all the water, and she was in pain from using muscles she'd never used much before, but at least she got to wear the same comfortable uniform as Salbee for a bit, and there had been dinner.

The next two days were the same, though each time Qi'ra managed to hold the tray a little bit longer before earning her beating for the day. Sarkin didn't hit her in the audience room after the first day. He made her wait for it, spending hours anticipating when he would catch her. The second night, he came into the kitchen. A fearful hush was her only warning before he grabbed her by the hair and slammed her down into the water she was using to scrub the dishes. She couldn't stop herself from fighting to breathe, and he'd punished her for that, too, grinding down on her knee with his boot after he'd smashed her to the floor.

"You don't want to be a kitchen slave, little girl," he told her before he kicked her in the back one last time. "I have more profitable plans for you than that. You should thank me for training you to be something better."

While she was gasping for breath in the aftermath of his attack, Qi'ra realized that whether he meant to or not, Sarkin had taught her a lesson: if she was going to fight, it had better be for her survival, because it was going to hurt.

On the fourth day, Qi'ra made it all the way to the final petitioner, a tall woman dressed in black and gold who wasn't so much a petitioner as an honored guest. Sarkin had food brought in for her, and a comfortable chair. The woman ignored both, only interested in her business.

"The credits are all here for you," Sarkin said, once somewhat strained pleasantries had been exchanged. "Qi'ra, take our guest her payment."

Qi'ra shuffled the tray off to the side table and then struggled to lift the box of credits with her exhausted arms. She managed, and made her way over to the woman.

"Qi'ra, is it?" she said, lifting the lid of the case and giving a cursory glance at the credits inside.

"Yes," Qi'ra said, her voice pitched low.

"You're new, I take it." Her eyes trailed over bruises and the split lip Qi'ra had no way to hide.

"Yes," Qi'ra said again.

The woman took the box and laid a hand on Qi'ra's arm when she would have retreated. Qi'ra looked up at her, alarmed. There was no pity in the woman's face, only a sort of acknowledgment that Qi'ra could take a beating and still be able to work the next day. The woman didn't care if she was defiant, only that she could be a punching bag and remain efficient.

"We'll take her, too," she announced.

"That wasn't part of the deal, Corynna," Sarkin said, an edge to his polite tone.

"I am empowered by my employer to make independent decisions," Corynna said. "And I have made one. She comes with me."

Qi'ra had no idea who this woman was, except that Sarkin had paid her the credits Proxima had given him after the Imperial job. He'd said something about Crimson Dawn at the time, but Qi'ra had been worried about other things besides galactic crime syndicates, so she had forgotten about it until now. It would explain why Corynna was treated as a guest, not as a supplicant.

Crimson Dawn was not something to be trifled with. They were too well organized and they had too many fingers in too many pies. Qi'ra wasn't sure she wanted to come to their attention, but at the same time, if it was a bigger organization, she might be able to get lost in it. Here, she was under Sarkin's gaze all the time. If she was taken into a large syndicate, she'd have room to breathe again. Maybe even enough room to make something better. Qi'ra pulled her mind away from optimistic thoughts. The only thing that mattered was opportunity.

"Fine," Sarkin said, after a long moment that was laden with the potential for violence. Unlike Proxima, he knew when he was overmatched. "She's next to useless anyway."

He rummaged in his pocket until he came up with the transceiver that controlled Qi'ra's chip. He tossed it to Corynna, who picked it out of the air like she was a Coronet salamander catching flies. She opened the box and removed three credit chips from the stash. It was more than Sarkin had paid for Qi'ra in the first place, and enough that he would be able to save face and say that he had sold her. He put the credits in his pocket and glowered.

"If you thought I was harsh, girl, you have no idea what's coming," he said. "You'll wish you were back here soon enough."

Corynna ignored him, motioning for Qi'ra to precede her out of the room. From the corner of her eye, Qi'ra saw Salbee pick up the tray again, but didn't spare her another thought. Yes, the girl had done her best to help her, but

Qi'ra felt no gratitude or obligation. Better Salbee carry the damn tray than her. If the girl wanted out, she could find her own way.

⊖

This time, the craft that Qi'ra boarded was heading off the planet. She followed Corynna up the boarding ramp and sat down where she was told. There were no viewports in the passenger area, but Qi'ra could see out the front of the ship through the flight deck. The seat she was in was remarkably comfortable for a small vessel. She realized that the only cargo this ship ever transported was people, agents of Crimson Dawn, carrying out jobs and missions on behalf of the syndicate. The ship was almost luxurious, at least by Qi'ra's standards, except that it was really only big enough for six people, and she was person number seven.

No one spoke to her as the preflight was completed and the ship took off. They cleared Corellia's atmosphere, and Qi'ra couldn't take her eyes off the stars. Corynna was watching her, taking her measure as she gaped out the front viewport with undisguised wonder, but Qi'ra didn't really care. The ship jumped to hyperspace so smoothly that Qi'ra barely felt it. She didn't know what was coming or how she should prepare for it, but for just a moment, she let herself enjoy the view. She hated herself a little bit, but she couldn't help wondering if Han had been as happy as she was to finally see what stars looked like when they passed you by, faster than light.

Without meaning to, she slid her hand to just above her belt at her hip, where she'd managed to keep the dice. When she realized Corynna was watching her intently, she pulled her hand back, reluctant to show more in the way of sentiment than she already had.

"I'm not saving you," Corynna said. Qi'ra was not surprised to learn this. Corynna hadn't been afraid of anyone on Corellia, which meant she was either high up in the syndicate or protected by someone who was. "Crimson Dawn is not in the business of helping wayward girls. I bought you because I know my employer. I have served him for years, as his concierge, and I know his tastes. You might do well, you might be dead by the end of the week. It's really up to him."

Qi'ra knew Corynna wasn't waiting for an answer, so she didn't give one. She stopped looking out the viewport, though. The time for fancifulness was over. Corynna turned her attention to reading something on the datapad she now held in front of her. The concierge had a calculating look on her face. Qi'ra wondered if it was her natural expression or if the woman was always plotting. Then she wondered who she might be plotting against. It wasn't very long before the ship slid out of hyperspace.

"Beginning docking procedures," the pilot said from the flight deck. "Five minutes until hard seal."

The little ship flew into a loading bay, and exactly five minutes later, the ramp was deployed. Corynna wasted no time and was halfway disembarked while the exhaust was still hissing around her. Qi'ra followed as quickly as she could. Already she could see the difference between Crimson Dawn headquarters and everywhere else she'd ever been. The loading bay was immaculately clean, the deck polished to the point that it was almost reflective. The people wore somber but well-made clothes and moved about their jobs efficiently. No one flinched away from Corynna, even if she walked close to them.

An Imroosian girl met them just before they entered the lift that would take them to the habitation decks of the ship. She was tall and hairless, her skin a mottled gray that looked like chalk. Her dress was simple and elegant, and she moved with the grace of someone who had never learned to shrink away from a blow. She handed Corynna a data rod and took three back in return. Then she turned her gaze on Qi'ra, and looked deeply unimpressed.

"Have her cleaned up, Margo," Corynna said. "And she's chipped. Take care of it."

"Follow me," Margo ordered.

Qi'ra followed. All three of them entered the lift.

Corynna didn't look at Margo again, like Margo was beneath her notice. Margo didn't look at Qi'ra, either, presumably for the same reason. There was a strange glint in the Imroosian's eyes, that calculation again. Maybe that was just how everyone in Crimson Dawn looked: always ready to jump if the chance to squash someone else arose.

They took the lift up several floors but got off before Corynna did. Margo took Qi'ra to a small room, where Qi'ra washed up and dressed herself in a set of clothing similar to what the deck workers were wearing. The shoes were a bit too big, which Margo noticed immediately, replacing them with a more suitable pair.

"Wrist," said Margo tonelessly.

Qi'ra held out her hand and winced as Margo extracted the chip from beneath her skin. It didn't make her free, she knew. They hardly needed a chip to control her if they were on a yacht in the middle of space.

Margo gave her another once-over, this time seeming more satisfied with the results. Now that she was clean, Qi'ra could feel her bruises and split lip more acutely.

"Come," Margo said.

With no further conversation between them, Margo took Qi'ra back to the lift and they went farther up into the ship. When the doors opened to the highest level, Qi'ra didn't let her attention be drawn to any of the shiny objects in the room. She made herself focus on the man who stood waiting, Corynna beside him, an attentive expression on her face. This, at least, was someone who Corynna felt deserved her full attention. Qi'ra felt Margo straighten beside her. It was definitely time to be on guard.

The man was tall and dressed in a black suit that was tailored so sharply it cut through the extravagant décor of the room like a knife. He was quiet, somehow, too, with a gaze that seemed able to pierce skin and see right down to the nuts and bolts of what really made a person. His face was marked by strange lines, unlike anything Qi'ra had ever seen before. They seemed to ripple beneath his skin as he moved, and they all shifted as his face split into a smile.

"Oh, Corynna," he said. "She's wonderful."

"She's uncouth and she has no idea what's happening," Corynna said. She sneered dismissively, but her eyes flicked over Qi'ra again, reassessing now that her boss was impressed. "But I thought you might like her."

It was as though his whole focus had narrowed down to where Qi'ra stood. She fought to stay still, not to squirm under his surveillance, and he knew it. A wicked smile curved across his face.

"Leave us," he said, not looking anywhere else but at her.

Corynna and Margo swept out of the room, leaving Qi'ra alone with him.

"My name is Dryden Vos," he said, suddenly too amiable. "I run Crimson Dawn. I am not a man to cross. What's your name?"

"Qi'ra," she said, a hint of defiance in her tone.

"Qi'ra," he repeated, rolling the letters around in his mouth like he was the only one who ever said them properly. "I look forward to our time together."

For the rest of her life, she would always wonder what made her say what she said next, how it changed her path and tied her future inextricably to Crimson Dawn.

"Sarkin couldn't break me. Neither could Proxima." It was mostly bluster, and she had a feeling he could tell, but she still had *some* fight left in her.

"My dear, I don't have to break you." Vos spoke in an amused tone, but the lines on his face flared a brief and angry red. "I just have to beat you."

Qi'ra didn't know which definition of the word he meant, but she knew with absolute certainty that she was going to find out.

CHAPTER TEN

The first time Qi'ra tried to escape Crimson Dawn, it was mostly to see if she could. She knew it was a long shot. Dryden Vos traversed his corner of the galaxy in an expensive personal yacht called the *First Light* and rarely docked it anywhere long enough for a true escape. Her better shot was to steal a shuttle, even though that required getting through several layers of security.

She failed, of course, and she was punished. She had never felt so driven to independence before. Maybe it was being away from Corellia. On that planet, it had always felt like there was nowhere she could run to. Now she could see the vastness of the galaxy out of any viewport. Or maybe she was just being reckless. She couldn't seem to stop herself, no matter how dire the consequences were. She was beaten by some of Vos's guards—not even particularly important ones—and Margo wore a thoroughly unimpressed expression when she came to check Qi'ra's wounds.

The second time, several weeks into her stay on the *First Light*, she made it all the way to the turbolift before she was caught. The *First Light* was actually docked this time, a brief stopover for cargo sensitive enough that Vos didn't want it on a shuttle. One of the Hylobon guards—it was a while before she learned to tell them apart while they were wearing their helmets—was exiting the lift as she was trying to get on, and he recognized her. The second beating, administered by the guard who had caught her, was almost impersonal for all its hurt.

It was foolish to try, and still Qi'ra caught herself planning escapes all the time. Her tasks on board were not particularly engaging, and even when she was busy doing something like serving drinks or cleaning up after one of Vos's parties, she had plenty of time to think. Most of the people who worked in visible jobs on the *First Light* were free. Vos liked to hide ugly things away, and it didn't get much uglier than trafficking. Yet Qi'ra was repeatedly called to the upper decks of the ship and shown all the things she couldn't have. It was enough to make her *want*.

The third time, Qi'ra didn't make it more than three steps away from the tiny room where she was confined. She'd been aboard the *First Light* for almost two months at that point. Corynna oversaw her punishments when it came to infractions during her work or training on the ship, and the concierge was light on patience. It was almost like she hated being made to remember that Qi'ra existed, even though she had been the one to bring her on board. She was particularly vicious when Qi'ra had recently done something that earned Vos's praise, as if the concierge thought the former scrumrat was overstepping. The punishments were rarely physical, and usually took the form of more work or less food, both things that Qi'ra could deal with. This time, Qi'ra had been confined to her quarters for taking too long to replace empty bottles on the sideboard in Vos's office. No one would come looking for her until Corynna sent them to tell her the punishment was done. Qi'ra didn't realize that a guard had been posted until he shouted at her.

Later, she would wonder if it was surprise, frustration, or some combination of the two. The guard—a human male roughly half again as big as she was—was charging at her, an electrified baton brandished above his head. She ducked under the blow, and the guard was carried forward by his momentum so that he rolled over her hip and went sprawling to the floor. There was a sickening crack when he landed, his neck at an angle.

Qi'ra checked the corridor for witnesses, but there were none. She knew there were probably cameras somewhere, but it didn't matter. She drew close to the fallen guard and saw that he was still breathing. She took the baton out of his limp fingers, turned the setting up as high as it would go, and pressed it right against the base of his spine. His body flailed like a drowning fish, muscles spasming into a horrible rictus, and then stilled when she removed the electricity. He wasn't breathing anymore.

Qi'ra wanted to scream. The guard would have hurt her and so she had killed him, and it was all so pointless. She was still on the ship and she still had no way out of Crimson Dawn, or any destination if she managed to free herself. She went back to her room and waited for whatever fate Vos or Corynna decided she would get. It was hours before the door opened, and when it did, the person standing there was Ottilie, one of Vos's servers. She was a human only a few years older than Qi'ra. It was a test. Ottilie was an easy target. Vos wanted to know what she would do.

"How do you do it?" Qi'ra asked. She watched dispassionately as Ottilie set down the tray that contained her dinner. All of her fire was gone, channeled out through the baton and into the guard. "How do you put on that smile and act like you want to be here?"

"I do want to be here," Ottilie said. She sounded surprised that Qi'ra would think otherwise. "I serve drinks and I'm good at it. I don't want to do anything else. And I certainly don't want to *be* anywhere else. I'm safe here."

Qi'ra wondered how it could possibly be that easy, how she could put away her ambitions for freedom and power without killing the part of her that craved both. If she could live inside the cage until she found a way to break out of it.

If she had a choice, or if the only other option she had was pain.

It was a game, not an adventure. She had to play by the rules. Vos was the strongest player, and she gained nothing by opposing him. She couldn't get out, but she could go up. She looked at Ottilie, her pretty face and her carefully neutral expression. Qi'ra could do that, scrape herself clean of everything that got in her way. She had to. She was going to play to win.

"Thank you for bringing me my food," Qi'ra said.

Ottilie gave her a smile so easy, Qi'ra decided that the body must have been removed from the corridor before she could see it. Ottilie picked up the tray from breakfast and left Qi'ra alone to eat. The door didn't lock behind her when she left, but Qi'ra was no longer interested in leaving. Just as she was cleaning her plate, the door opened again. This time, it was Dryden Vos.

"I am a patient man, I think," Vos said instead of saying hello. Qi'ra looked up at him. The red striations on his face were pale, so he wasn't particularly angry with her. "But you have reached the end of my magnanimity."

"It won't happen again," Qi'ra said.

"Oh, but it will," Vos said. "Maybe not the escape part, but you *will* kill for me again, as often as I wish it."

Qi'ra swallowed hard. Now that she had time to think about it, the death she'd caused was starting to weigh on her.

"But the important part is that you've gotten all this foolishness out of your system," Vos continued. "You will move to better quarters and you will be acting like you belong here. You are not enslaved anymore."

Vos declared all of this like she had graduated or passed some kind of test, and maybe she had. Whatever she'd done in killing a man and then returning to face the consequences had convinced him that she was beaten. It was what he'd wanted in the first place, and Qi'ra couldn't believe she'd been stubborn enough not to give it to him immediately.

Qi'ra wondered what the guard's name was. She never did find out.

◡

She served drinks with a smile. She carried messages efficiently. She did whatever Corynna asked of her as soon as it was asked. She pretended not to notice when Margo put in extra effort to make herself more visible to Vos. She watched the concierge play her subordinates against each other, but didn't get involved in the intrigues. She became a model citizen, at least by Crimson Dawn standards. She was rarely called to the uppermost decks, but when she was, she could feel Vos's eyes burning into her. He was trying to puzzle her out, untrusting of his victory over her spirit.

A little more than a year after Lady Proxima had sold Qi'ra to Sarkin Enneb, Qi'ra was summoned to Dryden

Vos's office. She didn't know why he wanted to see her. She just knew she had to be prepared for anything.

When the turbolift doors opened, she saw only two people in the office. Vos sat behind his desk, and a nervous-looking Quarren stood across from him. There was a blaster on the desk between them. Qi'ra came into the room and stood on the same side of the desk as the Quarren.

"Kill him," Vos said.

The Quarren reacted instinctively, spraying dark black ink in Qi'ra's direction as he backpedaled away from her. It was the wrong direction to move. Qi'ra lunged immediately for the blaster, and even with ink all over the floor and dripping down her face, she was able to get a clean shot off right away. There was a solid thump as the Quarren dropped to the deck. And then the only sound Qi'ra could hear was the rapid thumping of her heart in her chest.

"Thank you, Qi'ra," Vos said.

The ink hadn't reached him, but he had a handkerchief out anyway. He extended it to her, and she took it. He pressed a button, and a hologram of Corynna appeared in front of him.

"Bring up a janitorial droid," Vos ordered. "And Margo, as well. I would like more than one witness."

Qi'ra returned the blaster to the desk. There was never a question of shooting Vos. She wouldn't make it off the ship alive. She would need a much, much better plan if that was her intent, and there was no reason to scheme right now. She was his now. This proved it.

Vos pulled a device out of his desk and used it to suck up some of the ink that had splattered on the surface. It wasn't a cleaning device as far as Qi'ra could tell. It had a well for liquids, where the ink ended up, and a needle at the other end. Vos stood up and made his way around the desk, stepping gingerly to avoid the mess. He held out a hand to her, clawed thumb extended, and she let him help her step over the pool of ink at her feet.

The lift opened, and Corynna and Margo stepped out. Corynna's expression was strained, like something she both wanted and did not want was about to happen. Margo's face was as blank as ever. Vos had not let go of her hand yet, and Qi'ra didn't try to pull back. He flipped her arm over, exposing the sensitive skin on the other side, and pressed the device against her, needle first.

It stung, and then it stung more as the needle pierced her skin over and over again. Eventually the pain faded into a steady buzz, something she could ignore as she watched what was happening with a strange sort of detachment. It was a tattoo, the symbol of Crimson Dawn. Vos was marking her, and he was using something from a man she'd killed to do it.

It was over as quickly as it had begun. Her skin was red where he'd gripped her and pale around the tattoo. The tattoo itself was black, stark against her skin. It was unmistakable and permanent.

"Well, now that that's taken care of," said Vos, like there wasn't a dead body still warm on his floor, "I have an assignment for you. Margo will tell you what to pack."

Qi'ra's wrist throbbed, but she met his gaze without flinching. Wherever he might send her, she was Crimson Dawn now, for good. That mattered. And she was going to make sure she mattered, too.

CHAPTER ELEVEN

The planet Qi'ra was assigned to was called Thorum, a minor planet in a minor system in the place where people didn't really know for sure if they were Mid Rim or Outer. It had mattered a little bit under the Republic but much less so under the Empire, and not at all when it came to Crimson Dawn. The syndicate didn't care where you were; they only cared if you were useful. Thorum was a jungle planet, tamed. The cities were muggy, but there was no overgrowth of invading plants. Forestry was orderly, and agriculture was almost sustainable. The planet's ecosystem would fail eventually, caving to the pressures of an increasingly demanding population, but for now everything was stable enough.

Qi'ra was taken to a large house on a quiet street. The speeders parked on the roadside were shiny, and the pavement was clean. Most reassuring of all, the sewer grates were absolutely tiny.

"They're expecting you," her escort said before slamming the door of their vehicle closed and driving off without her.

Qi'ra's new clothing was much too warm for the humid air, but she wasn't about to complain. Margo had outfitted her with several different sets of clothing and three different pairs of shoes, including the nicest pair of boots Qi'ra had ever worn. After so long wearing whatever she could scavenge or the wretched uniforms during her brief time with Sarkin, her new wardrobe seemed endless. Qi'ra had once been able to pretend she had credits to burn. She wasn't quite there yet, but she was starting to close in on it.

Qi'ra walked up to the door of the house and rang the chime. She waited only a few moments before a protocol droid opened it and waved her inside. The droid left her standing in the vestibule while it went to fetch its master, and Qi'ra took the opportunity to look around.

This house did not appear to be in a wealthy section of Thorum's main city, and yet it was beautifully appointed. The floors were clean white marble with inlaid borders near the walls. The walls themselves were painted a vibrant blue that made everything feel extra lively. There was artwork here and there, paintings and sculptures and the odd vase. Qi'ra wondered how much of it was stolen. And if this was only the entryway. The rest of the house probably wasn't as opulent, at least outside the public areas, but it spoke very highly of this crew that their front hallway was this nice.

Qi'ra had always had a rough idea of what Crimson Dawn was. It was a large, powerful criminal syndicate, one of several that had been operating throughout the galaxy, though it was one of the newer ones. The syndicates all had individual reputations, but with only the White Worms for comparison, Qi'ra hadn't really understood what it meant when people said that Crimson Dawn was poised and deadly, an iron fist in a velvet glove. In this glittering foyer, she thought she might be getting a clearer idea of it.

It wasn't the first time Qi'ra had been exposed to riches. During the competition for Head, she had been thrust into the wealthiest parts of Corellian society. It had grabbed her imagination more than once, a distraction of shiny things that pulled her off mission. She had learned to avoid those sparkling diversions and keep her focus. She had won that competition because Han had been too foolish to seize his own victory, but she didn't think that made her victory any less valid. Knowing and exploiting someone's weakness wasn't flashy, but it was an effective way of winning. She would do no less here.

"If you would come with me, please." The protocol droid had returned and was gesturing her to follow.

The droid led her down another elegant hallway. Qi'ra made sure to do just the right amount of dawdling and gawk-ing. They would expect something like awe from a girl like her, and she could use the time to case the house.

"I can show you where all the doors are, if you want to

see them," said a light voice beside her. In spite of herself, Qi'ra jumped. "And the windows, too, I guess. There's a cat door, but even you might have trouble with that."

The girl who had appeared so suddenly beside her could only be described as pale, but not in the way Qi'ra was accustomed to. On Corellia, pale meant you never saw the sun because you lived in the sewer or worked in a factory. Here on Thorum, pale meant you never *had* to go outside. Your life was rich enough without your having to work too hard to add to it. She wore a bright green scarf around her head, and her lips were painted the same shade. Her dress was simple yet elegant, green with gold highlights, and she wore a large round jewel on a necklace around her throat.

"I'm Trinia," the girl said. "You must be Qi'ra."

It was a bit unnerving that this girl seemed to know her thoughts. Qi'ra was used to being a challenge to read, but that had been when her colleagues were scrumrats and Grindalids who didn't express emotions with their faces the way that humans did. Clearly, she would have to practice.

"I am," she replied. "Are you in charge?"

"Oh, no," Trinia said. She giggled. "I just like meeting people. I think we'll get on well."

There was something about her that was deeply off-putting, but Qi'ra couldn't put her finger on exactly what it was. She wasn't used to people talking to her so directly. Perhaps that was it.

"No one ever likes me at first," Trinia said, pulling Qi'ra farther down the hall while the protocol droid spluttered. "Don't worry. We'll both get used to it."

A vaguely familiar voice came from the room they were entering: "Trinia, I have asked you repeatedly not to do that. It makes our guests nervous, and we want this one to fit in."

"Fine, Cerveteri, I'll try to be normal," Trinia said. "Until I get bored, anyway."

"Go be bored somewhere else." The speaker was older than both Qi'ra and Trinia, but not by much. She was tall, and her long blonde hair fell down her back in carefully arranged curls. Recognition was right on the edge of Qi'ra's mind. Trinia giggled again, distracting her, and skipped off down the hallway in the direction they'd come.

"You do eventually get used to her," Cerveteri continued. "I'm Cerveteri Slane, crew leader. Come here and let me have a look at you. I've been to Corellia. I know what to expect."

Qi'ra crossed the room as slowly as she thought she could get away with. She racked her brain, trying to remember where she'd seen this person before. Qi'ra remembered everyone from the jobs she'd done, mostly because she'd thought she was going to have to spend the rest of her life on Corellia avoiding them.

Cerveteri turned around, still backlit by the window but with her hair behind her, and Qi'ra's flash of recognition was finally enough to identify her. She hadn't been in curls before. Her hair had been done up in a tight bun, and pinned under an officious hat.

"Manager," Qi'ra said. She didn't make it a question, even though it was apparent that Manager Veteri had no more been a legitimate presence at the shipyard than Qi'ra had been.

It took a moment for Cerveteri to put the pieces together.

"The navigation control boards," she said, a grim smile on her face. Now that she was close enough, Qi'ra could make out her face quite clearly. She looked more relaxed when she wasn't undercover, but that was probably true for everyone. "You were the Worm plant."

"I was," Qi'ra said. "And if you weren't actually an Imperial lackey, then I suppose you were the person with the antigrav unit who beat us to the warehouse that night."

"Not by enough." There was an edge to Cerveteri's laugh. She felt she had been shown up that night, and Qi'ra would do well to remember it. "I barely made it out and I only got a fraction of what I was after. I knew that Sarkin would be running a job, and his target is always credits. I was planning to use him as a distraction."

"There was a lot of that going around that night," Qi'ra said. "My boss used the stormtroopers to thin out her crew. If I hadn't made you run, you would have been stuck with us, like we were all in a garbage compactor."

Cerveteri did not look happy about it. Qi'ra doubted

that she was telling the whole truth, but there had been so many double crosses the night of the Corellia job, Qi'ra didn't really care to learn about more of them.

"Well, I suppose it ended up well enough for both of us," Cerveteri said. "You got off of Corellia, and I got to prove myself in the field, even if my cut was a bit smaller than I hoped. I already know you're good at basic scams. Now we'll see how good you are at everything else."

It was a challenge and a warning, both. Qi'ra nodded.

"Excellent," Cerveteri said. "I'll get Trinia back to show you up to your room. She's probably eavesdropping in the hall anyway. She knows things, and I'm never entirely sure how. Watch yourself around her. You'll get your assignments tomorrow, when we have our briefing. In the meantime, you're free to explore the house and yard. I would only ask that you not pick any locks or leave. Until we've got you sorted out, of course."

As Qi'ra followed a chattering Trinia up the stairs to the living quarters, she noticed that some of the walls were swelling under the paint, discoloration showing in track marks hidden by the vibrancy of the pigment. It was a faint smell, but it was one Qi'ra had spent her whole life with. There was no mistaking it, whether in a boggy swamp or a humid jungle. Under all the gilt and pretty words, Crimson Dawn had just as much rot.

CHAPTER TWELVE

T here was a lot to be said for being a low-level member of Crimson Dawn. For the first time in her life, Qi'ra slept through the night uninterrupted by someone pawing at her or loud sewer noises. Not only did she have a bed to herself, she had the whole room. There was a dresser and a chair and a rug. Attached to her room was a small bathroom, which she also had solo access to. She'd never had so much space to herself.

She wasn't entirely sure how to fill it. She didn't have any credits of her own thanks to her time with Sarkin, so she couldn't buy new items, and even if she'd had credits, she had no idea how to decorate a room. She liked it the way it was, though she'd never had strong feelings about paint color or curtain fabric before. The light green walls were offset by the deep purple of the chair. The bed was sturdy and so wide that she couldn't reach both sides of it at the same time. Her blanket was warm and her pillow was soft. It was much more than she'd ever thought she might have.

Qi'ra had spent most of her time alone since coming to the house. The bulk of the crew was off on some mission or other, and Cerveteri wasn't one to socialize, so Qi'ra decided to teach herself the basics of slicing while she waited. She found necessary materials in one of the workrooms on the main floor, and since no one told her to stop, she didn't. The house also had a cook and a housekeeper, as well as a small army of droids for cleaning and general operations. There was nothing in the way of visible security measures, but Qi'ra knew there would be cameras and sensors all over the place, and she thought the housekeeper looked a little too burly to have spent all her time doing the laundry. Speaking of laundry, she needed to acquire a lighter set of clothing. The items Margo had given her were a touch too warm for this environment, and Qi'ra wondered if she'd done it on purpose.

"I can take you shopping, if you like," said Trinia, appearing in the doorway.

There was a safe at the bottom of the dresser that was keyed to Qi'ra's handprint. All it held at the moment were Han's dice, because Qi'ra didn't have anything besides them that was valuable enough. Nothing in the room was secured. As a general rule, no one entered someone else's room without knocking, but Trinia liked to be a surprise.

"Shopping for what?" Qi'ra asked.

"New clothes, of course. Or pillows, I guess," Trinia said. "You've only got two, and neither of them are pretty."

The idea of buying another pillow because it was pretty seemed ridiculous.

"I suppose you've only got one head," Trinia said. "For now, at least."

She cocked her own head sideways, staring at Qi'ra like the second head might appear at any time and then the extra pillows would be justified.

"Did you need something?" Qi'ra asked.

"Oh, yes," Trinia said. "That. Cerveteri said that the others will be back in time for dinner."

"Thank you," said Qi'ra as politely as she could while still implying that she wanted to be left alone. She knew it would be a good idea to try to fit in, but Trinia made it difficult to want to open up.

Trinia took the hint and left. This time, Qi'ra shut the door, though she didn't activate the lock. She'd only been part of Crimson Dawn for a short time, but she could already feel herself softening. The bed was too comfortable and the house too secure. There was nothing to worry about, and so the parts of her brain that used to worry now did things like wonder if Trinia had a point about the pillows. Hopefully meeting the rest of the crew would change that. Every group of criminals was, by nature, a competition. Qi'ra would get her edge back as soon as she was part of the action again.

Despite its vastly better trappings, Cerveteri's crew functioned much the same way the Worms had. Cerveteri was basically Head. She received orders and handed out assignments—loan collection and protection payments mostly, though there were hints of more elaborate scams that Qi'ra didn't bother ferreting out yet—selecting each crew based on capability and what the job required. Above her were more senior members of Crimson Dawn. Like the Grindalids, it was probably better for Qi'ra if she spent as little time as possible coming to their attention. She might want to rise up in the ranks eventually, but right now she needed to get the lay of the land, and that meant sitting back, doing her job, and learning everything she could.

She heard noise in the hallway—several doors opening and closing, and bits and pieces of conversation over the tromp of at least a dozen feet. Her new crew was back. She wondered if they had been told she was there, or if she would be a surprise when dinner was served. It didn't really matter. Years of watching scrumrats engage in power struggles over food had made her an expert in reading people when it came to how they ate. Even if they were prepared for her, she would have an unexpected angle to work.

Qi'ra waited until it was a bit quieter before slipping out of her room and heading for the back staircase. Her boots made no noise on the rug. She'd left her coat in her room, which was a difficult choice for her. She didn't want to appear a grasping backwater thief, and she knew if she showed up to dinner in all of her clothes, that was what she'd look like. She felt exposed in just her red shirt, leggings, and skirt, but at least she wasn't cold. Thorum was too temperate for that.

The dining room had been rearranged so that all the small tables were pushed together. A giant tablecloth covered the long surface, and the chairs had been placed on either side. There was one chair at the head of the table, obviously for Cerveteri, but not one at the foot. Qi'ra saw no indication of where she was supposed to sit, so she chose a seat on the far side from the door, in approximately the middle of the table. If it was an issue, she'd negotiate. She had a moment to get settled, and then the door opened again.

There were about a dozen of them, from Qi'ra's quick count. Mostly human, but with a couple of Twi'leks and Rodians, what looked to be a Mon Calamari, and a Zabrak. Trinia was chatting with one of the Twi'leks, and Cerveteri brought up the rear. She took her seat and the others selected theirs, seemingly at random. Cerveteri cleared her throat and everyone's attention turned to her immediately.

"Everyone, as you've heard, we have a new addition," she said. "This is Qi'ra. We're still figuring out where she'll fit in, but I can personally attest to her skills."

She said it without so much as blinking, but she tightened

her fingers and wrinkled the tablecloth, which Qi'ra didn't miss.

"She is also vouched for, and you know how selective our superiors are," Cerveteri continued. "There's no point in introducing everyone at once because you'll just forget the names, but please feel free to talk as we eat dinner."

Qi'ra had never forgotten a list of anything, and she doubted that was an uncommon skill here. Cerveteri seemed determined to make the house feel like it wasn't the center of a criminal operation, for some reason. Qi'ra would play along.

Two droids came in with a selection of platters. The idea of serving herself and taking as much as she wanted was still new to Qi'ra. She wasn't quite able to eat a plateful of food without paying for it later, but her stomach was usually strong enough unless she ate something new or unexpected. Soon she'd be able to eat whatever she wanted. For now, she avoided the richer-looking items and reluctantly steered clear of the local spices, even though everything smelled fantastic. She'd regret it later if she indulged.

One of the human girls, Myem, was telling Cerveteri about the mission, but she was just too far away for Qi'ra to overhear without looking like she was trying. Instead, Qi'ra focused on the people who were sitting closer to her. Immediately across from her was Noyio, another human, whose black hair was cropped short. She had several rings in her left ear, each one pierced through the cartilage to highlight the shape. Thallia, the Mon Calamari, was talking to her about tattoos, advising the human girl on what color ink she should get based on Thallia's favorite colors. Not exactly a useful conversation.

The scrumrats hadn't talked much at meals. There was too much focus on getting food in their stomachs before someone else took it away. Qi'ra had to force herself to eat slowly. Two of the boys, one human and one Twi'lek, were engaged in a mock battle over the last dinner roll at their end of the table. Qi'ra felt her heart race as she watched them. She knew it was just in fun, but she had seen plenty of fights that looked like this one end in actual bloodshed.

A voice cut through Qi'ra's reverie: "Didn't you have siblings?" The Zabrak, Hilst, was talking to her. "You're staring like you've never eaten with other people before."

"I didn't, no," Qi'ra said. It was the truth, and if her new comrades believed that was the reason she was a little strange, then so much the better.

"You'll get used to it," Hilst said. "Uedan noodles?"

Qi'ra's plate was already too full, but she took a few of the fat noodles out of the offered bowl before Hilst passed it back down the table. The noodles were soft and warm. She ate them one at a time. It was interesting to enjoy the flavor of something and know that if she wanted to, she could simply put more of it on her plate.

Myem was still talking, but Qi'ra noticed that Cerveteri wasn't giving the girl her full attention. She was watching the others as surreptitiously as Qi'ra was trying to. At first Qi'ra wondered if she was checking them over, making sure they were all right after their mission, but then she realized that Cerveteri didn't care, as long as the mission was successful. No, she was watching for the same reason Qi'ra was. She was tracing the threads of conversation between speakers, determining who was in control and who was just along for the ride.

If she trusted these people, she wouldn't have to do that. She'd already know who worked well together and who was friends with whom. Qi'ra realized that Cerveteri was looking for cracks, any friendship that was on the rocks or any relationship that was going through a rough patch. If she could find a vulnerable point, she could exploit it. It was exactly what Qi'ra would have done in Cerveteri's position.

There was the edge that Qi'ra had been missing. Just like that, her sense of security was gone and her instincts were all piqued. This was how she liked to operate, sharp and precise. She would put up a front, she decided, a shy loner who was uncertain. It was just close enough to the truth to be useful, and far enough away that it wouldn't be dangerous. When it was time for the real Qi'ra to come out, no one would be ready for her.

CHAPTER THIRTEEN

C alda was the largest city on Thorum and it seethed with commerce. The wealthiest businesspeople didn't live there. They kept decadent apartments in the city for work purposes but actually lived in extravagant houses to the north, where a vast network of rivers kept things a bit cooler. The people who lived in the city itself were either poor or desperately trying to get rich enough to move north. The overseers had a tremendous amount of power, but only when the bosses were away.

Dozens of ships came in and out of the spaceport every hour. Under the Empire, Thorum's rate of exportation had increased, and a whole crop of new industries had grown up in the boom. Crimson Dawn wasn't interested in cutting down trees or couriering grain off-planet. They were on Thorum for the protection racket.

As more new businesses sprouted up, those who were most established tried to prune them back. Enforcement gangs and intimidation tactics seemed to be the favored practices, and Crimson Dawn had slid right in. They provided security for the lower end businesses, for a fee, and since there were a lot of them, Crimson Dawn was doing pretty well.

It was Cerveteri's job to ensure that collections were made on time. Most companies sent representatives directly to the house with their payment, but there was always somebody who was short, or someone who thought they could get away with skimming off the top. That was where the rest of Cerveteri's gang came in.

Qi'ra set out with Myem and Qorsha, one of the Rodians, to collect on an up-and-coming pulp enterprise whose owner had failed to appear at the appropriate time. They met Eleera a few blocks over as the Twi'lek was coming out of a café.

"I'm coming with you," she said shortly.

Neither Myem nor Qorsha complained. The two were mostly there to provide muscle, and Qi'ra had been a little nervous about leading a job so early. It felt a bit like Cerveteri was setting her up to fail. Eleera was the sort of person who looked slight and unthreatening, but Qi'ra could see the power in her arms and recognized the telltale signs of several knives shoved into her bodysuit.

"We're happy to have you," Qi'ra said, flashing a hesitant smile she didn't feel. Better that Eleera think she was nervous right away than discover it later.

Eleera made a short noise and didn't answer. The four of them continued on their way. Qorsha and Myem chatted quietly as they walked. Qi'ra had taught herself to understand Huttese since the job on Corellia. She hadn't liked that Han could speak to Tsuulo and she couldn't. She didn't tell anyone, and she still couldn't speak it very well because she didn't have practice making the sounds, but she understood it well enough. Qorsha was talking about some new blaster rifle he wanted, while Myem argued in favor of the reliability of the ones they already had, and saving their money for better things.

Eleera commanded a great deal of attention as they made their way through the streets. Twi'leks were common on Thorum, but Eleera's olive skin and tendency to wear bright colors reminiscent of a poisonous insect set her apart. She stuck out quite a bit, especially under an Empire that wanted everyone to forget the political powerhouse the Twi'lek people had been in the Clone Wars. She also made no attempt to conceal her disdain for everyone around her, or to hide the muscles in her arms if anyone got close enough to see them. Her confidence wasn't just in her looks. She clearly knew she could handle anyone who tried to attack her physically, as well.

Qi'ra didn't know if she'd ever be that strong. Her tactic had always been surprise, whether that was a language no one knew she spoke or a hideout in a part of town that no one liked. Eleera was terse and solitary, but she was loyal to Crimson Dawn. Qi'ra would never trust her, but she trusted her more than she trusted Cerveteri Slane.

"You know how to fight," Eleera said after a few blocks. It wasn't a question.

"Not really," Qi'ra said. "One of my friends had her own style of fighting and she would practice it, but I am more of a scrapper."

Eleera gave her a measuring look.

"No, you're not," she said.

Qi'ra gave a short laugh.

"You fight with everything, not just your fists or a weapon," Eleera said. "And you fight to win."

"I'm still alive, aren't I?" Qi'ra returned.

"I can see that," Eleera said. "If you ever want to learn about vibroblades, I am sure we can come to some kind of arrangement."

She said nothing further, and Qi'ra was left to wonder what sort of arrangement the Twi'lek would accept. She still had no money, and there weren't very many things she was willing to teach in return.

Myem and Qorsha had turned into a narrow alley, and waited for them in front of a nondescript door. At Eleera's nod, Qorsha rang the chime. The proprietor did not keep them waiting.

"Myem, my friend," said a human man with stooped

shoulders. He was sweating profusely, even though it wasn't that hot out and Qi'ra could feel the blast of cold air coming from inside the shop. "Please, please, come in."

The four of them followed him inside. Qi'ra automatically scanned for traps. It was not unheard of for a mark on Corellia to kill whatever kids Proxima sent to collect, and hope that no more came. She realized that this would not be the case today, though. There were too many witnesses, and the four of them were just too strong to confront.

"You're late, Tobin," Myem said. "So it really doesn't matter if we're friends or not. Cerveteri doesn't have that much patience."

"I was on my way over this morning," Tobin said, despite a total lack of evidence to the fact. "We had a shipment arrive late."

"And your comms were broken?" Eleera asked. Her voice was sweet and Tobin shuddered.

"Uh, no," Tobin said. "I, uh—"

"Just get the credits, Tobin," Myem advised. "Eleera's not much more patient than Cerveteri is."

Qorsha laughed and said in Huttese, "Probably even less." Neither Eleera nor Tobin looked like they understood him, but it was not the sort of laugh that lessened the tension. Tobin fumbled through his desk, and Qi'ra knew he was trying to buy time while he thought about where he was going to get money from.

"You should fire your secretary," Qi'ra said. Her voice wasn't quite as sweet as Eleera's, but she had always tended toward cold anyway. "They left your desk a mess, and with the credits you'd save, maybe you wouldn't be late next time."

"My niece is my secretary," Tobin said without thinking.

"Is she now?" Qi'ra asked. "Maybe you should consider all of your options when it comes to paying your bills, then."

She was bluffing, of course. But Tobin didn't need to know that, and he froze as he pawed through a drawer. The look Eleera shot her was thoughtful and approving.

"The credits, Tobin," Eleera prompted.

With a flurry of hands, Tobin found the credits that were secreted around his office and added them to the pile on the desk. Qi'ra could see them well enough to count. He'd make the payment, but she had a feeling he was cleared out.

"There," Tobin said finally, placing all of the credits in a camtono and handing it over to Qorsha. "That's everything I owe you."

"Much appreciated," Qi'ra said. "I look forward to see-ing you next month."

Tobin's hard swallow confirmed her feeling. They'd wiped him out.

"Maybe we should just get it over with?" Eleera asked. She drew a thin silvery flamethrower from one of her many pockets. Its flame was so hot it burned blue.

"No," Tobin said. "No, we're expecting several—I mean there's going to be a rush on—I mean—"

"Calm down, my friend," Myem said. "As long as you have the money, you don't have anything to worry about. And you've got a whole month to figure it out."

They left him in his office, looking overwhelmed and hopeless. Eleera had a definite bounce in her step as they walked back.

"Right for the throat," she said, nodding at Qi'ra. "Well done."

"You had him primed," Qi'ra pointed out. "I just pushed a little."

Eleera laughed and finally tucked the flamethrower back into her pocket.

"Do you think he'll run?" she asked Myem. "Or try?"

"He has nowhere to run," Myem said. "His whole family works for the business. He can't fire anyone because he already doesn't pay them. They're down to the wire."

"I thought pulp was supposed to be a good bet right now," said Qorsha in Huttese. Both Eleera and Qi'ra waited for the translation.

"Yeah, but his investments weren't good," Myem said. "He put too much company money in the wrong places."

"Our places?" Qi'ra asked. It would be very clever to get their marks from both sides.

"Of course." Myem laughed. "He didn't look closely

enough at the contract. Sometimes they do, and won't sign because they see the clause that says they aren't owed anything if the venture fails, but he didn't."

"Too much money, too fast," Eleera scoffed. "He forgot everything he learned coming up."

It was a lesson Qi'ra knew all too well. She'd seen it happen over and over again, and then it had happened to her. A canister of coaxium and the promise of a boy who'd always had stars in his eyes. It had been too easy to make the mistake, but the suffering after it had hardened her. She knew she wouldn't fall for something like that again, but she understood the temptation of things that seemed too good to be true.

"I'm glad I tagged along," Eleera said. "Cerveteri wanted you to flop, obviously, but you would have been fine if I hadn't been there. You didn't need me, but it was fun. We should definitely do it again sometime."

"There's collections every month," Qi'ra pointed out. "I'm sure we'll have the opportunity."

Eleera laughed, and this time Myem joined in, too. Qorsha made the rough barking noise that equaled laughter for a Rodian, and Qi'ra let them have another smile. She had learned a lot, and not just about how Crimson Dawn made money on Thorum. Eleera had Cerveteri's measure, too, and Myem and Qorsha were more concerned with hardware and bullying people than they were with advancement.

Someday she and Eleera might be adversaries, but for now they could work together. Sweet and cold was a good combination when it came to getting credits, especially when the mark knew that both concealed something else.

The Thorum crew was an odd mix. From what Qi'ra had been able to determine, the only two who had been recruited directly into Crimson Dawn were Cerveteri and, somehow, Trinia. The Rodians each had cousins in the organization, though they were unrelated. Hilst and Eleera had both come to the attention of Crimson Dawn lieutenants from the competitive fighting circuit—Hilst from logistics and accounting, Eleera from the ring. They had been sent to Thorum after a stint of rigging fights. Noyio had amused the Crimson Dawn pilot she'd highjacked enough that she hadn't been killed when they were nabbed, and Thallia had been "acquired" from a rival in much the same way as Qi'ra. The rest of them had stories that were variations on the same theme. All of them were on Thorum to prove something.

"Who's next?" Qi'ra asked. "Tobin can't be the only person late to pay."

Myem had a list of others who owed Crimson Dawn money, and Eleera made the selection.

"This is the third month in a row," she said, indicating the name. "Are we allowed to give a demonstration?"

"Cerveteri said it was up to us," Myem said. "So I'm thinking yes."

They didn't even go into the shop. Qorsha took a paint sprayer out of his bag and quickly sketched the familiar Crimson Dawn symbol on the front window. Inside, people seemed to realize what was happening, and Qi'ra could hear the commotion even from where she stood on the street outside. Myem had gone around the back. Eleera had her flamethrower in her hand again.

"Would you like to do the honors?" she asked, holding the contraption out to Qi'ra.

"Alley's clear," Myem said, returning. "Excellent job with the paint, Qorsha. You're really good at this."

Qorsha chattered his thanks, and Qi'ra took the flamethrower. The building was stone with glass windows, not exactly the first thing to burn in a fire. However, there was a large tree that grew in the center of the building and extended its canopy over the roof. She assumed it was a house symbol or some kind of conservation effort, but the important thing to her right now was that it was wood.

She aimed the flamethrower and shot three bursts of blue flame at the tree: one at the trunk near the roof and two into the leaves. Jungle damp or no, the flames caught immediately. It wasn't like electrocuting someone after incapacitating them by accident, nor was it like shooting a man without knowing anything about him, just because she was told to. This was about damage and fear. Qi'ra could understand those. She didn't mind inflicting them as much as she should.

She handed the flamethrower back to Eleera. They didn't stay around to watch the shop burn. They didn't have to. They could hear the crackle of flames and the shouts of people trying to escape for several blocks as they walked home.

CHAPTER FOURTEEN

After a succession of small jobs that essentially equated to running Cerveteri's errands, Qi'ra was finally given a real assignment more than a week after the fire. She hadn't let the time in between go to waste. Thallia was very open about her slicing skills, and even if she wasn't trying to teach, Qi'ra learned a lot. Eleera also made good on her offer of combat lessons, in return for Qi'ra's exhaustive description of how Grindalids had managed to take over the underbelly of a planet whose surface was deadly to them. Qi'ra was no stranger to bruises, but she didn't mind these ones as much. Like her new abilities with tech, they felt earned.

"It's not that I don't trust you," Cerveteri had said one morning when Qi'ra couldn't quite contain the huff of frustration at the inanity of her assignment for that day. "But you did start off rather aggressively."

Qi'ra didn't really care. She already knew Cerveteri didn't

like her, and Thorum was the best place she'd ever lived. There were three meals every day, her room and clothes were cleaned regularly, and she didn't have to worry too much about people stealing her things. She had received a portion of her first stipend the day after collections, along with a short note of commendation from whoever read Cerveteri's reports. Once, she would have hoarded those credits, or spent them on food and hoarded that. Now she could spend it on whatever she liked. Still not enough to burn, but enough to keep warm.

Hilst and Karil, a human boy who specialized in grifting, had taken her shopping. The Zabrak liked bright colors, and the human boy hated paying full price, so it was an interesting combination. Most of the items she ended up with were on the utilitarian end of fashion, but Karil talked her into a bright copper ring with a shiny blue stone. It was worthless and pointless, but it did make her happy.

"Also, if you ever punch someone with it, you'll draw blood," Karil said. That sealed the deal, as far as Qi'ra was concerned.

Today, Qi'ra and Lopie, the other slicer, were on their way to the local outpost of the Banking Clan. The clan had fared rather dramatically during the Clone Wars, and eventually there had been a significant leadership change, and now the Imperials were in charge. The current version of the Banking Clan was, however, a bit less centralized, which allowed them some flexibility when it came to investments. It also meant that the droids that were responsible for their communications were slightly more vulnerable, and that was what drew Crimson Dawn's attention.

Both Qi'ra and Lopie were dressed in jumpsuits that would let them fit right in with the myriad tech workers who filed into the Banking Clan compound every morning. The suits were gray and tedious, but they did have a lot of pockets. Qi'ra's were filled with blank code cards that Lopie could encrypt however he needed to. Lopie's pockets contained all of his tools.

"How many doors do you think we'll need to open?" Qi'ra asked, genuinely curious. She expected the Banking Clan to be fastidious when it came to security but was sure seven different types of slicing equipment would be sufficient.

"It's for eventualities," the light green Twi'lek said. "The Banking Clan used to be pretty streamlined, but now they use tech from all over the galaxy. It's not always easy to jump from one to the other, but I can make it work if I have tools that work for all of them."

"That makes sense," Qi'ra admitted. Her slicing was slowly improving, thanks to help from Thallia, but it would never be her strong suit. She preferred to talk people into doing things for her.

Cerveteri strode into the room where they were prepping, dressed in a jumpsuit of her own. Lopie raised a brow but said nothing. Qi'ra felt that Cerveteri was expecting a challenge, and decided not to give her one.

"I'm going to accompany you," Cerveteri said after a significant pause. Qi'ra had always been good at waiting people out. "I think three of us will have a better chance."

It was a thin excuse. She wanted to see Qi'ra in action.

"The more, the merrier," Qi'ra said.

The three of them took the speeder across the city. The Banking Clan was headquartered about as far from the Crimson Dawn house as you could get without going into the trees. Qi'ra hadn't been looking forward to the walk. The humidity increased every day, and the jumpsuits weren't exactly breathable. Cerveteri's inclusion meant they got to take a vehicle, which was good news, even if the block-shaped speeders that were popular on Thorum—because cutting blades could be attached to the front if there was jungle to be cleared—moved at decidedly un-speeder-like speeds most of the time. If that was the only benefit Qi'ra got from Cerveteri's being there, it would be enough.

Cerveteri drove the way she did everything else: determinedly, and with no regard for others. She wove in and out of traffic gracelessly, speeding up and slowing down abruptly as she misread the shifts. Qi'ra entertained herself on the trip by imagining what Han would say if he were sitting next to Cerveteri.

It was easier to think about Han these days. Her anger

with him hadn't faded, but the more time she spent with the rest of her crew, the more she understood what Han had enjoyed about working with people. His charm and blasé attitude toward danger got him in trouble, but they also got him out. And he thought that was *fun*. Qi'ra hadn't had time for that sort of thing on Corellia, not with several dozen children scrambling for her position and no guarantee that there would be food the next day, but now she was starting to understand the appeal of it. Being surrounded by so many people her own age at the house and not being in direct competition with them for anything—yet—had helped her acclimatize to her new surroundings. There were plenty of examples to follow, and there was always company if she needed it. She wasn't about to let herself rely on any of them, but talking was nice.

Cerveteri parked the speeder a few blocks away from the headquarters. Most techs wouldn't be able to afford that sort of transportation, so it would attract less attention if they arrived on foot. Lopie slid into the crowd to steal an access card and then encrypted one for each of them from the blanks that Qi'ra carried. They had no issues getting through the doors or onto the lift down to the tech level. They were only in the entryway for a brief time, but it was long enough for Qi'ra to catch Cerveteri staring hungrily at what few clients had arrived early. It was obvious she'd rather be one of them than what she was.

"We'll have to split up," Lopie said. "Our source was able to find out that the droids would be here, but not their exact location. I have four possibilities."

He brought up a map of the facility on his wrist holo-projector, though he kept it small and shielded the light with his other hand.

"I'll take these two rooms. They're close together," he said, indicating two dots three levels down. "Qi'ra, you take this one, and Cerveteri the other."

Cerveteri clearly didn't like taking orders, but she had added herself to this mission late, so she couldn't really complain about it.

"Fine," she said. "Let's get a move on."

The trick with stealing protocol droids was convincing them to come with you. They usually had full run of wherever they were so that if someone on the far side of the building wanted something, they could answer. Getting them out of the building might require some creativity, but once she got around their restraining bolts, she hoped they would be open to polite suggestions in place of commands.

Qi'ra made her way to her assigned destination. It was good to be back at this: in the field, in a disguise, on a mission. The little jobs she'd been doing since she arrived were fine, but they didn't excite her like this one did. Even if Cerveteri didn't trust her to do it alone, she still got to do it, and that would be enough for her today. She took the

lift down two levels and then found the color-coded hallway that Lopie had showed her. She'd committed the map to
memory, so she didn't need to call it up again as she made
her way to the correct door.

The code that had gotten her into the building was not
good enough for the door. Lopie had expected that and
given her a booster that would cycle her card until it found
the sequence that opened the door. It would take a few minutes, but there was no one in the area, and Qi'ra didn't see
any signs of surveillance, so she decided to risk it. It took less
time than Lopie had suggested before the door whooshed
open and Qi'ra could slip inside.

The room was full of droids, but all of them looked to
be squat and designed for menial tasks. She had some time,
so she did a thorough scan of the room. None of the droids
were active, and none of them were protocol droids. It was
a little bit like standing in a graveyard, but after growing
up near so many discarded freighters, Qi'ra was used to the
feeling of forced obsolescence. When she was absolutely sure
there were no protocol droids to be found, she exited the
room and sealed the door.

No sooner had she set out for the elevator than an alarm
began to sound. A helpful display on the wall told her where
the alarm was originating from, and she realized quickly
that it was Cerveteri's target area. For a moment, she was
tempted to leave. She could go to the rendezvous point and

pretend that she hadn't known Cerveteri was in trouble. It would be a perfectly acceptable excuse. But if Cerveteri was caught, they might dissolve the crew or bring in someone Qi'ra didn't know at all. No, she was better off with Cerveteri in charge, even if that meant sticking her own neck out to save her.

She didn't go to the spot where Cerveteri was meant to be looking for the droids. If the gang leader were there, she'd already be caught and they wouldn't need the alarms. Instead, Qi'ra began checking all the doors between that point and their designated exit, looking for a place that was big enough to hide in. When she opened the fourth door to check, she was greeted with a blaster to the face.

"I say!" came the familiar stuffy tones of a protocol droid from just behind the blaster.

"Cerveteri, it's me," Qi'ra said. The blaster was lowered.

"What are you doing here?" Cerveteri whispered. She stepped back to let Qi'ra out of the hallway and into the room where she was hiding. Like the room Qi'ra had found earlier, there were plenty of droids present, but only four of them were protocol droids, and Cerveteri had them clustered by the door.

"I heard the alarms and came to see if I could help," Qi'ra said. "You got them this far. What happened?"

"They followed me easily enough," Cerveteri admitted, "but someone must have noticed they were gone. When the alarm sounded, they stopped listening to me and insisted that we wait."

The four droids that Cerveteri had found were active, milling around in the room. The escape route was still clear, but they would have to move quickly. Qi'ra had an idea so terrible, she would have happily told anyone who asked that it was Han's.

"Go and check the door," she told Cerveteri. "Make sure we've got a way out."

Cerveteri nodded, and moved before she realized that she was being ordered around by a subordinate. Qi'ra didn't give her a second look.

"Hello," she said. "I'm sorry for all the noise. It's been that kind of day."

"It always is," one of the droids said mournfully.

"Well, I understand not wanting to go back out there," Qi'ra continued. She looked over her shoulder and saw that Cerveteri was still occupied. "But I came to give you an important message."

"Oh?" a droid asked. "What is that?"

"My employer has been told that you are the finest protocol droids that the Banking Clan has to offer, and that you're being absolutely wasted here." She tried to sound like she believed what she was saying and not like she was just trying to manipulate the droids. She had learned about the concept of droid liberation during the competition for head scrumrat. She thought it was a ridiculous idea, but it had opened her eyes to the fact that droids were capable of wanting things and could therefore be bargained with. "You'd have much better circumstances and more interesting work."

"What an odd idea," said the droid. "Though, now that I've thought about it, we are rarely challenged by our current owners, and the maintenance protocols leave a great deal to be desired."

"Yes," Qi'ra said. Betterment was always a tempting target, which was why it was so easy to use. And compared to freedom, it was easier to sell because it was easier to believe in. "You can work the same place I do. It's a much better working environment and you'll even have spare time to do whatever you want. We just need a bit of information from you in return."

The droids looked at each other, eyes flashing as they communicated.

"We find your terms acceptable," the talkative droid declared. Qi'ra almost laughed at them. No emotions beyond programming, yet they were still as malleable as any other being. "Though it will facilitate our progress if you remove our restraining bolts."

As far as negotiations went, it was pretty fair. Qi'ra didn't mind removing the bolts and did so quickly enough. Each protocol droid reacted to the bolt coming off in a different way, but none of them looked like they were even thinking about running off on their own. You didn't need that sort of thing with a protocol droid, if you were careful. You just had to make it easy for them to keep their promises, and their programming did the rest.

"There you go," Qi'ra said, detaching the last one. "Now, follow me."

She led them over to the door. They didn't move as quickly as she would have liked, but they might still be able to make it to the extraction point.

"Are we clear?" she asked.

"Yes," Cerveteri replied. She looked at the droids, who were following at Qi'ra's heels. "How—"

"We don't have time," Qi'ra said. "Come on!"

She led the way down the corridor, the droids in a line behind her like ducklings and Cerveteri bringing up the rear. Lopie was waiting for them at the door.

"Good job!" he said.

"Thanks," Qi'ra said. "The guards are probably right behind us."

Lopie needed no further encouragement. He opened the external door and sent the signal. Moments later, a transport appeared out of the jungle, and they hustled the droids into it.

"What an exciting morning," one droid said as they all disappeared into the trees.

Cerveteri scowled, but Qi'ra had to agree.

CHAPTER FIFTEEN

Qi'ra never learned the entirety of what information the protocol droids possessed. She assumed
it was financial records, or perhaps names and
useful account numbers. It wasn't really her concern. Whoever Cerveteri took orders from was very happy with their
success, however, and sent the whole crew a bonus. Lopie
and Qi'ra each received a lavish gift, as well, given out by a
tight-lipped Cerveteri as she reported how pleased her boss
was with their accomplishment. She didn't mention if she
had received something similar.

Qi'ra had never owned a necklace before, and certainly
not something so fine. It was Crimson Dawn's symbol, of
course, but in gold. It hung around her neck on stiff black
leather, highlighting both her collarbones and the symbol
itself. Lopie's was a headband, slightly less ostentatious but
no less finely made, with the symbol resting between his
lekku. Qi'ra put hers directly into the safe in her dresser.

She wasn't sure where she would wear it. If she ever got to meet Cerveteri's superior, maybe. She could already imagine what Hilst would suggest she buy to wear with it.

In addition to the rewards, the gang was given a new job. Since all communication went through Cerveteri, it was she who briefed them on it. Qi'ra disliked getting information secondhand, not to mention there was no telling what Cerveteri might leave out, but she didn't really have a choice in the matter.

"As you know, Crimson Dawn is not the only operation on Thorum," Cerveteri began. "We don't share the territory with another syndicate, but there is a local criminal organization here. They call themselves the Hammers, and they mostly limit themselves to industrial operations."

Qi'ra had seen them in the streets and had dismissed them as a threat. There were a lot of them, but they were called the Hammers because that was the best weapon they could afford. They had very little tech, and only the highest-ranking members had blasters. They busted unions and shook down low-level politicians. Nothing major, and nothing that affected anyone off-world.

"Lately it has come to our attention that the Hammers have acquired a large number of ships," Cerveteri continued. "They're underbidding our partners on transport contracts, and that makes it difficult for our partners to pay us. Crimson Dawn has decided it's time to make our presence on Thorum official, and that means no competition."

"We don't have the numbers for head-to-head conflict." Olio was human and mostly muscle, but he did know how to plan fights, and he knew better than to plan ones he couldn't win. "Are they sending reinforcements?"

"No," Cerveteri said. "The Hammers have a large membership because they're just workers from the industrial sector. If we wipe them out, then there's no one to do the work. We are supposed to make sure they leave off-world concerns to us. They can even keep their little hammers, if they want."

"Sabotage?" Thallia and Lopie exchanged looks. Something on this scale would be a lot of fun for the slicers.

"Sabotage," Cerveteri confirmed. "Obviously you two will take point. I want you to figure out what kinds of ships they have, and what the weak points are."

Thallia opened her mouth to ask a question.

"And no explosions," Cerveteri said. Thallia wilted a little bit. "We want to take the ships, if we can, not blow them up."

Lopie bent his head toward Thallia and whispered something that made her perk up.

"The rest of you will be getting your assignments over the next few days," Cerveteri said. "So don't go on any adventures. This is a bigger play than usual, and I don't have to tell you what that means about the higher-ups being invested in what we're doing. Stick close to home until this is over and we've locked down Thorum for Crimson Dawn for good."

If it was supposed to be a motivational speech, it wasn't a very good one, but that didn't matter. The crew was riding high after their victory with the protocol droids, and waiting around a few days wasn't going to kill any of them.

Qi'ra was restless, though, so when Eleera sought her out the following afternoon, she was primed for some action.

"We'll just take a look," Eleera said, leading the way out of the house. "I don't want to trust old holos. Who knows what could change."

The two girls were dressed nondescriptly, which for Eleera meant a blue bodysuit instead of a black one. Qi'ra had new leggings and a tunic that were better suited to Thorum's climate, and a wide belt that she could tuck all sorts of things into, should the situation require it. Her hair was long enough that it got in her face, so she tied it up before they left.

It was an easy walk to the shipyard where the Hammers were keeping their nascent fleet. They took their time. Qi'ra could almost forget that she was working and pretend that she and Eleera were just out for a stroll, maybe going to a café or concert. It was normal, and the strangest part was that this version of normal felt less and less strange. Qi'ra had settled in, and for the first time in her life, she was growing because she wanted to, not because she was being forced in one direction by someone much stronger than she was.

As they got closer to the yard, the shops thinned out and the buildings became more residential. It was clear that people who lived in this part of town were, if not members of the Hammers themselves, supporters of them. That made Qi'ra a little uneasy. Sabotage in the middle of a stronghold was a totally different matter than sabotage on the sly. It would be much harder to escape if the streets were full of angry gang members. She could tell by the calculating looks that Eleera was casting that the Twi'lek felt the same way.

"Cerveteri might have mentioned this," she grumbled.

"She always thinks it's need-to-know," Qi'ra said.

"Well, one day that won't be good enough," Eleera said. "But I'm not going to be the one who pushes her."

Qi'ra could agree to that.

The fence around the yard was just wire, but it was clearly electrified. It was also two meters high. At least Qi'ra could see through it. On the other side were the ships. There were about forty of them, all boxy transports. They could carry a decent amount of cargo, but they weren't very pretty. Qi'ra thought Crimson Dawn might be better served by better ships, but of course if everything went well, they'd get some of these ships for free.

"I've seen enough," said Eleera after a few minutes. "Let's get out of here."

Qi'ra might have stayed to clock the guard rotation or see if there was a weak place in the fence, but she had to admit that Eleera was right. It was almost end of shift, and that meant the streets would be full as they walked home. That was good cover. Standing here when that shift arrived was not.

Cerveteri didn't say anything when they returned. Three days later, when she gave the full team briefing, she did mention the fence and the location of the yard, but quickly followed up that the slicers had already found a way to deal with it. Qi'ra was paired up with Noyio, one of two pilots who were part of the crew. Their job was to make sure that the best ship in the yard was taken, no matter what. The other pilot, Drex, was with his fellow Rodian for a similar job with the other target ship. Everyone else would take orders from the slicers once they got inside, and sabotage vessels as directed.

The only suitable time for an operation of this scale was after dark, so they waited until a night when all of Thorum's moons would be rising late. Qi'ra and Noyio were in black flight suits, which were not the most comfortable things to walk around in but would be useful once they were on board their assigned vessel. Thallia got them into the yard quickly, funneling half through a hole she sliced in the electrified fence and the others through an opening that Lopie had made. Once inside, they all split off.

Qi'ra could hear the soft jungle night noises, as well as the hum of the lights in the yard. Soon she heard the hiss of boarding ramps, too. Olio and Myem had been dispatched to the guard post, and from there would go on to the control room to take care of any stragglers. No alarm sounded, so they must have done their jobs well.

"Good, because I hate rushing through a takeoff," Noyio said. "I can do it, obviously, but flying isn't supposed to be rushed. You're supposed to get to know the ship a little, not just run off with her."

It was the most Han thing Qi'ra had heard anyone say in a while, and in spite of herself, she smiled. He would have loved this. The thrill of flying was always enough for him, but when you added in the excitement of a job, he was absolutely ready to go. Noyio appeared to be the same way. Maybe it was a pilot thing.

"This is us," Noyio said, pointing at the hull of a nearby ship. "Oh, hello, you beauty."

"Do you need a moment alone?" Qi'ra asked, the smile still in her voice.

"Nah, we're good." Noyio grinned at her. "Let's get on board, though. I want to see the flight panels."

Around them, the Hammers' ships were clicking and wheezing as Thallia and Lopie's sabotage was executed on the less useful vessels that weren't worth stealing. Qi'ra had to admit that she was missing the explosions, but she understood why they had to be quiet about it. Across the yard, an engine flared to life. Drex and Qorsha must have been ready to go.

"Always in a hurry," Noyio said, strapping herself into the pilot's seat. Qi'ra took the copilot's chair, even though she didn't know what to do. "Hit that orange switch."

She did, and then watched as Noyio brought the ship to life. If this was the best ship in the fleet, it wasn't saying much, but Qi'ra knew that only a little while ago, such a ship would have completely changed her life.

The engines came on and the ship rose into the sky. Outside, someone finally set off an alarm, and the lights began to flash red. They couldn't hear it from inside the ship, but Qi'ra knew that it would be deafening. Most of her team would have already been on their way out when the alarm sounded, headed to their escape routes. She wasn't too worried about them.

The ship lurched as Noyio turned on the maneuvering thrusters, and then they were off. Noyio flew low, almost clipping the tops of the trees. They had no lights on, not even in the cockpit. Noyio was flying by touch and sight in almost total blackness, using the lights of the city to navigate. It was like watching an artist. Qi'ra wondered if Han would have looked the same way.

"We should download the navigational data," Qi'ra said once Noyio had brought them down in one of the small hidden ports that Crimson Dawn had built in the jungle. It would be a while before someone came to get them.

"What?" Noyio said. "Why?"

"Did you have other plans?" Qi'ra asked. "Besides, knowing where these ships have been might be important. If the Hammers have managed to make deals off-world, we should know who with."

Noyio was a good pilot and loyal to Crimson Dawn. It hung there for a moment while Qi'ra wondered how open Noyio was to going off book during one of Cerveteri's plans.

"All right," Noyio said. "Let's do it."

Qi'ra still had a few datacards from the droid operation in her pockets, so they loaded the records onto them. They watched the screen as the data flashed by, until they both saw something at the same time.

"Wait, that's—" Noyio said.

"Yes," Qi'ra agreed. "Yes, it is."

The Karthakk sector wasn't large or particularly profitable, but it *was* firmly under Crimson Dawn control. No local gang should have a basic map of it, let alone a detailed depiction of the hyperspace routes.

Qi'ra would probably have to go through Cerveteri to deliver this information, trusting her to pass it along the chain of command, but she almost didn't care. She'd make sure she got credit for it. Someone in Crimson Dawn was definitely going to be interested in this data. And in how the Hammers had managed to make a contact right in the middle of Crimson Dawn territory.

CHAPTER SIXTEEN

A team from Crimson Dawn arrived two days after the job, and Cerveteri was furious about it. Qi'ra had seen fury before. Lady Proxima was angry most of the time. Lady Proxima was also confined to a pool of water in the sewer, and while her species had a track record of inevitability when it came to revenge, it was still possible to run from her. Cerveteri's anger was hot and immediate and, most important, close by. The fact that she had been supplanted by senior members of the syndicate took away another chance to prove herself and earn full membership in Crimson Dawn. She was unable to argue with orders, though, and when informed that she was no longer in charge of the retributory strike against the Hammers, Cerveteri had no choice but to hand over leadership gracefully.

The Crimson Dawn team was led by a Mizi woman, a species Qi'ra had heard of but never seen before. The Mizi was tall and slender but clearly not fragile. Her long red limbs let her cover ground and reach for things in an uncanny manner. She wore bright colors but didn't look ridiculous in them. She took over operations smoothly and without sparing a single thought for what Cerveteri might be feeling, making it very obvious that she didn't care.

Qi'ra immediately gained a new appreciation for the organization of her Crimson Dawn crew. A demoted Grindalid or slighted Worm could retaliate against any kid and never be blamed for it. Qi'ra had done it more than once herself, most notably with Ema and the hounds. No one cared because none of them mattered. But here, on Thorum, they were more than allies with each other. They were, as hard as it was for Qi'ra to admit it, *friends*. There were people who would care if Qi'ra was hurt and who would be angry if Cerveteri went after her. The very bonds that Qi'ra had feared forming now worked in her favor, and all Cerveteri could do was accidentally spill water on her at dinner.

The Mizi worked quickly, and her team had a name and a place for the crew to infiltrate soon after they arrived. She called them together, the dining room being the only place big enough for everyone to gather, and laid out the plan.

"I like a loud operation," she started, "but this calls for a bit of finesse. The Hammers have made contacts in Crimson Dawn territory off-world, and you all know that this can't be allowed to continue. You've already taken their ships, so they know that Crimson Dawn has them in its sights. They'll be nervous, running scared. And we're going to run them down."

A projection of various faces and names appeared. Each was a member of the Hammers or close family. Qi'ra committed them all to memory automatically, and knew that everyone else in the room could probably do the same.

"We're going to infiltrate the gang," the Mizi continued. "Olio and Thallia will go in as low-level recruits. We'll place you in jobs where they'll invite you in. You'll familiarize yourselves with the habits of the people in this file, and be able to find them any time of day. Qi'ra will go in at the top, as a buyer, and see if she can identify how exactly the Hammers landed this deal in the first place."

"Qi'ra alone?" Cerveteri asked.

"Yes," the Mizi said, her tone cool. "Qi'ra has been here the shortest amount of time and is the least likely to be recognized. She has proved herself more than capable so far, and she is the reason we know about this at all."

Qi'ra shifted uncomfortably. Everyone knew it, but it was another thing to hear someone say it out loud.

"Once Qi'ra is finished, we'll dispatch teams based on Olio and Thallia's intel," the Mizi went on. "They will eliminate the targets, and that will be the end of it."

"There's no fear of reprisal?" Qi'ra asked.

"Not this time," the Mizi said. "This isn't two city gangs, remember. We are Crimson Dawn. The Hammers are workers first, and essential to Thorum's economy. They won't fight back, and we profit if they survive to keep doing their jobs. Crimson Dawn will probably end up hiring them, to be perfectly honest, and they'll forget their old bosses. You know that."

Qi'ra never forgot anything, but the first part was true enough.

"Right," said the Mizi, pointing to her team and the three crew members she'd named. "We've got work to do. The rest of you, carry on like normal, but stay away from anything too flashy. And no scrapping with the Hammers unless it can't be avoided."

Everyone but Qi'ra, Thallia, and Olio muttered their assent, Cerveteri obviously choking on hers, and filed out of the room. Once they were cleared out, the Mizi leaned against the table.

"I've brought my own slicer to get you all fake chain codes," she said. "It's not that I don't trust you, it's just that I like my own work and this style won't be traced back to you. Thallia, Olio, here are yours, along with your work orders and your new apartment."

The two stepped forward and took the forged bundles. Thallia scowled when she saw her name, but Olio only laughed and poked her shoulder.

"Congratulations on your wedding," the Mizi said dryly. "Newlyweds are always more appealing to recruiters, you know that. You wouldn't believe who I've had to pretend to be married to."

Thallia looked slightly mollified.

"My slicer will get the pair of you settled in," the Mizi said. "Qi'ra, you and I need to talk."

They set off to work out the final details for their covers, and Qi'ra sat down in the chair the Mizi pointed her to.

"Vos thinks you can do this, so I think you can do this," she said. "But have you ever done anything like it before?"

"Yes," Qi'ra said shortly. When Qi'ra had competed for Head in the White Worms, she'd had to infiltrate the upper class of Corellia. She knew the working-class people on Thorum would be awed by any persona that had enough credits attached to it.

"Good," the Mizi said. "We'll need to get you outfitted. No one's going to believe you have enough money to buy the Hammers if you look like that. Being small and vulnerable is a good tactic for a lot of things, but you're going to need to run this like you own it."

Qi'ra straightened her shoulders. The Mizi looked at her appraisingly.

"Have you ever even had a professional haircut?"

⊜

Elesa Norre was a wealthy grain buyer from Galara, a distant but reasonably wealthy planet in the Mid Rim. Her shoulder-length brown hair was always done up in some kind of braid, and her makeup was always immaculate, even in the jungle. She dressed with an effortless sort of style and dared anyone to question her about it. She made up for her lack of height by being absolutely unmovable when it came to negotiation. She didn't even travel with guards, preferring her own delicate blaster and the strength of her reputation.

Qi'ra had never felt more intimidating in her life. It was almost magical, stepping into Elesa's skin. She was entirely a construct, invented by the Mizi and made real by a slicer, but Qi'ra felt strangely powerful in the role.

She exuded power, too, if the reaction of the Hammer secretary was anything to go by. When she arrived at the office—unannounced, of course—she was shown immediately to the nicest sitting room and given some of the local iced fruit to drink. The poor girl apologized profusely for the time it was taking her employers to arrive, but Qi'ra didn't even look at her.

The head of the Hammers had been in lumber before he was head of a gang, and it showed in his muscles. The trees on Thorum were mostly felled and hauled by droids, but a common cost-cutting method was to use living labor, and that was clearly how Dennet Clyde had made his name. As gang leader, he was intimidating—or he would have been if Qi'ra hadn't known that Thallia had already pinned down his whole schedule.

"My lady, I apologize for my tardiness," Clyde said. "Our appointment must have been erased somehow."

The secretary turned white as a sheet, and Qi'ra felt a surge of anger toward this man who would so easily turn the blame to someone who couldn't possibly fight back.

"I like to be a surprise," Qi'ra told him, her accent as polished as it had ever been. "I don't make appointments."

"Well, then," Clyde stumbled, clearly having expected the conversation to go differently. "May I ask what you've come to talk about?"

"I want the delweed crop," Qi'ra said, naming a minor grain on Thorum that was popular off-world. "All of it."

"All of—" Clyde's surprise got away from him before he checked himself. "I see. Unfortunately, we have had some issues with our transports. I'm not sure we can guarantee a delivery."

"I don't want a delivery," Qi'ra scoffed. "I have ships of my own. I want the delweed, and I don't want to have to buy it through a broker."

"Of course, now," Clyde said. "That's the very foundation of our business. Direct sales. None of those payoffs. We're happy to work with you."

"Charmed," said Qi'ra, her tone dropping the temperature in the room by at least four degrees. "Have the sale drawn up. Do not bother trying to cheat me. I am well aware of the market price, both here and off-planet."

"Right away." Clyde turned to his secretary, but Qi'ra interrupted.

"I would appreciate if you did it yourself, Dennet Clyde," she said. The voice she had practiced left no room for argument, and he gave none. She smiled. "Direct sales, you know."

Clyde left the room, a bit shocked, and the secretary floated near the door.

"Oh, sit down," Qi'ra said. "I know he probably doesn't even give you a lunch break, and this fruit ice is very good. He can scramble for a bit while you sit here with me."

The girl sat down and took a glass off the tray Qi'ra's drink had come from. It shook a little in her hand, but after a few sips, she calmed down.

"I hope he's not your father or uncle," Qi'ra said.

"No." The girl almost snorted her juice out her nose. "Brother-in-law."

"Ugh, that's even worse," Qi'ra said. "Though I suppose at least you don't have to live with him."

"It's a good job," she said. "And he treats my sister well. They actually like each other. He's just different at work."

In Qi'ra's experience, no one was *that* different at work, but she'd leave the poor girl her illusions.

"It is nice to be served a drink by a person every now and again," Qi'ra said. "Most places use a droid, and I find that lacks the personal touch."

"Our droids are all offline," the secretary said. "There

was a data breach a few weeks ago, something to do with the Banking Clan. Nobody really explained it to me. I just got all the extra work."

"Typical," Qi'ra said, oozing sympathy. She'd been worried that a person would be harder to crack than a droid, but the secretary was very accommodating.

"They're all in the tech unit until we can check them over," she continued, blithely unaware of Qi'ra's interest. "Hopefully it won't take too much longer."

Qi'ra stood up, causing the secretary to jump to her feet, as well.

"I think I am done here for the day," Qi'ra announced. She set her glass down.

"My lady, Dennet will be back soon with the contract," the girl said. "He'll have it ready for signing, I'm sure."

Qi'ra looked at her. Once she would have given anything to be in her position. A stable job, a family. Probably a good home, though her sister's taste in men left a lot to be desired. Once she would have done everything in her power to become that girl. Now she only felt pity. It was a trap, just as sure as the White Worms were a trap. Crimson Dawn was probably a trap, too, but at least Qi'ra got to make some of her own rules. This girl was no doubt going to be replaced by a droid, and thrown away without a second thought.

"I'll come back tomorrow," Qi'ra said, readying herself to sweep from the room. "It won't hurt to make him sweat."

She left, already plotting her return, while the girl gaped like a fish. She was going to have to get closer to those droids. She knew she could get what she needed out of them. Then the hits could start, and Qi'ra would be back to being herself. She was a little bit surprised at how much she was looking forward to it.

CHAPTER SEVENTEEN

Qi'ra's ploy with Dennet Clyde worked out extremely well for everyone—except the Hammers, of course. Those on surveillance got to watch the gang leaders in near panic as Dennet tried to figure out who Elesa Norre was, why she had so much money, and why she hadn't stuck around to finish the deal. Several caches of credits and stock were uncovered, each marked on the Mizi's master copy of the map of the area. Everyone was in a good mood, except Cerveteri, who was forced to watch as more and more control was taken away from her.

It was only a matter of time before Cerveteri would snap, but Qi'ra couldn't help enjoying the moment. The other crew members were boisterous and cheerful, and even the Mizi's team cracked the occasional smile.

When the dust had settled a bit, Qi'ra donned the Elesa persona again and went back to finish the job. She strode into the office like she owned it, unannounced once again, and was pleased when the secretary actually smiled at her.

"Right this way, my lady," she said. "I'm sure my brother-in-law will be quite eager to speak with you again."

Qi'ra smirked and followed her to the familiar waiting room. She would bet a large number of credits that Clyde had been absolutely insufferable over the past few days, and he was definitely the type to take it out on his underlings. The secretary was probably looking forward to watching Qi'ra take him down a peg or two, and Qi'ra was more than happy to oblige.

"I apologize," the girl said after showing Qi'ra to her chair, "but the droids are back in operation, and I've been told not to leave my desk, so they will be in charge of your comfort until Dennet gets here."

"That is quite all right," Qi'ra said graciously. "I appreciate that you were able to give me a bit of your time."

The secretary was beaming when she left, decidedly lighter in her step. A droid came in shortly afterward with a tray. It looked at Qi'ra for a moment and then set a glass down within easy reach. Qi'ra didn't see a restraining bolt on its chest.

"You are Elesa Norre, I am told?" the droid asked.

"I am," Qi'ra said. "Thank you for the drink."

"You're welcome," the droid said. "Do you sometimes have another name?"

"I do," Qi'ra said cautiously.

"Someone matching your description came to the Banking Clan a few weeks ago and liberated some of the droids who worked there," the droid said. "One is curious to know why you are here now."

"I have many dealings," Qi'ra said. "And I believe in proper payment. Those droids had something I wanted, and I offered them something better than what they had. They received new identification codes and an exterior redesign so the Banking Clan can't claim them back. They work in my house now. We don't even put restraining bolts on them."

It wasn't her house, but the droids were grateful to her, so she felt that the lie was permissible. They did good work and were allowed to wander when they weren't busy. That was what they thought freedom was, and they seemed as content now as what droids were capable of.

"Do I have something you want?" the droid asked.

"You do." Qi'ra smiled. "I would like to know how the Hammers managed to secure a trade deal in the Karthakk sector."

"Ah," said the droid.

"I cannot promise you very much, but if you can get out of the office, I can take you to the others," Qi'ra offered. This wasn't exactly part of the mission, but if anyone asked, she'd say the droid had figured out what she was up to so she had to take it home to keep it quiet. She didn't waste things that were still useful.

"That is sufficient," the droid said. "I do not know the details, but I understand that someone from inside Crimson Dawn leaked the trade routes and suggested the Karthakk sector because it was of low importance. Not low enough, apparently."

Qi'ra blinked. The droid didn't know that *she* was Crimson Dawn, though it would figure it out pretty quickly if she took it home.

"Might I make a request?" the droid asked.

"Of course," Qi'ra said, her mind still spinning through her options.

"I would like the information regarding the Karthakk sector to be removed from my memory," the droid said. "I do not want to be completely wiped, just that information taken out. I do not wish to compromise anything before I am able to leave this place."

Qi'ra smiled. This was perfect. She didn't even feel that bad about knowing she'd shave out a little more of the droid's memory than it had asked for.

"Of course," Qi'ra said. "Now?"

The droid came within reach, and Qi'ra quickly deactivated it. Her basic slicing skills made it easy enough for her to do what the droid asked. She didn't pause before she continued to work, wiping the last few moments of its memory, erasing all knowledge the droid had about her and their conversation, including all information about Qi'ra's previous dealings with protocol droids. It was more than the droid wanted removed, but Qi'ra didn't hesitate once she was granted access to the programming. She wouldn't risk the job for a droid when she could simply erase the knowledge.

"My lady. I am so pleased to see you again." Dennet Clyde, red in the face and puffing for breath, came through the door. He paused, looking at the inactive droid that stood in front of her. "Is there something wrong with the droid? They have had strange malfunctions lately."

"It kept repeating the same question over and over," Qi'ra said. "I turned it off because it was getting on my nerves."

"My cousin bought them secondhand," Clyde said, shifting the blame again. "They have been nothing but a headache ever since."

"I didn't come here to talk about your family or your droids," Qi'ra said, brushing off his obsequious behavior. "Do you have the contract or not?"

Clyde seemed to be wrestling with what passed for his conscience but eventually set down the contract for her to read and sign.

"I must warn you that Crimson Dawn operates in that area," he said. "We will not be in a position to help you once you leave Thorum or replace anything that gets, er, lost."

"Yes, I can read that," Qi'ra said in a bored tone. "Did

you think I wouldn't do my homework before I came? Which broker do you think I was trying to avoid?"

That seemed to settle him down a bit, and he let her read the rest of the contract in peace. It was pretty standard. He wasn't even trying to cheat her. The Hammers might very well price themselves out of the organized crime business on their own in a few years, but Crimson Dawn wasn't going to be patient about it.

She signed and authenticated the contracts—meaningless, since her name was a fake—and pointedly avoided him when he tried to shake her hand. He stood awkwardly as she rose to her feet.

"The credits will be transferred in a few hours," she said. "There's no institution on this planet big enough for the sum, and I certainly wasn't going to carry it with me."

"We look forward to working with you," Clyde said.

She narrowed her eyes at him, and he took a step backward.

"Yes, I suppose you do," she said. "I will be in touch."

Qi'ra left the office, offering a small wink to the secretary as she passed by her desk. She walked to the apartment that Elesa Norre was renting and carefully shed the identity. It was almost a relief to put her own clothes back on. She sealed everything in a bag and then dumped it in the building's incinerator before letting herself out the maintenance entrance and heading for home.

The house was quiet when she arrived, but the Mizi was in one of the lounges, so Qi'ra went straight to her with her news. It was safer to tell her, a Crimson Dawn insider, and let her deal with it than it was to trust Cerveteri. There was no telling what *she* might do with the knowledge before she passed it up the chain. And if the leak was one of the crew members, then it made sense to go to outside help as quickly as possible.

"Qi'ra, you've returned," the Mizi said, lifting her glass in a toast. "Come, celebrate a job well done with me before your sniveling boss gets back and ruins the mood."

"Where is Cerveteri?" Qi'ra asked.

"Out with the hit squads," the Mizi said. "She said she wanted to make sure it was done properly, but I think she just wanted to yell at someone."

Qi'ra froze, the glass halfway to her lips. A horrible suspicion solidified in her chest, and she fought to keep her face or voice from giving away her feelings.

"The squads have gone out?" she asked.

"They started right after you left the office," the Mizi said. "Cerveteri reported that the funds cleared, so I gave the order."

"Look," Qi'ra said, trying to be polite with the woman while observing the Mizi's preference to remain unnamed. "Someone inside Crimson Dawn leaked the trade routes to the Hammers and told them which one to target."

The Mizi sat up and reached for her comlink, but Qi'ra knew it would be too late. Most of the crew had been cooped up for days and would have come out swinging. She knew how efficient they were. She'd helped make up the strike teams, based on who worked best together. And they were about to wipe out the evidence she needed.

"Dammit," the Mizi cursed after a few moments. "Dammit, they're already done."

"There's one person who wasn't on our hit list who might know something," Qi'ra said. "The secretary, Dennet Clyde's sister-in-law. She trusts me. Elesa. She might be able to tell us something."

It was a stretch of the truth—the secretary only knew something was up with the droids, not any of the important details—but Qi'ra would rather give up the girl than explain her proficiency with droids. She needed the Mizi to believe her about the leak without giving away too many of her own secrets.

"Dennet Clyde was killed by a bomb in his office," the Mizi said. "His secretary was collateral damage."

Qi'ra put her head in her hands, her mind whirling. Distantly, she knew that she should feel bad about the secretary, but at the moment all she could focus on was the inconvenience of her death. So far, only she and the Mizi knew there was a leak at all. The droid was wiped, and Qi'ra hadn't had time to tell anyone else. She didn't know if she could trust the Mizi to keep a secret this big, especially since someone high up in Crimson Dawn was the one issuing her orders. Qi'ra's mind locked on to that thought: the Mizi knew how to get in contact with Crimson Dawn via different channels than the one Cerveteri used.

"I can tell you're planning something," the Mizi said. "You'd better hurry. They'll be back soon."

"You need to tell whoever ordered you to do this job about the leak," Qi'ra said slowly. "If you tell them, you won't look like a suspect because you didn't try to hide it."

"You'll look like a suspect, Qi'ra," the Mizi reminded her. She didn't sound concerned about it.

"Yes," Qi'ra said. "Which will probably make whoever it really is get cocky and do something we can actually pin on them. Will your superior believe you if you tell them it wasn't me?"

"No," the Mizi admitted. She leaned back in her chair. Qi'ra took her relaxation as a good sign. "But he will take it under consideration if it's a convenient way to ferret out the truth."

"That's good enough for me," Qi'ra said.

The Mizi raised her glass in a mock toast and then drained it in a single draw. Qi'ra mirrored the toast, but not the drink. Her stomach was roiling too much to think about putting something in it.

"How did you find out, anyway?" the Mizi asked, a little bit too casually. "About the leak, I mean."

"The secretary," Qi'ra said without hesitation. She was going to need an ally going forward, especially if this went back to the heart of Crimson Dawn. She would be as honest as she could be with the Mizi for now and maybe the Mizi would give her a bit of cover. "She was very friendly to anyone who put Clyde in his place, and I did it right in front of her. That's why I thought she might know more, or be aware of something without realizing what she knew."

"They always ignore the girls in the back," the Mizi said, looking thoughtfully at her. "Right up until they can't."

Qi'ra didn't trust herself to reply, and the Mizi didn't seem to expect one anyway. They sat in silence until the front door crashed open and the first of the strike teams made their victorious entry. Qi'ra screwed on a smile and went out to celebrate with them. Strangely, it helped to think of Han. He would have liked this part, too, and never cared if there was something deeper going on, because it wasn't his problem yet. So she smiled, and she laughed, and she watched the other faces closely, to see if they were hiding anything beneath their mirth.

It did not escape her notice that Cerveteri was doing the same.

CHAPTER EIGHTEEN

D ryden Vos sat in the largest chair in the receiving room at the Thorum house like an absent king, never directly issuing a command but being obeyed instantly all the same. The members of the crew were all assembled, some looking confused and most looking nervous. Cerveteri looked smug and Qi'ra looked apprehensive, but she knew that they were both pretending.

"I haven't been to Thorum in a while," Vos said. Every eye in the room immediately snapped to him. "As a matter of fact, I don't know if I've ever been to Thorum. It's not really my kind of place."

His complete disregard for the health and well-being of everyone in the room was unspoken but unmissable.

"You lot have had a marvelous run, lately," he said, clapping his hands together and leaning forward in a suddenly friendly way that Qi'ra found deeply off-putting. Thallia actually flinched. "Collections on time, thefts completed without a trace of evidence; it's remarkable, and you should be proud of yourselves."

No one relaxed, though Cerveteri couldn't help puffing out her chest a bit. Qi'ra wondered how she could have gotten so far when she gave away so much of what she was thinking. If Qi'ra kept too many secrets, Cerveteri didn't keep enough.

"I am especially impressed with your intuition," Vos continued. The smile on Cerveteri's face faltered. "It takes a clever mind to know when the orders they are given can be safely exceeded. I want very much to be proud of all of you. But, alas, I cannot, can I?"

He didn't expect an answer and no one gave it, though a few of the confused faces became more confused.

"Someone in this room is a traitor," Vos said. "Someone has given up our information, *my* information, for another gang to use. That is not the kind of intuition I want to see. Not at all. And yet it is so blatant here that I can't be happy about the good things you've done."

He looked genuinely sad about it, but something simmered underneath his skin, a rage so volatile that any trigger would unleash a deadly torrent. The red lines on his face darkened slightly, but he held them under control for now.

"Cerveteri, this is your operation," Vos said, looking directly at her for the first time since his arrival. "Have you any idea who it might be?"

Cerveteri swallowed hard, and Qi'ra saw the exact moment when the other girl's plan solidified, confirming her suspicions. Cerveteri was going to frame someone on the crew. Qi'ra already suspected her for being so eager to go out with the hit squads when they didn't really need her, but now she was certain. Cerveteri was the leak, and she was going to sacrifice someone else to cover it up. Qi'ra had no real evidence, though, certainly not enough to stop what was coming. There was nothing she could do about it without endangering herself. She just had to hope Cerveteri didn't decide to point the finger at her.

"Both of our slicers have the ability to set something like this up," Cerveteri began. Everyone started to react at the same time, but a single look from Vos froze them all in their seats. "But only one of them has the ability to cover it up. And she had a whole week of pretending to work for the Hammers to do it."

Thallia was on her feet, even as Vos's guards closed in around her. There was nowhere she could run, and it was blatantly obvious that no one could appeal to Vos for pity. She turned instead to face the rest of them.

"Cerveteri," she said, her hands held out. "Cerveteri, please."

Cerveteri said nothing. The guards had her by the shoulders now and were starting to drag her from the room.

"Qi'ra!" she called out. "Qi'ra, you know it wasn't me!"

Qi'ra set her face in stone and said nothing. If she intervened, Cerveteri would immediately label her a suspect, too. She would be forced to admit how she got the information from the droid, and she didn't want to reveal her hand yet. She wasn't even sure the truth would save her. She didn't think Vos would accept her story about dead secretaries as easily as the Mizi had. There was nothing she could do.

Silence fell over the room as Thallia was dragged down the hall and out into the little courtyard in the middle of the house. Qi'ra closed her eyes when the blaster fired, and when she opened them again, Dryden Vos was staring right at her.

"The operation on Thorum is over," Vos announced, not breaking his gaze away from her. "A different level of supervision will be required now, and I have use for all of you somewhere else. Gather your things, and if you have affairs to set in order here, do so. You will all depart tomorrow."

There was a beat of silence, and then they all rose to leave.

"Qi'ra," Vos said, not looking up from the knife he was twirling in his fingers. "Stay a moment, would you?"

Eleera caught her eye with a worried glance, but Qi'ra shook her head. It was a nice gesture, but none of them could run any more than Thallia could. And Qi'ra didn't think she'd need to, no matter how menacing Vos was.

"Our Mizi friend has excellent taste," he said when they were alone. "She speaks very highly of you, you know, and she doesn't like very many people."

"I like her, as well," Qi'ra said. She wasn't entirely certain what he wanted, which set her off balance.

"Yes, I'm sure," Vos said. He leaned back in his chair almost as if he were relaxing, but both of them were coiled as tight as springs.

Qi'ra met his gaze. For the first time, his smile seemed real.

"We both know that poor slicer was not the leak," Vos said. "And I imagine we both have suspicions as to who the leak is, but can't prove them. I can dispose of anyone, as I have just proven, but before I do, I want to know how far this goes. I think we will make an excellent team. Assuming no one pins this on you and I have to have you taken care of, of course."

Qi'ra had been recruited into the White Worms after failing to pickpocket Moloch, and had been promoted by shows of brute force. It looked like she'd get upward mobility in Crimson Dawn through subtlety, which played to her strengths anyway.

"I see we are of the same mind," Vos said, reading her silence as well as he might hear any words she'd spoken. "The others will be your underlings, of course. It makes no sense to break up a team. You'll come with me back to the *First Light*, and there will be some more training to undergo."

"I look forward to it," Qi'ra said, because she didn't think he was the sort of man who liked to be thanked.

"Go and pack, my dear," he said. "We are leaving quite early."

He had to know she barely had anything, but she appreciated his veneer of politeness. It gave her something to work with. She got the feeling he was looking for a protégé, and that was a position she could fill. He would know she kept secrets; he already knew it, and he didn't seem to care. She could work with that. She could work with him.

◕

Every time Qi'ra packed up her things, it took more time. Even with Trinia's assistance, she was still surprised by how many belongings she had now. She'd been on Thorum for only a short while, but she had accumulated knickknacks and additional clothing. She didn't need a second bag, but it was a near thing. Trinia had to sit on the bag for her to get it closed.

Qi'ra looked around the first room she'd ever had to herself. It wasn't a bad start. There were better things in her future now. It was still dangerous and unpredictable, but if Vos was taking an interest in her, it could only mean good things about her future with Crimson Dawn.

She almost went without them, but at the very last minute, right before she left the room, she pulled the pair of dice out of their secure spot in the safe and shoved them into her pocket.

○

It was her own fault for not checking the hallway when she went down to the kitchen for a snack after nightfall. Dinner had not been a particularly comfortable meal, and Qi'ra hadn't been able to eat, but now she was hungry. She'd gotten used to eating when she felt like it, so she thought nothing of going downstairs. She forgot that there had been a power shift since that afternoon and not everyone would be happy about it.

"I should break your face right open," Cerveteri said, body-slamming her into the wall and then holding her up with her hands around Qi'ra's throat. "See if Vos still finds you so interesting then."

Qi'ra didn't struggle. She was stronger now than when Ema had attacked her, thanks to decent food and her workouts with Eleera, but she was in no hurry to let Cerveteri know how strong. Her airway wasn't restricted yet, and she would choose her moment to fight back.

"I have been trying to get promoted higher up into Crimson Dawn for years," Cerveteri hissed. "You ruined my operation on Corellia. It took me months to set that up.

It's not easy to manufacture a whole identity with no backup, but I did it, and you screwed it up."

Considering that she'd been waiting for Cerveteri to crack, Qi'ra felt extra foolish for not seeing this coming. She'd gotten too comfortable on Thorum. With friends instead of people she happened to work with. Now one of them was dead in the courtyard, and another one had her hands around Qi'ra's neck.

"Then you show me up here, over and over again," Cerveteri ranted. "These were *my* operations, and my way upward, and you stole them, too."

Han would have said something like *Well, we are thieves*, and then gotten the crap kicked out of him, but Qi'ra couldn't take that kind of beating. Cerveteri's hands spasmed, like she wanted to close her fingers but was waiting for something. Maybe she wanted Qi'ra to beg for her life. It wasn't going to happen.

"I'm going to find out how you know so much, and then I'm going to pin all of this on you, and then I'm going to throw you out the airlock myself," Cerveteri said. "No one will ever suspect that I framed you."

It took everything Qi'ra had not to laugh. Cerveteri wanted the wrong things and always had. The only way she could frame Qi'ra was if she knew the details Qi'ra didn't, which she could only know if she was the leak. Of course, because Qi'ra didn't know the details, she couldn't accuse Cerveteri of anything. It would be too easy for the other girl to wriggle free. Qi'ra swallowed, pushing her throat out toward Cerveteri's palms, almost asking her to squeeze. Instead, Cerveteri threw her sideways, and Qi'ra stumbled into a decorative table a little harder than she needed to.

"Sleep well, Qi'ra," Cerveteri said, and left.

Qi'ra stood for a moment in the hall, no longer hungry but not quite ready to return to her room. A flash of movement caught her eye, and Dryden Vos stepped into the hall from the shadows of the courtyard. He must have been watching Thallia's body in the dark for some reason and heard the scuffle.

"Well, that was interesting," he said. "You don't look surprised, but at least now you know you're starting in the right place."

Han would have bragged, told him it was nothing he couldn't handle. Thinking about him gave her courage, returned the feeling to her skin when she had felt so cold. It was strange, to have anger change one so much, but there was no point in fighting it. Qi'ra only raised her chin, as though to ask how Vos expected any less of her.

"Yes, I chose well, I think," Vos mused. He reached out and placed a gloved hand on Qi'ra's shoulder. The squeeze was possessive, his clawlike thumb digging into the sinew of the joint, and made her flesh crawl ten times more than Cerveteri's hands had. "You'll get to the bottom of this, if only to save yourself."

With an unwavering gaze, Qi'ra looked straight at him. There were no words he wanted to hear, and so she didn't give him any. Instead, she thought about Han. She remembered stolen moments and stolen vehicles, a reckless exuberance that not even Lady Proxima had been able to quell, and she smiled.

And Dryden Vos smiled back.

*T*he new boy is loud, and for a whole week all Qi'ra wants is for him to shut up. He flirts with her, even though they are too young for it and barely even understand the concept. He mimicks what he's seen in dive bars while she avoids him like he has Corellian pox. It doesn't deter him, though he does dial it back when he realizes he has been making her uncomfortable.

That is the first loose plate in her armor when it comes to Han.

Qi'ra is prepared for violence and cruelty. She can handle neglect and pain. She is used to hunger and wanting something she can't even imagine properly. She has no defense against genuine kindness. And Han is kind to everyone.

He does it without a reason, without expecting anything back. He isn't nice to her because he thinks she's pretty. He's nice to her because he can't help it. He jokes with the younger kids and makes the older ones feel important. He charms the Grindalids when they are angry, often taking blows that are meant for smaller targets. He seems to fear nothing, and lets everyone see straight into his heart.

She will learn later that it is part of his defense. She is getting better at being cold and unresponsive, but he has never mastered it, so he leans hard in the other direction. He uses his charm and gregariousness as a shield as much as she uses her quiet control and her stone face. It is just a different way of fighting back.

For a while, she thinks that everything he says is false, but it soon becomes apparent that there is a seed of truth to all of his behaviors, and the one he gave to her is sprouting into something else. Slowly, they become a team. He learns to trust her silence, and she learns not to flinch when he laughs loudly or draws attention. They complement each other very well, and as they grow up, they work together more and more frequently, because they always get results.

When he ensures that she becomes Head, he expects nothing in return. She would have, had their positions been reversed and had it been anyone but him. Yet she knows he will always be at the front of the dinner line, unless he lets someone cut in. And she won't stop him, if he does. It is the closest they can come, in the White Worms, to true friendship. And in the end, it is not enough.

When he drags her out of the sewers, the coaxium burning in her pocket, she is already concocting the lies she will tell if they get caught. Han has no backup plan; he jumps from scheme to scheme without looking at the landing pad. But Qi'ra plans ahead. She thinks of all the outcomes and tries to find solutions. They work together so well, but when they are separated, both of them falter.

Han leaves with a promise on his lips that she knows he will break himself fulfilling, but she isn't that naive. He's forgotten what they are, pieces of a moving engine that burns hotter than either of them can control. But Qi'ra never has. Han thinks it's a game that they can win, and he has risked it all. Qi'ra knows that the odds are stacked against them, and from now on, she will only play to survive.

In spite of everything—the differences between them—they have been a good team. But the most important lesson Qi'ra has learned is that teams are for breaking when times get tough. In the end, it doesn't matter how strong your partner is, because they can't help you. The only person you can rely on is yourself.

Qi'ra takes those lessons with her into the final weeks in the sewers with the Worms and then out into the galaxy with Sarkin before being given the dubious shelter of Crimson Dawn. She never lets herself forget, even though she wants to, for a moment, on Thorum. She knows better. She hasn't always known better, but she's learned. And anyone who makes her feel otherwise is dangerous and has to be removed from her life before they can hurt her. Every time her defenses are almost breached, she thinks of those horrible hours waiting to see if Proxima was going to let her live, and she shores up the walls she has built around her heart.

And still, no matter how hard she fights or how strongly she resists, every time Han crosses her mind, she smiles.

CHAPTER NINETEEN

Qi'ra landed heavily on the hard deck of the sparring room and rolled immediately to avoid the follow-up strike she knew was coming for her head. The baton missed her by a fraction of a second, but the boot that found her neck was right on target. She froze, the weight of the sole no more comfortable than it had been the last hundred or so times this had happened.

"I didn't hit you this time," Dryden Vos said above her. He applied the slightest bit of pressure to her throat. Qi'ra fought off the panic more successfully than she'd ever been able to fight off him. He was much, much faster than Eleera, and Eleera was pretty fast. "So you are improving, slightly."

He leaned back and retreated to his own corner for water and a towel. Qi'ra hauled herself off the deck without assistance. She felt like one giant walking bruise. Vos had turned her over to various other denizens of Crimson Dawn for her training in things like slicing, etiquette, and poison detection since she'd come back on board the *First Light*, but for some reason, he oversaw her physical combat practice himself. She was a complete novice at studied forms of fighting, and teräs käsi wasn't kind to beginners. But she could feel herself getting stronger, moving faster, and so she went back every day for her lesson.

She didn't really have a choice in the matter, of course, but Qi'ra didn't care. The upper decks of the *First Light* were far superior to anywhere else she had ever lived, or ever imagined living, even when she'd had quarters on the decks below. The gilded ship left Corellian glamour in the dust, and nothing outside of the Old Houses could match Dryden Vos for style. She was out of her depth and completely at the mercy of her teachers, but Qi'ra knew an opportunity when she saw one, and she seized it with both hands.

"Margo tells me you are doing well," Vos said conversationally while Qi'ra drank some water and tried to soothe her aching knuckles. She still held on to the batons too tightly, and it wore on her after a while.

"I am glad to hear it," Qi'ra said. Margo was less openly dangerous than Vos, but she was still a harsh teacher. The concierge's assistant had not warmed up to Qi'ra during her absence, and now that she was responsible for all of Qi'ra's etiquette training, she liked her even less. She'd already poisoned Qi'ra twice as part of her security training protocol, though at least Qi'ra had known it was coming, so she'd had the appropriate antidotes available. Vomiting that much still hurt, though. At least Qi'ra could trust Margo not to improvise too much. The few times she'd had lessons with Corynna, the concierge had been creative and vicious.

Vos laughed. He had a way of speaking and laughing like he actually cared. It was by far the most intriguing thing about him. Qi'ra knew he was dangerous, knew he would kill her in a moment if he thought she was even a minor inconvenience, but sometimes he seemed so *normal* that she would almost forget. No wonder he had held on to Crimson Dawn for so long. People genuinely liked him, even as they were scared of him. It was a gift, and Qi'ra was going to learn it from him, if he would let her close enough.

"There's no one like you, my dear," Vos said. "So much potential, ripe for molding. I'm lucky I found you and not someone else."

It was flattery, and Qi'ra knew better than to accept it at face value, but she let herself react like she was pleased to hear his words. She was still figuring him out, trying to test boundaries without getting herself killed, and to see how much he really knew and how much she could actually conceal from him. She was rebuilding herself in the image Dryden Vos wanted, but she was hoping to keep some parts just for her.

The door to the sparring room slid open and Aemon came in. Generally, Vos did not like to be interrupted when he was training with Qi'ra, but the head of the Hylobon guard held special privileges on board. In the general hierarchy, Aemon was the one to worry about after Vos. Their violence manifested in different ways. Of the two, Aemon's was the most physical and straightforward, which meant he was the one Qi'ra was the least equipped to deal with. Even without his helmet, Aemon was intimidating. Qi'ra had heard stories about children who owned furry creatures for comfort, but every furry species she'd ever met had been just as cruel as everyone else. She mostly tried to stay out of his way.

"Ah. I am sorry, Qi'ra. We must end early this morning." Vos sounded truly apologetic. "The Empire has little regard for the scheduling of others, unfortunately. It is something I am working slowly to correct, but in the meantime, I must be available to them when they call. You do understand."

"Of course," Qi'ra said. She understood on every level. Vos hated it, which was probably why his Imperial contact did it. She didn't think it would end well for him if Vos ever felt confident enough to object. "I appreciate that you are able to train with me at all."

"My dear, there is no one I would rather teach to potentially be my match in a fight," Vos said. The smile in his voice indicated that he didn't think she'd ever be his match, and she intended to make sure he always thought that, no matter how proficient she got.

He crossed the room, touching her face to look at her bruises before he left. She would cover them up when she got dressed, but he always checked before he left. Aemon, who never bothered to conceal his disregard for anyone he viewed as an opportunist or climber within Crimson Dawn, glowered at her before following his master from the room. When the door slid shut, Qi'ra finally let her shoulders relax a little bit. There was always someone watching on the *First Light*, but that didn't mean she had to be tense all the time. It would do her well for everyone to think she was capable of letting go.

She cracked her neck and spun the batons in her hands. Eventually, they would move up to electrified ones. Vos had a set of personalized weapons she'd only seen briefly—most who saw any set of Kyuzo petars didn't survive very long, so she was in no hurry to see them again—but for now he was content to pummel her with the batons. She was better at the forms than he knew, but she wanted to move up to the harder weapons on her own schedule, not his. If she was more wounded from training with him, she would be less responsive training with the others, and she could not afford that right now.

Trinia was waiting for her in the little room where she changed. Instead of being sent belowdecks with the rest of their crew, Trinia had been brought on board as Qi'ra's attendant. At first, Qi'ra was worried the other girl would be resentful, but Trinia had given no indication of that. She got to watch all of Qi'ra's training and she didn't have to endure whatever the Hylobons were doing to hone the abilities of the rest of the crew, so it probably worked out better for her anyway. Qi'ra didn't exactly trust her, but it was nice to have a familiar face around when so many other things were new, even if Trinia was still a bit off-putting.

"The Mizi is here," Trinia said, helping Qi'ra out of her training robes. None of her bruises were purple, which was a good sign. Qi'ra tried to poke the large green bruise on her side, but Trinia grabbed her hand. "None of that. It'll only make it worse. The steam bath is ready, if you want to go in, and I've set your clothes out."

"Thank you, Trinia," Qi'ra said. The steam wasn't curative in the real medical sense, but it stopped her from stiffening up. The rest of the *First Light* was cold, and that was uncomfortable when she was bruised.

Qi'ra went into the bathroom and shut herself in the sauna. It was warm, warmer than anything she'd ever experienced on Thorum. She was used to associating dampness with the misery of sewer living, but this was an entirely appealing way to spend a few minutes after getting beaten into the floor. She felt her muscles loosening as she rolled her shoulders and did her best to rub down the worst of the knots in her arms and legs. She didn't have much time to luxuriate, but she made the most of it, and by the time she was pulling on her black shimmersilk trousers and the wide-necked red blouse Trinia had selected to go with it, she felt much better.

The necklace that had been her reward after the droid job was laid out, as well. She now knew that it had come from Vos, an early sign that his eye was on her. Lopie had received one for the same reason, but they both knew that it didn't mean the same thing. The metal lay cool against her heated skin, a reminder of what life was like on the rest of the ship. A long black wrap completed her outfit, and then she sat down to do her hair and makeup.

Trinia came in to help. There was a bruise on Qi'ra's back that the shirt revealed, even with the wrap, and Qi'ra couldn't reach it on her own. The makeup went on quickly, restoring her skin to its porcelain perfection and adding a blush of color to her cheeks. Her hair was still long, and she had decided she liked having it swept up the way the Mizi had shown her when she was posing as Elesa Norre. Vos had given her a set of decorative pins that she'd quickly discovered were actually tiny stun grenades, and Trinia carefully added them to secure any loose hairs that might escape.

"Where is the Mizi?" Qi'ra asked as the last pin slid into place. The figure in the mirror was almost unrecognizable. The silk of her trousers alone would have bought enough food for every scrumrat in the White Worms for a week. Her cheeks were fuller, her hair a shiny brown instead of the dull, muddy color she'd always seen when she caught her reflection before.

"She's with Corynna," Trinia said. "They know you were with Vos, so there's no hurry. But I assumed you would want to at least say hello."

Qi'ra definitely wanted to see the Mizi. Corynna was less of a reason for excitement, most days, but it was no use trying to avoid her. Being Dryden Vos's special project made it hard to be in Corynna's good graces, but Qi'ra still had to try. The woman was simply in charge of too many things to cross. And Qi'ra needed as much flexibility as possible while she worked on tracking the leak. Giving Corynna an excuse to monitor her closely wouldn't do her any good.

The *First Light* required a vast staff. Vos lived on the ship, having turned it into his home and base of operations. It was certainly easier to secure than some stationary asteroid outpost or a stormy island hideaway. In addition to the Hylobon enforcers, who could be found patrolling every level, there was a large domestic staff. Some of these were droids, but many of them were organic beings, because Vos did business deals on board, and those business partners didn't want to look at droids.

The absolute authority on the domestic side, as feared as Aemon was on the security side, was Corynna, Vos's concierge. Margo was one of her apprentices and did not conceal the fact that someday she wanted to take over the job entirely. Corynna tolerated her ambition with a sort of careless scrutiny, as though she didn't think Margo had it in her. Qi'ra knew better. Until then, Margo was tasked with bringing Qi'ra up to snuff, a job neither of them really enjoyed but both endured because the end benefits were obvious. If Margo relished the parts of the regimen that were uncomfortable for Qi'ra—poison detection, for example—a little too much, no one pointed it out. Even though she was an Imroosian, from a planet where heat was normal, Margo was uncharacteristically fond of the cold, which drove Qi'ra to distraction. It was a constant battle of wills between them, with Margo holding the upper hand for now.

Qi'ra told Trinia to go back to their room and then took the turbolift up to the second highest level of the ship. One deck above her, Vos was entertaining the Imperial representative, but someone like the Mizi could relax a little bit lower down. She was in one of the small receiving rooms, with Margo pouring tea just as Qi'ra came through the door. Corynna reclined on a lounge and didn't sit up when Margo passed her a cup. Qi'ra didn't feel like she was interrupting an important conversation, but she also got the distinct impression that Corynna didn't want her around.

"Qi'ra, you look fantastic," the Mizi said, standing up to give her a quick hug. "I knew life up here would suit you. Only four months and you already look like you've never lived anywhere else."

"It does suit me, thank you," Qi'ra said. She took a cup of tea from Margo and sat down. The sensor she had added to her ring didn't go off, so she was pretty sure it was safe to drink.

"I was just telling Corynna that I have to go up and talk to Vos," the Mizi said, still on her feet. "But I'm glad you made it before I had to go. It is good to see you."

"Safe travels," Qi'ra bid her. If Vos wanted her to know what the business was about, he would tell her. She wasn't yet in a position where she would try to find things out on her own.

The Mizi left the room, cheerily whistling as she went. Corynna went back into her office without giving either Qi'ra or Margo even a look.

"They'll call you up eventually," Margo said, delicately stirring sweetener into her own drink. "I wouldn't stray too far while you're waiting."

Margo didn't usually give her tips like that, so Qi'ra's curiosity was definitely piqued.

"Thank you," she said, and took a long drink. The Imroosian watched her closely and then drained her own cup.

CHAPTER TWENTY

As Margo predicted, the summons came less than half an hour later. Although there was a perfectly functional intercom on the *First Light*, the message was delivered by one of the droids. Qi'ra took a moment to make sure her makeup hadn't smudged. Vos wouldn't want his guests to see the bruises. At Margo's sharp nod of approval, Qi'ra pulled the wrap around her shoulders and headed for the turbolift.

Like everything else on the *First Light*, the lift was a perfect combination of form and function. Repulsor bolsters allowed it to glide smoothly and quickly between floors, ferrying guests and employees to their destinations at Vos's behest. A second, less decorative lift ran on a parallel shaft and carried out the more utilitarian tasks on board, like laundry and moving droids around. Qi'ra strongly suspected that Vos had a third lift that he kept secret. There was no way he didn't have an emergency exit from his offices.

The *First Light* was his own personal yacht, but there was a smaller craft stored down by the engine room. Qi'ra would bet the secret lift took him there if he needed a quick escape.

For now, she put thoughts of the hidden lift out of her mind, adding it to the list of things she would investigate when her position was more secure. It was a long list at the moment, but she looked forward to checking things off of it when the time came.

The doors opened into the heart of Crimson Dawn, at least as far as the public was concerned. Vos held court in a room that took up most of the top deck of the ship. It had windows all the way around, each decorated with the Crimson Dawn symbol, and was full of what Margo called Vos's conversation pieces. Qi'ra knew they were trophies: valuable things he'd won or been paid with or bought under extremely questionable circumstances. Each display was arranged to catch the light, showing off Vos's achievements before anyone ever got close to him. Sometimes Vos would bring in a musician or entertainer if he was trying to set a client at their ease, but Imperials received no such treatment.

He was sitting at his desk when Qi'ra exited the lift, the Imperial officer sitting on the other side of it, flanked by four stormtroopers. Their conversation appeared to be wrapping up, since the officer stood and held out his hand. Vos rose slowly. The desk was too wide for him to reach across without bowing, and the officer realized his error just in time, withdrawing the hand. His uniform boots clicked together at the heels, a seemingly instinctive response to projected authority.

"We'll see it done," said the officer.

"Excellent, Lieutenant Veers," Vos replied. "We look forward to working more closely with someone in possession of such singular vision."

The lieutenant nodded and strode to the waiting turbolift, the troopers close behind him. None of them looked at Qi'ra as she stepped out of their way. Vos waved her over as the door to the lift shut, indicating that she sit on one of the lounges in the center of the room. He stopped to pick up a glass for each of them, a small line of amber liquid at the bottom of the fine crystal, and settled down beside her.

"He's very clever, that one," Vos said, handing her the drink and leaning back to cross one long leg over the other. "And smart enough not to join the Imperial navy. Ground troops are always easier to manage, and you can do that from relative safety if you want. He's more hands-on, I think, but still. He'll be promoted soon, I'm sure of it."

Vos preferred to own governors and cooperate with officers. It was easier, for one thing, and officers had a much shorter life expectancy. Owning one was simply a poor investment. Whatever Lieutenant Veers was worth in the future, it would be a connection to exploit, not a neck to squeeze.

"You sent for me?" Qi'ra asked. She took a sip of her drink and managed to keep her reaction to a blink. The first time she'd tried, she had taken a whole mouthful and coughed. Vos had laughed and told her to remind Margo that she needed to learn more than just polite greetings. Her subsequent tasting sessions with Margo had been unpleasant, leaving her tongue numb and her stomach frequently rebellious, but she did learn what kind of alcohol she liked and how to pretend to enjoy strong spirits when she didn't. Qi'ra would never enjoy the feeling of dulled senses that alcohol led to, but she had learned how to drink to put others at their ease, and make them more likely to dull themselves in comfort.

"Yes." Vos's free hand landed on her shoulder, delicately missing the bruise he knew was there. "There is going to be a party when we reach our destination. Several of the other syndicates will have representatives in attendance. I want you to accompany me."

Qi'ra blinked again, this time in genuine surprise.

"Oh, you're quite ready for it," Vos said. "Margo is without question the most judgmental person in my organization, and she hasn't said anything negative about your progress. Even Corynna only grinds her teeth a little bit when I mention your name in conversation. This is an informal gathering, really. It's nothing you can't handle."

Qi'ra fought down the urge to be pleased at his faith in her.

"How long do I have to get ready?" Qi'ra asked, looking down at her outfit. While more elegant and expensive than anything else she'd ever owned, it was still almost casual by Crimson Dawn standards.

"Oh, this will do nicely," Vos said. "As I told you, it's an informal meeting. I do have one thing to add to your ensemble, however. An accessory, if you will."

He reached behind him and took a gold-wrapped box off a nearby table. He handed it to her, looking at her like he was excited to see what she'd do next. She peeled the wrapping off and then slid the box open. Inside, on a bed of red velvet, were two small batons. It was clear that they were the proper electrified version of the weapon. Though they weren't full-sized, they were the real thing.

"I told you I knew you were ready," Vos said.

She knew he didn't mean the party. He'd been able to observe more of her progress than she wanted to show him, but she couldn't be surprised by that. He was better at playing the game than she was. That was why she wanted to learn from him, not someone else on the *First Light*.

"It wouldn't do for you to be unarmed where we are headed," Vos continued. "They'll be confiscated at the door, of course, but letting you show up with nothing would be a misstep on my part. It would make it look like I didn't trust you, and I do trust you, Qi'ra."

"Thank you," Qi'ra said quietly.

He was never angry with her little deceptions. If anything, they amused him, hence the gift. He liked to catch her off balance by suddenly letting on that he knew exactly what she was capable of, or exactly what she had been trying to hide. That was the main reason she kept doing it. She knew eventually he'd lose interest in the game, thinking her an unworthy opponent, or she would become proficient enough to actually be successful. It didn't really matter which. The important thing was that she wouldn't be punished along the way.

Dryden smiled at her, the wide, toothy grin that looked oh so genuine unless you noticed the fire smoldering beneath his skin. She had no idea why his face was like that, and she wasn't about to ask. He could control his facial expressions to a degree, but the seething red heat that lurked beneath his skin gave him away, and she was learning how to read even the subtlest shifts. His hand moved to the back of her neck, this time pressing into the bruise there. She didn't falter.

"Come," he said, emptying his glass. She did the same, not appreciating the burn in her throat the way she knew she was supposed to. "We should be dropping out of hyperspace any moment."

He had no sooner finished speaking than the ship

lurched back into real space. The stars were once again fixed points, but the planet in front of them blotted them from the sky. It was a world she didn't recognize, green like Thorum but with more purple than any jungle she was used to. She hoped it wasn't humid. She didn't miss the humidity at all.

Vos held out his arm, and she took it. He led her into the turbolift, and they headed down to the disembarkation level. Another person might have taken a shuttle and left his ship in orbit, but Vos liked to make an entrance, and that began with the great knife of the *First Light* descending from on high. If there were clouds to pierce or mountains to shadow, it only added to Vos's grandeur. If the planet was not equipped for a ship of this size to dock, then Vos simply had no interest in hosting guests there.

That he had deigned to come to Thorum via shuttle all those weeks ago spoke to the severity of the situation. He preferred to entertain his guests on board the *First Light*, even if he had to dock it somewhere during the meeting.

Aemon and three other helmeted Hylobon guards joined them as the ship completed the docking procedure and began preparations to open the shuttle door. Aemon was still scowling at her. The others probably were, too, but their helmets were shut. Vos raised his eyebrows in Aemon's direction, an unvoiced question that he didn't need to speak to ask. Aemon shut his helmet immediately, and the Hylobons took up formation behind Vos and Qi'ra. A moment later, they were joined by Corynna and Margo, both in elegant black, designed to fade into the background the same way that Qi'ra's outfit was designed to draw attention.

The door opened, letting in a rush of planet-side air. Qi'ra breathed it in, a welcome change after being on the ship for so long. On Corellia the air had been damp and disgusting, while Thorum had been verdant and green. She had missed the changeable nature of air, since the *First Light* had no weather and was always the same. You could change the environmental settings, to a degree, but there was no match for the real thing.

"It's nice, isn't it," Vos agreed, his nostrils flaring. "I imagine you're accustomed to air that is a certain amount of—pungent."

He rarely mentioned her upbringing directly. He alluded to it all the time, when he was giving her a backhanded compliment or trying to put her off balance, but he didn't usually say the actual words. She had no idea where he came from or what his upbringing had looked like, and she was fairly certain she never would. That part of Dryden Vos was off limits. But he liked to remember her origins, from time to time. It made him feel important, she supposed, or maybe accomplished for having turned her into someone else so quickly after taking her out of the gutter.

Lady Proxima had made the same claim once, that she

had pulled Qi'ra out of the Silo and given her a home. It was what Proxima wanted her to believe, because it meant that Proxima was important in Qi'ra's life. The truth was that Qi'ra had gotten out of the Silo on her own. If she'd been better at picking pockets, Moloch might not have noticed her, but when she was caught and showed enough intiative to defy him to keep what she'd stolen, she impressed him enough that he brought her back.

Vos was the same way. He gave himself credit for shaping her, when it was she who had done all the work. He thought she was a tool, an instrument waiting to find its place in the orchestra. And to a degree, he was correct. But she had brought herself to this place. She had made it this far by fighting for everything she had, and even her failures and shortcomings were tools she could wield if she had to. He had given her the opportunity, just like Han had when he pushed her into the Head position, but she had made sure she was in a place to be pushed, and that was not nothing, even if other people thought it was.

Vos treated her like a pet, like one of the trophies in the displays in his office, there to show people how cultured and accomplished he was. And for now, Qi'ra was happy to play the part. Pets got fed after all, and she needed a full belly if she was going to plan for her own future.

CHAPTER TWENTY-ONE

Nightsend was a planet of extremes. Far from its star and slow in its rotation, the days were long and hot and the nights were dark and very, very cold. The party was hosted on the nightside of the planet, but the *First Light* was docked under the blinding sun. It was too bright and too hot for them to be outside. The fresh air Qi'ra had inhaled so eagerly was an illusion, piped in from a hostile desert to greet travelers exiting the cold of space.

As a security feature, having the spaceport so far from where the party was actually taking place was quite clever. It was an efficient way of controlling access, and even though the cost of maintaining facilities that would be constantly bombarded by unrelenting solar radiation or freezing without it was high, the safety was undeniable. Their party was escorted to a shuttle by a protocol droid, who also warned them not to look outside too frequently until they crossed to the dark.

The landscape sped past as the shuttle took them the last few kilometers to the relative safety of the darkness. Here, instead of heat being the killer, it was the cold, but at least cold could be defended against more easily. Qi'ra didn't look out the window. She spent the journey listening to Vos and Corynna chat quietly about ship affairs. Corynna appeared to be frustrated by Vos's nonchalance when it came to the day-to-day details of running the *First Light*, but Qi'ra had a feeling Corynna knew Vos was more involved than he let on. Margo didn't say anything, and Qi'ra followed her example. There was nothing she could have added anyway, but at least with Margo there, she didn't feel awkward sitting in silence.

At last they crossed the boundary, a hard line between one and the other, to the black night of the planet's dark side. The shuttle docked shortly afterward, and they were escorted, again by a droid, to a small room to refresh themselves if they required it. Vos was beginning to get annoyed about the whole process, thin red lines webbing across his face. The droid picked up on it immediately, gesturing them toward the final door.

All five major crime syndicates would be in attendance, but the party was officially hosted by Black Sun. As Qi'ra entered the room on Vos's arm, she saw immediately that a large number of Falleen made up the population in attendance. Some of them had Black Sun tattoos clearly visible, but most chose subtler ways to express their allegiance, the way that Qi'ra's gold necklace marked her as Crimson Dawn.

"We appear to be early," Vos said as a tall Falleen female came over to greet them. "How gauche. Verelea, I do apologize."

"You are fashionably late as ever, Dryden," Verelea said, looking over their party with a piercing gaze. "Everyone else is now unforgivably tardy."

"You are too kind," Vos said. He followed Verelea's gaze to where it had landed on Qi'ra, the corner of his mouth turning up. "Ah, yes, allow me to make introductions. Verelea, this is my newest lieutenant, Qi'ra. Qi'ra, my dear, this is Verelea Xhorrun, of Black Sun."

"Charmed," said Verelea, extending a hand.

"Thank you for the invitation," Qi'ra said, accepting the light handshake and hoping she wasn't making a fool of herself. "Dryden's ship is wonderful, of course, but I do like to get out and stretch my legs every now and again."

The look she directed at Vos was sufficiently doe-eyed that he smiled like he was fond of her.

"Yes," he agreed. "I always take advantage of opportunity."

"Please, settle in," Verelea said. "I am sure the others will be along soon enough, and we can get this over with."

Vos laughed, the edge in his tone more obvious than usual, and led them to an alcove on the far side of the room. Even though she knew Aemon was doing the same thing, Qi'ra immediately scanned for exits and potential danger.

It wasn't a particularly solid position. Going outside any way other than the way they'd come would mean death, and even though they could see the door, the vaulted ceiling was made of glass so that partygoers could admire the starlight.

"Aemon, don't growl, I can hear you," Vos said. "You know this is the safest place I could be. It's probably safer than my own bed."

Qi'ra wondered what it was like to feel safe, and then wondered how Vos could possibly feel safe here. She hated not knowing reasons for things but couldn't come up with a way to ask the question that wouldn't reveal her ignorance.

"Relax, Aemon." Vos was still talking, though his voice had lost the ennui of his previous words. He turned to Qi'ra. "Aemon has been with me for a while, and he remembers the old days. Back then, I would have had three times as many guards at a party like this. But that was when the five syndicates worked against each other. Now that we are allies, we cooperate."

Now that they were allies, they didn't kill each other openly, he meant. They'd gotten more creative, but the balance to be maintained was absolute.

"I suppose he misses the good old days, when we could operate however we wanted," Vos continued. "It certainly had some benefits. But our current overseer does encourage some independence, as long as we don't go against his rules about infighting and vengeance. His methods for business got enough of us rich that he silenced most of the protestors. And anyone else, well, he had a method for silencing them, too."

It wasn't the first time Qi'ra had heard rumors of the mysterious figure who ruled the five syndicates with an iron fist. No one seemed to know very much about him, and Vos was reportedly the only person in Crimson Dawn who had ever spoken to him. It was strange to think about Dryden Vos reporting to anyone, but he seemed to have made his peace with it. Or at least, he was biding his time.

It did explain why Vos was not concerned for his safety. Anything that happened to anyone at this gathering would be punished severely, and so it was very unlikely that someone would take the risk. The days of jockeying for power were over. Centralized power could be vulnerable, but if one was strong enough to hold it, then everyone down the chain had to fall in line. It was a difficult path to follow. Whoever commanded Vos would have to be extremely powerful. Qi'ra wondered what that sort of person would be like. Then she decided she didn't want to know.

A serving droid came over with a selection of drinks. Vos handed one to Qi'ra and nodded to Margo that she should take one, as well. Corynna left to make arrangements for future meetings, taking one of the guards with her. The remainder of their party stayed in the alcove, the Hylobons at attention and the rest of them reclining on the sofa that was provided. Margo had the space at the end to herself, but Vos had made sure Qi'ra was sitting close to him.

Members from the other syndicates began to arrive, and Vos kept up a steady narration in her ear as the different representatives met with Verelea and came into the room to mingle. The Pykes were the next to join the gathering. With Vos's whispers as a guide, Qi'ra learned to read the uniforms and discern the rank and relationship between the various members. Black Sun operatives often wore their allegiance openly, even when they were moving through the more legal side of the galaxy. They feared little and trusted their syndicate to back them up. The Crymorah were a mix of species, and even droids. The humans among them were the least formal of those in attendance. They called for drinks as soon as Verelea greeted them, and even though their host was poised, Qi'ra could see her annoyance. Last were the Hutts, unmistakable and unmissable. Qi'ra had heard all sorts of things about them. Everyone had.

"Nothing quite prepares a person for their first encounter with a Hutt," Vos said. He sat back from her a little bit, giving them both space to take a drink. "What do you think?"

"I'm glad it's Black Sun who is hosting," Qi'ra said. As she had hoped it would, the comment amused Vos, and he laughed. His arm came around her shoulders, his clawed thumb under her chin so he could direct her gaze where he wanted her to look.

"Watch them with each other," he instructed. "And watch them with me, if any of those buffoons manage to find us. You'll have dealings with all of them later, or with ones just like them. This will be your introduction."

Qi'ra nodded, and his hand retreated to her shoulder. She watched and listened while denizens of the other syndicates came to speak with Dryden Vos. She quickly realized that he *had* been early, and moreso, he had done it on purpose. His arrival had allowed him to set up a little kingdom in this supposedly neutral territory, and if anyone wished to speak with the leader of Crimson Dawn, they had to come to him. While the others mingled around the room, Vos managed to hold court, almost exactly the way he would on the *First Light*. Even the Hutts sought him out, dragging themselves across the polished floor to say a polite hello and ask a few seemingly innocent questions about his profit margins.

While Qi'ra focused on the people in front of her, Margo scanned the room in general. Qi'ra wondered if it was habit, like for Aemon. She didn't think Margo was old enough to have been in Crimson Dawn when it ran independently and could get away with more indiscriminate killing, but Qi'ra had been in the Worms from childhood, so maybe Margo had a similar backstory. Eventually, Qi'ra realized that Margo was looking for the concierge, who had left her without any instructions. At least Qi'ra's tutor was right beside her. Margo sat alone on the end of the sofa, and even the serving droids took no notice of her when her glass was empty.

"Are you still getting on well?" Verelea asked, making rounds of the room to ensure her guests were comfortable. "I know this is a small affair, but these things are so difficult to arrange."

The look that passed between her and Vos was the final piece in the puzzle that Qi'ra was trying to solve. The party felt strained and random because it *was* strained and random. Someone had ordered Verelea to host it, and then ordered everyone else to attend. All of these former enemies and competitors, forced into a room together to eat and drink and pretend that everything was business as usual.

It was a power play, and the player wasn't even in attendance. Whoever pulled Vos's strings, and the strings of the other syndicate leaders, had made them drop everything and play nicely together, just to prove that they could force cooperation.

"You've done a marvelous job, Verelea," Vos said. "Really, I can't imagine a better place to introduce Qi'ra to everyone."

Vos was pretending that the party was to his benefit, when Qi'ra knew he'd rather be on his own ship. Faced with the idea of sitting down with his enemies, he had elected to use her as a distraction. And it had worked. Everyone who came up to them, even a representative from the Hutts, had inquired about her. Then, while Vos introduced her, they had tried to take her measure. They would have assumed all sorts of things about her, about them, and Vos let them do it because it shifted them away from thinking about Crimson Dawn.

"I am having a lovely time," Qi'ra said. She forced herself to dredge up a memory of Han, and then turned the resulting smile on the Falleen woman with nothing held back. It caught Verelea off guard, and she smiled back before she could regain control of her emotions.

"I must see to my other guests," Verelea said. She sounded slightly flustered, and turned away from them without waiting for Vos's farewell.

Qi'ra leaned back into the sofa and took a drink. Vos raised his glass to her in a mock salute and went back to work.

CHAPTER TWENTY-TWO

Even though no one was present by their own choosing, Verelea had managed to put together a very nice party. The food, of which there was plenty, was delicious, each dish delicately prepared for specific species, with room for crossover where digestion and adventure allowed. There was more than enough to drink, though Qi'ra would not have been surprised if the real alcohol was replaced with a less intoxicating substitute to keep the Crymorah humans and Pykes under control. She only held her third glass, but she felt none of the usual effects two of Vos's drinks would have had on her. Even the musical entertainment was well received, with burly Black Sun members discreetly in place to deal with any Hutt who got too close.

The longer the party went on, the more tightly Vos seemed to be wound. His hand, placed possessively on her knee or shoulder every time someone came close to talk to him, grabbed her harder, and he stopped being mindful of her bruises. Corynna returned but, after giving a short report and taking a seat next to Margo, did not attempt to draw anyone into conversation. Qi'ra was not by any means running out of people to observe, but the façade was starting to wear thin. There were no other syndicate leaders present, and Qi'ra realized that Vos was there—if somewhat reluctantly—only because he wanted to see what she was capable of. He could have sent Corynna on her own, but he'd chosen to come because he wanted to see Qi'ra in action for himself. At least she didn't have to worry about impressing someone really important. Still, there was never a good reason to overlook apparent underlings. You never knew where they might end up.

After several hours, Vos apparently decided his time was done, because he stood up and looked around for Verelea so that he could make their good-byes. Qi'ra was still on his arm, with the others ranged out behind them, as he scanned the crowd. Qi'ra had lost track of their hostess several minutes ago, but as she leaned over to tell Vos the last place she'd seen her, all the lights went out and the room crashed into darkness.

No one in a crime syndicate screamed just because it was suddenly dark, but there were a few gasps and curses, and the unmistakable noise of several dozen people reaching for weapons they had been relieved of and then remembering they were unarmed. Vos's grip on Qi'ra's arm hardened, but he didn't pull her in any direction yet. Margo and the concierge were pushed close behind them by the Hylobons, who were all growling now.

Verelea's voice rang out: "It's all right." She did not sound all right. "The life support system is intact, and there hasn't been a containment breach. We merely have a few uninvited guests."

The lights came on, and Qi'ra blinked as her eyes readjusted. Verelea was surrounded by six Falleen mercenaries who had not been present before. A seventh, a male dressed in clothes fancy enough that he could have been a party guest, stood apart from them, pointing a double-barreled blaster pistol straight at Verelea's head.

"I want to be very clear," said the intruder with the blaster, "that this is not inter-syndicate violence. I have no interest in anyone who is not the leadership of Black Sun. This is a self-contained coup, and there is no reason for any of the rest of you to be worried. When we're finished reorganizing our management, you will be taken to your ships and allowed to leave."

One of the Hutts protested loudly, and everyone in the room who understood Huttese winced when they translated the threat made to the Falleen's physical safety. Even Qi'ra, who was too distracted to remember to conceal her understanding of the language. Fortunately, no one was paying any attention to her.

"Oh, come now," said the intruder. "Surely even the Hutts have enough patience to wait a few moments."

He turned his attention back to Verelea. At his nod, two of his men grabbed her roughly by the arms and shoved her to her knees.

"Good-bye, dear sister," he said. "Thank you for all the work you put into restoring this place. It will serve me well as a base of operation."

"It will serve no one if I'm dead, fool," Verelea said. "The emergency environmental systems are keyed to me. If you kill me, the whole thing crashes, not just your trick with the lights. It's going to be very cold for at least six more hours out there, brother, and I don't think you'll like it very much."

The intruder paused, then brought the butt of the blaster down on her head, knocking her to the ground. Qi'ra flinched. A blow like that could easily kill someone, but Verelea must have survived, because nothing turned off. There was a rush of noise as the people in the room again started to protest being held in place.

"Everyone shut up!" the intruder shouted.

"If you truly don't want the other syndicates to be harmed, the best course of action is to let us go, Alorium." Dryden Vos had a soft voice, but it carried well when he wanted it to, and everyone in the room heard him speak.

"Dryden?" Alorium asked. "I thought everyone was

sending lackeys to this party. What the hell are you doing here?"

"There's no need to be rude, Alorium," Vos continued. "Everyone here is important, in their own way. Even you might be, if you pay attention."

"He keeps us under his boot, and you know it," Alorium hissed. "Once we were great, all of us, and now we wait for instructions like academy cadets. Black Sun will be independent again!"

"Oh, Alorium," Vos said, his patronizing tone pleasant enough to be disarming, even though no one in the room relaxed. "I might have suspected you were foolish enough to take out your sister, but for that reason? Oh, you should ask me to shoot you right now, to spare you the suffering he'll want if he catches you."

The green of Alorium's face turned a bit sickly. He had clearly been expecting someone in the room to take his side, but even knowing what little she did about the mysterious person who controlled the five syndicates, Qi'ra knew no one would go against him so brazenly.

"Well, I can't have witnesses, then, can I?" Alorium said.

Moving so swiftly he was almost a blur, Alorium turned back to his unconscious sister and fired the blaster into her midsection. Then he barked an order at his guards that Qi'ra couldn't hear over the rising tide of panic sweeping through the room. Alorium and the other Falleen with him left Verelea where she lay and pushed their way back to the door. Alorium must have bribed the door guards, because they offered no resistance, and the door shut behind them, effectively sealing everyone else in as the emergency lighting began to fail.

Qi'ra looked at the blood pooling under Verelea with growing understanding. Alorium had bought himself time to escape by shooting her not quite fatally. She was bleeding out, and that would give him enough time to get to his escape craft. The rest of them, sealed in, would be at the mercy of the elements as soon as Verelea's heart beat for the last time.

The Hylobons formed a tight circle around Vos's party, though already the crowd was starting to be too unpredictable for them to hold everyone together. They were jostled around, eight people being too many to control and too few to fight.

"Get me to her," Qi'ra shouted.

She wasn't sure if she was talking to Vos or Aemon, but at Vos's nod, Aemon began to press forward. It was up to them to keep up with him, but Qi'ra wouldn't relent. They reached the crumpled body, and Qi'ra knelt down beside her, feeling for a pulse and soaking her clothes in blood. Verelea's pulse was thready, but it was there.

"Help me," Qi'ra said, struggling to turn the semiconscious woman onto her back.

One of the other Hylobons knelt beside her, and they turned the body as softly as they could to prevent further injury. Qi'ra didn't think Verelea would feel more pain than she already was, but a sudden movement might hasten her death. Chanting an old Corellian skipping song under her breath and hoping like hell that Falleen anatomy was similar enough to a human's that this would work, Qi'ra began compressing Verelea's chest, stopping every eight beats to breathe directly into the woman's mouth. She couldn't press the dying woman's nostrils closed, and had to plug her nose with her fingers to force the lungs to inflate. Vos watched her for a few cycles, his surprise obvious and genuine, and then turned to the Hylobons.

"Find a way back to the shuttle!" he commanded.

They split off into the crowd. Were it anyone else, Qi'ra would doubt they'd come back, but she knew they were completely loyal to Vos, and as long as there was a chance Vos would make it out, they would fight for it. She couldn't spare much thought for them, though. The skipping song filled her mind—eight beats down and then breathe, eight beats down and then breathe. She was positive that Verelea's heart would have already stopped beating if she hadn't intervened, and this rhythm was all that was keeping everyone alive.

She lost track of time—eight beats down and then breathe—but at some point Vos leaned down to speak to her.

"How long will this last after you stop?" he asked.

Qi'ra couldn't reply—eight beats down and then breathe—which he took as answer enough. He paced uncomfortably, waiting for his bodyguards to return, or for Qi'ra's luck to run out.

"We have a path to the shuttle," Aemon said, appearing between one "eight beats down and then breathe" and the next. Qi'ra was only half listening to him—eight beats down and then breathe. She'd saved all their lives, and they were absolutely going to leave her behind.

"Give us ten seconds, girl." It was the first time Aemon had spoken directly to her. His helmet was open, and he was looking at her with something like respect. "Then follow us. Same way we came in."

He took his helmet off—his fur sticking up in tufts that would have been amusing under different circumstances—and put it on her head between cycles, leaving the visor open. She'd have to close it while she was running—eight beats down and then breathe. It would protect her head from the cold, and maybe her body would last long enough to make it.

"Come on," Vos said, and they left her.

Qi'ra had never felt so alone in her life. Not when she was dragged away from Han. Not when she was locked in the dark on Proxima's orders. Not even when she was a child, starving to death in the Silo without a single person who even knew that she existed, let alone cared if she died.

Eight beats down. And then breathe.

Qi'ra stumbled to her feet, shoes sliding in blood that wasn't hers even as she reached for the helmet controls. The seal that formed around her was claustrophobic and smelled horrible, but she'd never been so glad to be contained. She sprinted for the door, ignoring the ripples that ran through the remaining crowd as they realized that she had stopped doing whatever it was that had been keeping Verelea alive. Hands reached for her, but she was already running too fast. She'd gotten so much stronger since the days when running had been her only option, and now she was even better at it.

She peeled down the hallway to the shuttle. Aemon had found a blaster somewhere and was shooting people who were trying to push their way on. They had waited for her. She could hardly believe it. She got to the shuttle door, and one of the Hylobons dragged her inside. Vos was yelling at Margo, who was doing something with the wires that controlled the door. They hadn't waited for her. They couldn't get the door shut.

Margo finally crossed the correct wires, and the door closed so quickly that they ended up with several extra limbs in the shuttle with them. Qi'ra almost threw up in her borrowed helmet, and tore at the controls to get it off. Aemon pushed the arms and legs to the side of the shuttle and pulled his helmet off of Qi'ra's head.

"Thank you," she said.

Her skin was cold, white in some places, which she knew was bad. But the helmet had let her keep her focus and finish the job.

Margo couldn't meet her eyes, whether out of guilt or shame about the door. Corynna was piloting, because the Hylobons had all been needed to hold the door. Vos sat on a bench, breathing hard. This time, when Qi'ra met his gaze, she actually felt like he believed she was his lieutenant and not just a playing piece he could lose and still win the game.

CHAPTER TWENTY-THREE

The fallout from Verelea's death was minor and did not impact Crimson Dawn very much. She had led a small faction within Black Sun, and her vacancy was filled quickly enough. Not by her brother. Qi'ra didn't care enough to find out what exactly happened to Alorium, but she assumed it was grisly. Either Black Sun would clean up its own mess, or they would disavow him, and then he would be fair game to the other syndicates. Vos had been the biggest player in attendance, but that didn't mean there weren't a lot of very angry criminals who were interested in what happened to their attacker.

The death toll aside from Verelea had been fairly high. Although a few people had managed to get out of the room when Vos did, no one who was behind Qi'ra had lived. A lot of fairly senior spots in the other syndicates had to be filled quickly, and Vos made no secret of the fact that he was very pleased not to be in the same position. He never quite came out and said that Qi'ra had saved his life, but he did allow that she had saved him a great deal of datawork.

Trinia had been unable to get the blood out of Qi'ra's clothing, even with assistance from the high-tech cleaning droids aboard the *First Light*. Replacements appeared, all sized perfectly for her, along with a new version of the Crimson Dawn necklace, which had also been damaged. Qi'ra hadn't even noticed until they were back on board Vos's yacht, and then he'd put his fingers on her collarbone and said he didn't think it was salvageable. The red lines on his face were still bright, and everyone had been concerned that this would push him over, but he only apologized to all of them for not protecting them properly and disappeared into his office.

Margo was slightly kinder to Qi'ra now, especially once Vos emerged from his office after several days of conferences to report that no one who had harmed someone from another syndicate during the escape would be held accountable. The Imroosian had closed the door on several people, undoubtedly killing them, and was relieved to find out there would be no consequences. Corynna still treated her coldly, but now when she looked at Qi'ra it was with a sort of calculation instead of dismissal. Aemon didn't say anything, but Qi'ra was pretty sure he was glad, too. For her part, Qi'ra was just as happy to pretend the whole thing had never happened, except that three of the most high-ranking people on the ship—plus Margo—now owed her their lives. She didn't like the attention. But she did appreciate the Hylobons opening doors for her. It made everyone treat her like she could hurt them, if she wanted to.

When Qi'ra was summoned to Vos's office after the conferences were done, she wasn't entirely sure what to expect. The turbolift doors opened on a subdued version of the room. The windows were half-covered, so even the starlight couldn't get in. The artificial lights limned everything with a golden halo that should have been warm but only served to highlight the stark emptiness of the room. The only people present were Vos and a Falleen woman, and there was none of the usual background buzz of talking or music. This business was not for the glamour of a party or to show off Vos's power. This was private, and probably deadly.

"Qi'ra, this is Tallaria," Vos said. He waved her into a seat. No one held a drink, which was also unusual. Vos considered himself hospitable above everything else. Qi'ra looked at the decanters, and Vos shook his head. "You have met both her sister and her brother, and will be happy to know she is more of the former's character. She is also the one who has taken over."

"Your sister did her best to save everyone," Qi'ra said. "I am glad she could be succeeded by someone worthy of her."

"My sister only wanted to save herself," Tallaria said. "And you are all lucky that my brother is an excellent student of anatomy. If he'd been off in any direction, she would have bled out much more quickly."

"Still," said Vos. "None of us are entirely displeased by the way things have turned out."

It was nothing less than Qi'ra had expected. Vos hadn't lost anything, and Tallaria had gained a great deal of power.

"Qi'ra, you recall the situation that brought you to my attention in the first place?" Vos asked, steepling his fingers and leaning forward with his elbows on the desk.

"Yes," Qi'ra said. "I had uncovered a leak of Crimson Dawn trade intelligence. It went higher than we expected, but the source of the leak was plugged."

It was a cold way to describe Thallia screaming all the way out to the courtyard and being cut off only by the blaster bolt that killed her, but it was the story that was best told for public consumption.

"Indeed," Vos said. "Your admirable work in that incident elevated your whole crew within Crimson Dawn, but I am afraid the leak isn't quite as plugged as we thought."

Qi'ra's blood froze. She knew Vos was pretending ignorance, but if he was openly searching for a scapegoat, she herself was still the easiest person to blame. She hadn't found anything yet to identify how far up the leak went, and therefore couldn't expose Cerveteri because then Vos wouldn't be able to use the other girl to source the leak. Qi'ra had been too busy trying to carve out a place in Crimson Dawn to work on that mystery. She'd barely thought of her old crew, except for Trinia, at all. She shouldn't have spent so much time focused on her own stability without taking into consideration the group she had started her climb with.

"I also lost some money in the Thorum dealings," Tallaria said. Vos's eyebrows rose. "Not directly, of course. That was a Crimson Dawn territory. I did have some tertiary investments that were affected, however."

Vos chose to accept that explanation, and some tension left the room.

"At the time I was too low down in the operation to get an audience with Dryden Vos to speak about it," Tallaria continued. "But, as you know, circumstances have changed."

"Indeed," said Vos. Qi'ra had a suspicion he was considering which of them would be easier to kill, and she didn't like how his calculations might turn out.

"I know it was someone involved in the Crimson Dawn operation, obviously," Tallaria said. "They would have to be. That crew was strangely competent for a group of adolescents, and it wouldn't surprise me at all to learn that the leak had outside help."

"Have you been able to track anyone down?" Qi'ra asked. "Communications were monitored in that house, and there were other forms of surveillance, if the contact visited in person."

"I have been looking into it," Tallaria said. "I didn't have the resources until recently, and now I am reluctant to go digging around in the private information of an ally without permission."

"Very prudent," Vos said. "As far as I am concerned, you may look into whatever you like. I have just as much to gain if you find the culprit, but it's not easy to run an investigation on your own team. Feelings get involved."

"I do not suffer from an overburden of feelings," Tallaria said. "I will begin my examination as soon as I return home."

"How are you settling in, Tallaria?" Vos asked. It was the slow, overly genuine drawl he used when he was trying to say something else without actually saying it out loud. Qi'ra understood him immediately.

"It's a bit rocky," Tallaria said. "There are a lot of things that require my attention. My sister keyed many things to her DNA, it turns out, and sharing half of it is not helping as much as I might like."

That meant Qi'ra had some time. Even if Tallaria went straight home, there would be other things that required her attention. It wasn't much, but it was a window that Qi'ra could use, either to finish off Cerveteri and find out who was helping her, or frame someone else if she was desperate.

"It happens when there's a shift in power, no matter who you are," Vos said. "When I succeeded, my predecessor had left all sorts of nasty surprises. Sometimes our programmers still trip the traps, and then someone has to clean up the mess."

Tallaria grinned, her teeth showing white against the deep green of her skin.

"I know exactly what you mean," she said. "But I am confident that I'll have it sorted out soon. I do appreciate you seeing me on such short notice. I know you are busy, too."

"I have an obvious interest," Vos said. "I respect your loss of funds on Thorum, but I could lose a great deal more. It behooves us to work together. And, whatever her true motives, Qi'ra is correct about your sister. In trying to save her own skin, she saved ours. The least I can do to honor her is aid you in being her replacement."

"I look forward to working with you, Dryden Vos," Tallaria said, rising to her feet and inclining her head almost imperceptibly. Vos returned the gesture, and Tallaria went to the lift, which would take her down to her guards and her vessel.

Vos waited until the doors slid shut before he stood up and went over to the table where the decanters sat. He only held one glass.

"I don't need to tell you what I wish to happen, do I?" he said, filling the glass with dark green liquid. He took a sip and then looked at her over the rim.

"You do not," Qi'ra said. She still couldn't accuse Cerveteri directly, not until they knew who was pulling her strings. Tipping them off by going straight after Cerveteri might allow an escape, and Vos did not want to waste time and resources running the traitor down. "This is a bit sooner than I expected, on account of involving Black Sun, but I will be prepared by the time Tallaria gets the information she seeks."

"I am sure you will," Vos said. "But out of generosity, my engineers have informed me that something has malfunctioned on Tallaria's ship. She will be able to use her hyperdrive for only short bursts until it is fixed. They imagine it will extend her journey home, but, alas, we do not have the facilities to repair it."

"Thank you," Qi'ra said. "I will not waste the time you have given me."

Vos nodded his dismissal, and Qi'ra went back down to her room. Trinia was out, so she had her quarters to herself. She sat down on the edge of her bed, trying not to panic. Up there, in the stark light of Vos's office, it was easy to think about framing someone if she couldn't blame Cerveteri directly. Down here, it was much more complicated.

"They're not your friends," she whispered to herself. "When it's them or you, it always has to be you."

She stood up and looked into her mirror. The scrumrat was gone, her body filled out to a healthier weight and her eyes no longer instinctively looking down into the muck. She was Crimson Dawn. She had saved Dryden Vos, and he knew it. When he named her as his lieutenant, it might have been a lark for him at first, but she was going to make it mean something. No matter what it took.

The door opened and Trinia came in. She was carrying a tray piled with food. Qi'ra smiled by way of greeting, pretending to fix her hair.

"You look a little stressed," Trinia said. "Do you think we'll see old friends soon?"

As always, her comments were a little too close to the mark for comfort, but this time Qi'ra didn't care. She had work to do, and there were people who were going to help her, even if they didn't realize it. Because that was what power meant. Day by day, she was gathering more power around her, and day by day, she was learning how to wield it.

CHAPTER TWENTY-FOUR

The members of Qi'ra's crew from Thorum had changed since her time there, almost as much as she had. They were hard now, beaten into shape from training with the Hylobon guards. Even Hilst had lost the uncharacteristic softness in her Zabrak features. She was still focused on logistics and comms, the way that Qi'ra was focused on politics and commerce, but both of them had been honed sharp to the killing edge.

The change was most obvious in Cerveteri. Losing the privileges she'd enjoyed as crew leader had clearly been hard on her, though her newly acquired muscle and bulk made her a match for even Eleera. They all had a few more visible scars, but for whatever reason, the rest of them looked pleased to see Qi'ra and Trinia when they arrived in the barracks on one of the lowest inhabitable decks on the *First Light*.

"Do they even let you down here in shimmersilk?" Eleera

said, giving Qi'ra a quick and surprising hug. The violent Twi'lek had gotten much faster.

"You lot get to go around visibly armed," Qi'ra pointed out. "I have to defend myself with whatever pretty thing looks appropriate in polite society."

It wasn't quite true. Vos had given her a new set of batons after hers had been left in the weapons check at Verelea's disastrous party. They were nicer and hung from her waist almost unobtrusively enough to pass for a strangely decorative belt.

"Well, I'm pretty enough for polite society," Karil said, his grin far too carefree for someone who'd been going hand to hand with a Hylobon guard every day for weeks. "I'll defend you."

Qi'ra's laugh was genuine. The idea that any of them could defend her against what she faced now. Well, maybe Cerveteri could, but not in a way that she would like.

The room sorted itself into little groups as Qi'ra sat down, some to talk with Trinia, some with Qi'ra. A few were even indifferent. Lopie and Myem clearly had their sights on new career paths now that they were on Crimson Dawn's flagship, and neither of them wanted it to look like they were being favored because Qi'ra said so. The group that Qi'ra took special note of was the one that formed around Cerveteri. Both Rodians, Olio, and Noyio were with her. It was a strange group. Noyio and Olio were both connected to the slicing on Thorum, having been present at the time, and the Rodians were always a wild card. She could imagine what Cerveteri had been telling them.

"It hasn't been all bad," Karil said. "I can take a punch now."

"You cannot," Eleera said. Karil looked deeply offended, and she laughed. "You're getting better at dodging though. And getting up when you get decked."

"That's what taking a punch means," Karil said. "But no one wants to hear about our training regimen. We want to hear about everything that happens on the upper decks. We've barely been allowed higher than the engines. Does Vos really have the crown jewels of Mandalore up there? Have you seen them?"

Qi'ra let Trinia do most of the talking, trusting her not to give away too many secrets. Trinia had excellent judgment and was a fantastic read of character. As reluctant as Qi'ra had been to have her around all the time, perceiving all too much, she had to admit that of everyone she might have kept close from her life on Thorum, Trinia was the smartest bet. The only person who might be more useful was Margo, and Qi'ra still hadn't figured out how to win her over.

"Finally back with the scrumrats?" Cerveteri said, elbow digging hard into Qi'ra's hip as she sat down next to her. "We didn't think you'd ever come all the way down here just to see us."

"You were never a scrumrat, Cerveteri," Qi'ra said. "And you know as well as I do that only a few people can go everywhere they want on the *First Light*."

Let them imagine Vos had forbidden her from coming down. Let Trinia not say anything that indicated otherwise.

"Of course," Cerveteri said, disdain dripping from every pore. "We've all been so busy."

Qi'ra did not want to engage with her any more than she absolutely had to. The Rodians were clearly beyond her reach, but she still might be able to convince Noyio and Olio that she was worth being friends with. If Cerveteri had let anything slip, it would have been to them.

"Do you have any idea when we'll get to do something real?" Noyio asked. "This is the longest I've ever gone without flying something. They'll only let me and Drex use simulators, and I can only fly cargo pods around for so long before I lose my mind."

Drex agreed with her, but Qi'ra let Noyio tell her about it instead of revealing that she understood what he'd said.

"I think you might get an assignment soon," Qi'ra said. "I have been on one. We accidentally witnessed two factions in Black Sun trying to overthrow each other. The new leader of the faction came to thank Vos personally for her advancement."

She wasn't sure if Cerveteri knew that Black Sun had been involved, or if that had been above her head. From the rapid blinks that Cerveteri managed to quell after three or four repetitions, Qi'ra would guess that she did know, and that she understood that a Black Sun representative would only come here to get more information from Vos himself.

"In any case, I am sure you'll be able to get out soon," Qi'ra continued. "The Hylobons gossip, and I've heard them saying that you're all about to be better than them. They don't want anyone showing them up, so they'll just say you're ready."

Even the Rodians laughed at that, though she could tell none of them really believed her. Olio still hadn't said anything, and he was looking at her with resentment on his face that she didn't think had anything to do with her not visiting.

"I'm sorry I can't stay any longer, but I have duties of my own to attend to," Qi'ra said. "I think we'll see more of each other now, though. So at least there's that."

"Just like old times," Cerveteri muttered.

"Tell that to Thallia," Olio replied.

Qi'ra didn't think either of them had meant her to hear, and she gave no indication that she did. She and Trinia finished their good-byes and headed back to the lift.

"Are they really all right?" Qi'ra asked once they were alone.

"Yes," Trinia said. "It's just different. Cerveteri spent a lot of time trying to make them jealous of what you had, but none of them really cared. None of them expected to rise up in Crimson Dawn, and you got them a prime position with excellent training."

Qi'ra was glad most of them saw it that way. She was also glad that Cerveteri was shortsighted enough to try flipping the crew by making them jealous. If she had any sense at all, she would have spent all her time reminding them what Qi'ra had done to Thallia. It would have upset them, and eventually it would have convinced them that Qi'ra couldn't be trusted. It was such an obvious choice, and it took her a moment to realize that Cerveteri had made the mistake. Cerveteri had chosen to prey on what *her* biggest resentment was, not what everyone else's would be. And it was going to cost her, as soon as Qi'ra figured out how to make her pay.

"Olio will never like you, though," Trinia said. "He feels like it could have been him, and you wouldn't have cared about that, either."

This was Trinia's value. Her uncanny insight that seemed almost supernatural. It also offered up a solution to Qi'ra's problem. She didn't have time to draw Cerveteri out, and she wasn't sure how much collateral damage there would be to herself if she did. Olio was an easy target. He had been with Thallia that week, in the same apartment, working the same job. It would be very, very easy to make it look like he had done more.

Qi'ra didn't relish the idea of getting rid of him, but it had to be someone, and he had made it clear that he disliked her for the real reason, not Cerveteri's manufactured jealousy. By the time the lift reached their floor, Qi'ra had a plan. She made a few requests of Trinia, mostly designed to keep her away from their room for as long as possible, and then got to work.

She didn't have a dedicated workspace, because what would have been an office functioned as Trinia's bedroom. They did have a small table, though, so she got together all the gear she would need and went to work. She'd kept a copy of the slice she'd uncovered, both from the navicomputer and from the unfortunately helpful droid before she'd wiped its memory. It already looked like Thallia had done it, no thanks to Cerveteri's manipulations, but it was fairly straightforward to add a second set of digital fingerprints.

Olio wouldn't be good at slicing, so Qi'ra had to scale back what she wanted to do and leave much more evidence behind than a real slicer would. It also had to seem normal that no one had looked past Thallia's alterations in the code until they had a reason to examine it more closely. A fine line of clumsy to walk, but her recent training gave her enough skill to do it, especially with the top-of-the-line tools that were available to her now.

She elected to have Olio give away Crimson Dawn fleet schedules. There was no way he could have known them, but her proof would be undeniable. Where Thallia supposedly had given up the routes and customers that Crimson Dawn would notice the least, Olio would give away the schedule that allowed the Hammer ships to avoid Crimson Dawn altogether.

It was a death warrant. Every line in the code, every new bit of data that she sealed, was a nail in Olio's coffin. But Vos wanted to know who was pulling the strings, and he would absolutely sacrifice Qi'ra to find out, if she didn't make a move first. He was invested in her enough to give her time and a chance, but that was all. The rest was up to her.

She finished the programming and had hidden everything away by the time Trinia returned. There was a party tonight on Vos's level, and both of them had been included on the guest list at the last minute. Trinia was thrilled. She hadn't spent much time up there, and she loved the art and jewels in the collection. Qi'ra knew the truth. This was the end of Vos's timeline for her. She would have to hand over her evidence, or face the consequences.

Less than an hour later, and immaculately put together in black and red and gold, Qi'ra arrived at Vos's gathering. The music was already blaring and the drinks were flowing. How he'd found so many people on short notice was a mystery to her, but she supposed every planet had a criminal element, and all of them were probably as curious about Crimson Dawn as they were afraid of it.

"Qi'ra, my dear," Vos said, halfway across the room and

not bothering to modulate his tone. "Come here, come here, there are so many people to introduce you to."

He looked almost recklessly pleased with her, the sort of carelessness that led to blood. And tonight, it would. Leaving Trinia to get a closer look at the displays, Qi'ra stepped into the center of the throng, her face haughty and her posture relaxed. Vos handed her a glass off a tray and pulled her close, wrapping his arm around her shoulders. His lip curled when she slipped into his pocket the datacard with all the incriminating information he'd need to stop Black Sun from getting too far into his business.

"Now," he began, "first and most importantly, there is Dok-Ondar."

Qi'ra gave herself over to Crimson Dawn.

CHAPTER TWENTY-FIVE

Waiting for the summons felt like an eternity. Qi'ra guessed that Vos and Tallaria were negotiating who got what payout before moving on to the final deed, and wondered what exactly casual murder was worth to Dryden Vos. She'd never seen him lose control, but those lines on his face told of a truly terrible rage.

At last, word came down, and Qi'ra and Trinia returned to the top level of the *First Light*. This time, Qi'ra was all in black, the gold gleam of the new Crimson Dawn necklace the only color on her person. Trinia was dressed the way she always was, in a simple blouse and trousers with a scarf around her head, but today she, too, was in black. A set of Crimson Dawn earrings Qi'ra didn't know the origins of were her attendant's only concession to color. They made a striking pair. There was no doubt to whom they belonged.

The turbolift opened to the brilliant light of Vos's office on full display. They were in a planetary system, and the light of the stars shone through the uncovered windows. The interior lighting provided the rest of the illumination, breaking up the stark contrast that the starlight would have provided on its own.

Standing in a line down the center of the office, from just beyond the lift to the windows on the far side, were the members of Qi'ra's Thorum crew. They had been given uniforms, at last, marking them as agents and operatives of Crimson Dawn. The design was not exactly the same as the black-and-gold uniform worn by the Hylobon guards, but the effect was similar. They looked unified and deadly. Even Cerveteri couldn't help standing up straight, with authority pulling at her shoulders.

They were all looking forward, to Qi'ra's right, at Vos's desk. He was seated behind it, clearly waiting for her entrance. Tallaria's image glimmered blue as she watched via hologram. When Qi'ra drew near, Trinia on her heels, Vos stood and held his hand out to her. Nodding at Trinia to stand aside, Qi'ra went to him. As usual, he took her hand, this time raising the other to hold her chin between his clawed thumb and forefinger. She held her expression like she had at the party where she'd given him the datacard: confident and sure, a Crimson Dawn lieutenant who knew what she was worth.

"Qi'ra, my dear, thank you for joining us," Vos said. He released her face and slid the hand holding hers up to her elbow, drawing her close to him. "And Trinia. We haven't spoken frequently, but I am pleased with your work since you joined us here, as well. Qi'ra has benefited greatly from your support. The earrings suit you."

Trinia gave him a small smile and glanced nervously at Qi'ra. Perhaps she expected jealousy. It was strange for Trinia not to have a perfect read on the situation. If anything, Qi'ra was relieved that Vos thought Trinia was valuable enough to keep close. Qi'ra knew for certain that she was. She returned the smile before turning back to Vos.

The members of her crew looked confused. Most of them were decent at keeping their faces neutral, but this was overwhelming for them. They weren't sure why they had been summoned to Vos's office, and they were not expecting him to treat Qi'ra the way he did. Perhaps they had been imagining her position was more like Trinia's, an attendant or perhaps someone who served drinks and overheard conversations. What they saw instead was someone who was a full-fledged operative of Crimson Dawn.

Cerveteri was seething. She clearly hadn't expected to see Qi'ra in such a position, but now that she had, she was right back to wanting it. Qi'ra let a small smirk show, knowing it would only enrage the other woman. She wanted Cerveteri as off balance as possible for whatever was about to happen. She might let something slip. Vos still wanted to know who the higher-up leak was, and any one of his provocations might flush them out, but there were only so many crew members Qi'ra could sacrifice before she ran out of candidates.

Vos let go of her and stepped out from behind his desk. He was all in black, as always, his pale face not yet revealing the strange striations he bore. He looked almost avuncular, or like a proud teacher, pleased to see how well his students had turned out. And maybe that was part of the truth. Whatever else they were, they were his, and he was about to put them on display for Tallaria and Black Sun to see.

"I am so pleased that all of you are here," Vos said, his hands held extravagantly wide. "You haven't been on board long, but by now you must have realized that there are dozens, hundreds even, of hardworking, loyal members of Crimson Dawn who will never see this place. Not this office, though that is reserved for an even more select few, but this ship."

No one moved. Qi'ra wasn't even sure they were breathing anymore.

"The *First Light* is my home," Vos continued. "I needed a place that I could take with me, a place I could keep secure. That means I have given up many things, like sunlight and fresh air. I know you must miss them, too, cooped up here, but I also know that you are aware of the honor you have been accorded."

Myem glanced sideways at Qi'ra, trying to figure out what Vos was building up to, but Qi'ra didn't give anything away.

"You have been taken from your little operation on Thorum because you excelled there," Vos said. "And you have been brought here, to the very heart of Crimson Dawn. A privilege that so few are given. You should be proud of yourselves. You have done well."

Cerveteri was fighting to keep her shoulders still. She knew that something was up, that Vos was being much too effusive, but she had no idea what he was trying to lull them into and it was making her twitchy. Qi'ra watched her struggle and kept her own face straight with some satisfaction, letting Cerveteri see the gleam of confidence in her eyes.

"And yet," Vos said quietly. The temperature in the room plummeted. "And yet I cannot be entirely happy for you."

He reached again for Qi'ra, and she went to him. He put his hand on her shoulder and squeezed. Her bruises had mostly faded, since she hadn't trained with him for several days, but he still caught one with his claw. She let them see a bit of her pain, which she assumed he wanted. It put them on edge, and she felt the beginning of panic rise in them.

"Qi'ra has worked tirelessly to make sure that I don't regret bringing all of you here," Vos said. He squeezed again. She let more discomfort show and saw them draw the easiest conclusions. They were wrong, but that didn't matter.

They believed, and after this, no matter their shock, they'd remember how they thought she'd bought what they had.

Vos released her suddenly and she stumbled away from him. Trinia started forward to catch her, but Qi'ra gave the smallest shake of her head and the other girl withdrew. Qi'ra was sure there was about to be violence, and she didn't want Trinia caught up in it. She had no one to replace her with.

"Yet despite her efforts," Vos continued, "I am uneasy. Because although I have shown you every advantage, given you the very best I had to offer, another one of you has betrayed me."

Any good feeling left in the room dissipated immediately. All of them remembered Thallia's screams, but they'd taken comfort in thinking it was over. Learning that it wasn't was an ugly shock, especially now that they had been on the *First Light* long enough to hear all sorts of rumors about Dryden Vos's temper. To their credit, none of them moved. There was nowhere to go, and Crimson Dawn had taught them dignity. Also, every single one of them believed they were innocent—except the one who was actually guilty—and they thought that would protect them.

Vos turned away from them, looking out the viewport. It faced away from the suns, so he had full view of the planet beneath them. It was white with ice, as inhospitable as the void of space, for all its breathable atmosphere.

"It will not be tolerated." Heat crept into Vos's voice.

From her vantage point, Qi'ra could see his skin begin to turn red. The marks darkened, bathing his face in a red glow that seemed to emanate from them. "It will not be. I will not have disloyalty in my organization, much less my own ship. My home."

He shifted, reaching into his jacket for something shiny that Qi'ra couldn't see clearly from her angle.

"And so it will be wiped out," Vos said. "Driven from the ranks of those around me, so that only those who are loyal, who are true members of Crimson Dawn, remain."

He spun with the inhuman quickness of one who had studied teräs käsi much longer than Qi'ra had. To those who didn't know the forms, it looked impossibly fast and agile. A red arc extended from his hand as he threw one of his petars toward the line of soldiers assembled unknowingly for his judgment.

Olio didn't even have time to scream. The petar pierced his eye, burning with a sickening sizzle and smell, and found root in his brain. He had been standing at attention, his body locked upright. The speed at which the petar hit him was enough to propel him backward, a dead weight that crashed to the floor before anyone in the room had time to fully realize what had happened.

Drex and Lopie had been on either side of him, and both turned sideways to watch him fall, shocked to silence by the suddenness with which the so-called justice had been dispensed. The rest of the line wavered as they came close to the emotional breaking point. Several of them looked at Qi'ra, and the look she returned to them was calm, if not comforting. They held their positions.

"I knew I was right to be proud of you," Vos said. His face was returning to normal, his rage spent. "You really have done well, and I look forward to seeing what you'll do as you continue with Crimson Dawn. You will not be returning to the recruit barracks. Other quarters have been assigned to you. Please check with Corynna, my concierge, and she will ensure you are all seen to."

No one moved. No one knew what to say or do. Vos walked back to his desk and sat down, reaching for a cloth to wipe his hand.

"Oh, and leave the body," Vos said. "I will have it dealt with. You have much more important things to concern yourselves with now."

Qi'ra cocked her head toward the turbolift, and Karil and Eleera understood instantly. Karil inclined his head to Vos, and Eleera began to shepherd the others to the lift. Qi'ra waited until the room was empty before she turned to look at Trinia. Her attendant was paler than usual but still on her feet. No one was ever prepared for Vos's true face. Their eyes locked together, and a promise was exchanged. It was still everyone for themselves, but up to that point, they would do their best to help each other. Or, at least, Qi'ra was reasonably sure Trinia would anyway.

"That went well, I thought," Vos said. "No fuss, and barely any mess. Everyone seemed to accept the outcome."

"You made sure they were trained," Qi'ra said diplomatically. He still wanted results, but they both knew patience was the best play after a move like this.

Vos laughed, and then went to retrieve his petar from Olio's eye. It had stopped glowing, so the burning smell was dissipating a bit thanks to the air-filtration system. The hole in the burned ruin of Olio's face was cauterized all the way to the occipital.

"Tallaria, is that enough for Black Sun?" Vos continued conversationally.

"We are impressed with your management style, as ever," Tallaria said, her voice distorting slightly through the hologram. "Thank you for inviting us to observe."

"If there's anything else to pass along, I'll send a message," Vos said. He deactivated the hologram, then looked up at Qi'ra and Trinia. "Please, Trinia, take one of the meat puffs from that tray by the door when you leave. Eating will make you feel better."

Trinia dutifully picked up the morsel as they walked past, but as soon as they got back to the safety of their room, she threw it down the trash compactor.

CHAPTER TWENTY-SIX

I t took Cerveteri three whole days to learn the layout of the decks she was now permitted to access well enough to plan and execute an ambush on Qi'ra. Qi'ra even made it easy for her, taking the same route every day to the training room, even though she had no set schedule. Cerveteri was smart enough to attack her after she'd been sparring, at least, when her bruises would be fresh.

Qi'ra could have prevented the body slam into the bulkhead, and she could have broken Cerveteri's hold in any number of ways, but she had killed a boy to get here, so she was going to see it through. She did stop the blow that would have landed on the side of her head, though. Only Vos was allowed to bruise her face.

"Are you happy now?" Cerveteri hissed. "How many of us are you going to let him kill before you give up and die?"

"I don't let Dryden Vos do anything," Qi'ra said. "The sooner you learn that, the safer you'll be."

"Oh, I'll be safe," Cerveteri said. "I have connections you can't even dream about. Much better than being someone's pet. So he'll just keep killing, until there's no one left but you."

How she had ever thought Cerveteri Slane was clever, Qi'ra did not know. She was so angry, so hotheaded, that she missed the most obvious clues. She hadn't used the right reason to turn the crew against Qi'ra. She hadn't seen the walls closing in on Thorum. And now she didn't understand that Qi'ra was the one who had chosen Olio for death. Cerveteri thought Vos had, and that she herself was still in the clear. Most important, Cerveteri didn't realize that Qi'ra had no intention of being dislodged from her position for anyone.

There were a hundred things Qi'ra could have said to seal her victory. Pinned to the wall, she still held all the power, and Cerveteri was about to know it. But she decided not to say anything. Instead, she did what she always did when she wanted someone off balance. She remembered a reckless boy who wanted to fly, who had promised her the galaxy and truly believed that one day he would be the one to give it to her.

The smile that broke across her face was wide, and Cerveteri stumbled away from it as if it were a blow.

"It's all for nothing, you selfish hag," Cerveteri hissed, the death throes of a dying predator determined not to die alone. "I don't know who it was. The messages just appeared.

There was no name or origin. Nothing. Your precious Dryden Vos could cut me open with that fancy knife of his, and there is no way he'd learn anything from me."

Qi'ra kept the smile but let her eyes turn cold.

"So you are worthless to me, then?" she asked. "That was the only reason I was keeping you around."

Cerveteri wound up like a spring, releasing a desperate flailing blow that Qi'ra would have been able to dodge even before she'd started sparring with the leader of a criminal syndicate. It was easy to evade, grab Cerveteri's hand, and turn her energy against her. The movement ended with Cerveteri on her knees, Qi'ra's arms on her shoulders pressing her down, her hands at just the right places on her neck.

"Do it," Cerveteri spat.

Qi'ra took a moment to consider her options. Death was easy, relatively speaking. If Cerveteri was taken out of the equation, Qi'ra would have one less reason to look over her shoulder. Her life would be mildly simpler. She didn't know how the crew would react, but she was sure she could come up with a way to conceal the corpse long enough to provide herself with an alibi. Vos would know, but once she told him that Cerveteri was a dead end, he would be understanding, even if he would be frustrated over not discovering the identity of Cerveteri's associate. It would certainly be the most justified Qi'ra had ever been when it came to murder.

She remembered lying to the Mizi back on Thorum

that the secretary might know more about the leak, as a way to deflect attention from herself. If Cerveteri was good at one thing, it was *attracting* attention. Left alive, she might be viewed as a loose end, especially now that she was close to Vos. That would make her a target, and the people who came to take her out might be the lead that Qi'ra needed. Vos trusted her, but if she brought him this answer, she would fortify her position.

Picking up one foot, she kicked Cerveteri over onto her side. The landing was hard, air rushing from Cerveteri's lungs as she crumpled.

"I think you're late for mess," Qi'ra said sweetly. "I know you're new to the way things run up here, but it's always best to be punctual. It makes the right impression."

Cerveteri tried to say something but didn't have enough air for it, so all that came out was an angry croak. Qi'ra stepped over her and walked off without even looking back to make sure that her foe was still down.

◠

No one was more surprised than Qi'ra when Aemon caught Corynna in the act of poisoning the meal about to be served to Vos's guards. It was a desperate act from a desperate woman. Qi'ra must have frightened her half to death for her to do something so foolish. The Hylobon enforcers ate the same food that the non-Hylobon guards did. Maybe they would have died first, giving enough time and warning for the Hylobons to be cured, but it never got that far. Aemon caught her in the kitchen with poison held over the serving dishes, and that was that.

Qi'ra had arrived in the mess just as the commotion was starting to die down. Aemon had Corynna on her knees in the middle of the room. The guards, Hylobon and otherwise, were seated at the tables. They looked orderly at first glance, but Qi'ra could tell they were spoiling for some violence. Corynna had betrayed Dryden Vos himself. This wasn't a petty power play to gain status within Crimson Dawn. Corynna had wanted it all. And she hadn't been good enough to pull it off. Qi'ra looked at the presumably former concierge's face and saw only angry resignation. Everyone knew there was no getting out of this. There were only two options in a coup of this magnitude. Corynna might have come close, almost close enough to touch it, but she hadn't made it all the way.

Vos came down to the mess himself, rather than Aemon having to drag Corynna upstairs. Margo, looking terrified, arrived shortly after he did, on his summons. When she realized what her superior had done, she immediately denounced any involvement.

"Don't worry, Margo," Vos said without looking at her. "This had nothing to do with you, and I know that. You may sit, if you wish."

Margo did not sit, but she did calm down.

Corynna looked defiantly up at her doom. Vos didn't even give a speech this time. Now that the traps had drawn his quarry out in the open, he only wanted the kill. His face was cold and pale as he activated the petar. More than one of Qi'ra's old comrades flinched at the sound. It was not easy to forget the smell. Qi'ra had been right about not wanting to see those weapons up close.

Vos took two steps toward Corynna—who was clearly expecting the opportunity to explain herself, even if she didn't expect to survive for long after the explanation—and then slashed his petar across her neck. A normal blade would have opened her throat. She would have reached for the wound reflexively, trying to hold the blood back as her life gushed out of her. But the petar didn't cut like a normal blade. Instead, the wound immediately sealed over, cauterized with a heat stronger than fire. She fell to her knees and tried to scream, but the burns went deep enough that her vocal cords were damaged, and she couldn't.

"Margo, do you have a moment?" Vos asked, still not taking his eyes off of the woman in front of him.

"Y-yes, of course," Margo replied. Her voice was strong, considering, and Qi'ra knew she was deploying all the tricks she'd taught Qi'ra.

"You have been in charge of part of Qi'ra's training. Would you say she is sufficiently ready for what her position in Crimson Dawn will offer her?" Vos leaned forward and sank the petar into the concierge's shoulder, right at the joint, where the bones rubbed. The horrible not-a-scream rattled again.

"Yes," Margo answered. She looked sideways at Qi'ra, but Qi'ra couldn't read her expression. "She is a quick study, and she has worked hard."

"Excellent," Vos said. He took a handkerchief out of his pocket and mopped his forehead with it, like his work was a great exertion. "You will no longer have time to be her teacher. I want you to go to your office and make sure everything is in order there. You and I will have a meeting later, to ensure that certain files are secured properly. Do you understand?"

Dryden Vos's new concierge straightened her shoulders, the smallest satisfied smile creeping across her chalky face. She looked at Qi'ra again, and this time, Qi'ra saw that Margo had a complete understanding that her sudden rise in fortune had been due to machinations that Qi'ra had set in motion. Margo nodded to her. It wasn't much of an accord, but it was the start of one.

"Of course," Margo replied. "I am happy to serve Crimson Dawn, and I am at your disposal."

"Go, then," Vos said. "I will be along shortly, after I have dealt with a matter of housekeeping."

Chin high, Margo glided out of the room, heading

for her new office. Qi'ra silently wished her well. Margo's loyalty to Vos was thus far unimpeachable, but with some time, Qi'ra would find a way to win her over. Technically, she was Margo's superior, but she decided that polite deference would be the best way forward for a while. Corynna had treated her assistant as more of a tool than an ally, and Margo didn't seem to be aware of what the concierge had been up to. Qi'ra would be wiser and utilize all of Margo's talents.

"Lunch will be delayed, with my apologies," Vos continued. "You may remain here until it is served. I will personally ensure that the cooking is up to the proper quality."

Corynna was no longer able to hold herself upright. She was in too much pain, and breathing was too difficult. She started to fall to the side, and Vos waved off the Hylobons who would have held her up for him. He stepped close and then ground the heel of his polished boot into the petar burn on her shoulder. She couldn't even draw enough air to croak anymore, and Qi'ra realized he intended to let her die like this, choking on her own throat while everyone she'd tried to murder watched. If she was lucky, she'd pass out from pain first.

"After lunch, you are to take the afternoon at your leisure," Vos said. "We will be doing some reorganization, and it's possible that some of you may be shifted around as a result. My new concierge is highly skilled, however, and I have complete faith in her ability to see to everyone's needs."

Corynna held her hands up like claws, pleading for mercy or air, Qi'ra didn't know which. It hadn't been a particularly original plan, undermining from within by exploiting greedy underlings, but it could have been effective. As concierge, Corynna was privy to a great deal of information. No one in Crimson Dawn trusted anyone else completely, and Corynna had been perfectly placed to play those strings of distrust. She might look like she was nothing more than a glorified steward, but with her access and ambition—and her ability to conceal the latter when she needed to—she should have been able to come up with a more cunning idea. Or at least one that didn't fall apart the moment one of the underlings was exposed. Qi'ra looked at Cerveteri, who was white as the ice planet they were still orbiting. She felt Qi'ra's gaze on her, and they locked eyes.

This is what I can give you, Qi'ra promised silently. *This is what waits for you, the moment I decide you deserve it.*

There was no mistaking the understanding in Cerveteri's eyes. Or the fear. She was Qi'ra's now. Eventually she might recover enough to plot again, and her anger would always burn hot, but for now, she was nothing to worry about.

"Qi'ra, my dear," Vos said. "Will you accompany me? Everyone here is sorted, and I wish to speak with my new concierge as soon as possible."

He wiped the petar on his handkerchief and returned

both of them to their places, concealed on his body. He held out a hand for her, demanding. And like always, she took it.

He led her out into the corridor. Behind them, the mess was totally silent, except for a pair of desperate heels, kicking against an uncaring floor as a set of dying lungs exploded and an ending finally came.

*S*he knows it's destined for failure before they even start, but she can't resist the allure. How could anyone, with a smile like that flashing out of the grim sewers only for her (and maybe a little bit for the speeder), and a vial of the most valuable thing in the galaxy tucked into her jacket? It's a siren song, attracting the doomed, and she has no defense against it, even though part of her screams to leave him, to run.

They have had wins before, days of heady victory and nights with full bellies, but nothing quite like this. The adrenaline surges through her, like the wind rushing over the front of the speeder, and she feels like they might be unstoppable. She's not thinking about an angle or a way out. She's only thinking about flying, and the way he'll look at her when he sees the stars up close.

It goes sideways so quickly, and quite literally at that. The speeder comes so close to making it through the gap. If he'd held the accelerator a bit longer, or if their momentum had been just a little bit greater, they would have made it. Those extra seconds would have bought them enough time at the spaceport instead of throwing them at the mercy of an uncaring bureaucrat and a door that closes much too fast, with her on the wrong side of it.

He hammers on the glass, but she already knows it's pointless. He'll stay and be noble and get caught, and they may not even bother to take him outside before they shoot him. She does the only thing she can think of to save his life, and he finally goes, self-preservation kicking in much too late to do her any good.

The dice are hard in her hand, still warm from his skin. He's always had *them close by, and now they're stuck in the spaceport with her. She wants to think that she tucks them away because she's saving them for him, for when he comes back to stage a glorious rescue. She wants to think that it's sentiment that drives her, as it would drive him.*

But it isn't.

The dice are small and they are hard. They are not much of a weapon, but she is not in a position to throw anything away. They are small enough to hide. Small enough to keep. She's never going to give them back, not in any of the futures that she's seen, but they're still something that's hers. She puts the dice in her mouth as they drag her away. Han is already lost in the crowd.

CHAPTER TWENTY-SEVEN

Considering all the excitement it took to get there, being a high-level operative in Crimson Dawn was a relatively staid experience most of the time. Qi'ra sat in on more and more of Vos's meetings, her hand on his arm as a show of support, or his hand at the small of her back as she leaned forward to feign interest in whatever their associate was saying. She signaled when it was time for drinks to be refilled. She announced when it was time to celebrate a well-struck deal. She laughed at all the right times. She flattered their visitors with breathless compliments or calculated appreciation, whichever they would most prefer. And every time Vos smiled at her, the edge on his possessiveness sharpened.

One of her crew members was always on guard in his office now. The role was largely ceremonial, but the honor did not go unnoticed by anyone on board. The Hylobons knew they weren't under threat, so they didn't care. Noyio and Drex were taught to fly the shuttle. Hilst worked with Margo. Karil and Eleera were occasionally invited to Vos's parties, to play the crowd like Qi'ra did, though their targets were of decidedly lower status. Lopie was recruited to the engineering department. Myem and Qorsha split command duties between them, an unspoken agreement that worked out well for everyone.

Cerveteri was largely overlooked. She spent the most time on guard duty in Vos's office, a blessing on the surface, but she had no secondary role aboard the *First Light*. Even Trinia was involving herself more in ship operations at Qi'ra's request. Cerveteri knew it was being done deliberately, but all she could do for the moment was show up for her shifts. Vos looked right through her when she was in his office, even though he casually chatted with the others if there was no business to be done. She wasn't worth gathering information about. He knew everything about her that he cared to, and she was only alive because Vos had left her fate in Qi'ra's hands.

By the time Qi'ra was finally given what she considered a real assignment, she was worried that she had gone soft from ship living. It was like Thorum, she realized. Being in a comfortable position that she got used to in spite of the constant fear that something was coming down on her. Vos laughed when she told him, pointing out that her body had never been a finer weapon, but that wasn't what she meant.

Teräs käsi kept her in peak form physically, but it had been some time since she'd put her mind to any significant test.

"I know it might seem trivial," Vos said. "But this job is important. Not because of what you are after or the credits it's worth, but because of who the client is."

The serious bent to Vos's tone and the lack of any additional information filled Qi'ra in on the rest. This mission was at the request of their mysterious controller. Her success was mandatory.

She requisitioned a slightly nicer version of the uniform her crew wore when they were on guard duty. Since they would all be going together and since the mission was probably going to involve getting her hands dirty, Qi'ra dressed for practicality. Trinia was coming with her. Qi'ra met with Margo a few times to arrange the finer details. They never spoke of Margo's new office or how she'd got there, but the current of it threaded its way into all of their conversations.

At last Qi'ra called her team together to give them the mission briefing. She had carefully selected what she wasn't going to tell them but otherwise would be generally honest about their objectives and plans. She had them assemble in the mess, rather than somewhere more formal. They knew who she was. She didn't have to remind them.

"On the surface, it's a simple retrieval job," Qi'ra said. "Nothing we haven't done before. The scale is a bit larger, mostly because we'll be traveling between planets instead of just sticking around like on Thorum."

The memory of their time on Thorum was what bound them all together, so reminding them about it never hurt. Whatever splinters had been driven between them by Thallia and Olio's deaths, some of the wounds had healed now that Corynna was dead. They hadn't been given a full explanation. As far as they knew, Corynna had tried to poison Vos's guards as part of her plan to supplant him, fearing that they were too loyal to him to switch over to her. The rest of their reconciliation with Qi'ra was the result of the increased privileges and training they now enjoyed. Only Cerveteri knew it wasn't over, and continued trying to turn them against Qi'ra, but most of them recognized a good ride when they were on it and weren't about to mess it up.

"Noyio and Drex will split piloting duties, but then both will join us on the rest of the mission," Qi'ra said. "The planet we are headed to is uninhabited, so we are able to leave our ship unguarded. What we are after is no trifle, but it is only worth credits to a select few. I do not know the details, but I am told that the retrieval will test us. I, for one, am looking forward to it."

They grinned at her, and she knew they were, too. Vos had been right when he said that being cooped up on the ship was a trial for them, even though it was also an honor. All of them were planet-born, and even Qi'ra, whose part of Corellia had been a glorified garbage pile, was eager to get outside. If nothing else, that fact would have tied them all to her cause, but they were also proud to be agents of Crimson Dawn. Vos had flattered them right into it, and training with the Hylobons had given them the confidence they needed to pull it off.

"If you have any final preparations, I suggest you make them," Qi'ra concluded. "We leave in three hours. Noyio and Drex, be on the ship in two."

They all nodded—even Cerveteri, who was, at least, glad to be getting off the *First Light*. Qi'ra watched them break off into groups, excitedly talking about what they were about to do. She and Trinia headed directly to the ship, since they were already packed and Qi'ra wanted to go over the vessel before they left.

"You worry about them, but not for the reasons they think," Trinia said.

"If they knew what I thought, then they wouldn't need me, would they?" Qi'ra replied. The key to Trinia, she learned, was answering with a question.

"I suppose," Trinia said. "Cerveteri will be armed."

"And dangerous," Qi'ra agreed. "But nothing to be concerned about. She'll strike when she strikes, and I'll stop her."

Trinia didn't say anything, but her small smile indicated she had no doubts as to who the victor would be.

The hauler was not large, considering how many of them would be making the journey. At least the actual trip was relatively short, a matter of hours by hyperspace. It was the planetary expedition that was expected to take up the bulk of their time, and they had packed accordingly. The hold was full of camping gear and survival equipment. Qi'ra was not exactly looking forward to roughing it, but after so long in the luxury of the *First Light*, she admitted it would be good for her.

Trinia took their bags to the cabin they would share, and Qi'ra continued her explorations. The cockpit was just large enough for the pilot and copilot. No observers would be able to sit with them. There was a bunk for whichever pilot was not on duty, and a small head. She knew that Noyio and Drex had been practicing on all manner of craft in the simulators, and she had flown with Noyio enough on Thorum that she did not doubt either of their abilities to make the journey safely.

The hauler had one gun turret in the aft section. The goal was not to need it, but Qi'ra determined that the controls were easy enough that any of them could fire it, if required. Since Cerveteri would be on board, Qi'ra keyed in a security code. Cerveteri could probably break it, but at least Qi'ra would have a warning if she decided to do something drastic.

The cabins were cramped and the head even more so.

There was no real galley or common area. The ship was made for cargo hauling, and people were an afterthought.

"Does this ship have a name?" Trinia asked.

"You know, I didn't think about it," Qi'ra replied. "Is there anything in the registry? I didn't see markings on the side when we boarded."

Trinia stepped to a panel and typed quickly. She scanned through several files and then found the one she was after.

"*Crimson Reach*," Trinia reported after a moment. "It's fairly new, so nothing's been retrofitted. The maintenance manual is up to date, if you want to look?"

Qi'ra waved her off. Trinia's assessment was enough. Her life would rely on the ship, too, so there was no reason for Qi'ra to doubt her report on it.

"The others will start arriving soon," she said.

"It hasn't even been two hours yet," Trinia told her. "You gave them three."

"Yes, but I think they'll be excited to get underway," Qi'ra guessed.

"Cerveteri might wait until the last moment," Trinia said. "No one could say she wasn't following orders."

"I don't think she will," Qi'ra said. "As tempting as malicious compliance is, she's more afraid that we'll leave her behind."

"She's not going to have many chances to prove herself to Vos," Trinia said. "She has to make the most of this one."

"Exactly," Qi'ra said. "So she won't be late, and she won't cause trouble. She will definitely try to kill me, but it won't be the first time."

"The Hylobons didn't even bother setting up a betting pool," Trinia told her. "Well, about that, at least. There are bets on a bunch of other things."

Qi'ra had no wish to know what Aemon thought her odds of success were, or what minute details the guards thought fodder for betting. She had no problem being their amusement, but she didn't need to know everything about it. She already ignored most of what was said about her and Vos—for a crime syndicate that relied on secrecy and subterfuge, there was a tremendous amount of gossip—so it was easy to ignore everything else. She knew the truth, and the lie had its uses, so she didn't try to set the record straight.

As she predicted, her entire team showed up just after the two-hour mark, Cerveteri scowling at the end of the line as the pilots raced ahead to finally get their hands on some real controls. They stowed their personal gear efficiently and took a few moments to familiarize themselves with the contents of the hold. When Qi'ra was satisfied that they were all settled in, she commed *First Light* control and asked for permission to make an early departure. She expected an automated reply, but instead, the familiar voice of Dryden Vos filled the ship.

"I am thrilled you're all so excited to be off," he said. She could imagine him pacing in his office, thinking faux paternally about the mission his people were about to embark on. "It is a sign of your quality and loyalty, and I am honored to have both from you. Your permission for an early departure is granted. I hope all of your tasks go so efficiently, and that you return to us successfully before we've even had time to miss you."

He probably wouldn't think about them the entire time they were gone, except maybe to wonder where his usual guard was or to ponder what their mysterious leader could possibly want with an ancient trinket from a dead world.

"Farewell, my friends," Vos said, winding down his speech. "And safe travels."

The comm clicked off, and Qi'ra made her way up to the cockpit. It was crowded, and she had to hold on to the wall in order to stay stable, but she wasn't going to be anywhere else when the ship launched.

"Take us out," she said, once she was securely installed behind the pilots. They worked in perfect concert on the controls, and *Crimson Reach* slid into space as smoothly as if they'd done it a hundred times. "Set a course when we're clear."

Noyio began the calculations while Drex piloted them clear of the *First Light*. They put enough space between the two ships for safety, and then Drex turned *Crimson Reach* in the right direction. They floated there, awaiting the results from the navicomputer.

"Course laid in," Noyio reported. Her hand hovered above the controls, her excitement palpable. Qi'ra could sympathize entirely.

"Let's go, then," Qi'ra said.

Noyio finished the sequence, and *Crimson Reach* shot into hyperspace. The stars streaked by, and Qi'ra was caught up in the beauty of them. Noyio was also staring, but turned back to the controls when Drex coughed to get her attention.

"Well done," Qi'ra told them. "Notify me ten minutes before our arrival."

She descended into the hold, ready for whatever was to come.

CHAPTER TWENTY-EIGHT

The planet was entirely empty of signs of habitation, current or otherwise, save for one giant mountain of a construct that rose high enough out of the forest that they could see it from orbit. Qi'ra did not have to tell the pilots that it was their destination. They were already scanning for the closest available landing site.

"There," said Noyio. "It's just a clearing, but it's as close as we're going to get, unless you want us to drop you in."

"No," said Qi'ra. "We'll go in together."

The decision wouldn't save all of their lives, but it would save some of them.

Since they still had no real idea what to expect, Qi'ra called Myem and Qorsha up to walk at the front of the group with her. She highly doubted they would be attacked from behind, but the building in front of them was large enough to house all kinds of surprises. They picked their way through the trees, crossing the pine-needle-strewn ground quickly since there wasn't much in the way of undergrowth. The forest was strangely quiet. The jungle on Thorum had always been full of birdsong at the very least, and even in the shadows of the shipyards of Corellia, what few trees there were attracted wildlife. Here there was nothing. The forest was empty.

At last they came to the base of the building's outer wall. Its four walls reached upward at an angle that would have almost been scalable, except the black stone was polished smooth and there were no handholds. Where the walls met at the top of the pyramid, there was a point that looked impossibly sharp, even from the ground tens of meters below. There were no markings, no windows. Nothing cut into the stone that gave any indication what they were looking at. There was no sign of a door, either.

"Eleera, take Noyio, Myem, and Hilst, and go that way," Qi'ra said, pointing along the wall. "Everyone else will come with me and go the other way. Whoever finds a way in first, notify the others."

Eleera nodded, and her party set off. Qi'ra's party reorganized themselves and began to trek along the wall in the opposite direction. It seemed to stretch on forever.

"These blocks are huge," Lopie said. "And they're fit so closely together that you couldn't squeeze a Hosnian termite between them. How did they get put in place?"

Qi'ra wasn't inclined to spend a lot of time thinking

about construction, but she had to admit the building was impressive. By sheer size alone, the technology needed to build it would have been substantial. Each stone in the wall had been ground down after it was put in place and then polished, to give the angle and shine. The black rock shone in the sun, and looking at the top was difficult, because the gleam was so bright.

Eventually they turned a corner and came to a spot in the wall where some damage had been done to the stone. There were scrapes and blaster marks, like something had tried to cut through the blocks and then got annoyed when it couldn't.

"Qi'ra!" called Trinia, who had stepped into the trees for some shade. "You had better come see this!"

Qi'ra walked briskly to see what she'd found, and was not entirely surprised to discover a corpse on the ground at the bottom of one of the wide-trunked trees. A closer look made her realize that *corpse* might be too strong a word. The body was long gone, and even most of the bones had been dragged away by scavengers. All that was left was unfamiliar-looking body armor. A few meters away, where it would have rolled or been dragged by some no-longer-present scavenger, was a helmet. The skull was long gone, too, but Qi'ra took a closer look at what was left.

The helmet was a design she didn't recognize, either. It was black, and fit closer to the skull than a stormtrooper or clone helmet would. It had been designed to look sleek, with a silver front piece that still glistened in the dappled sunlight under the trees. Lines had been carved in a grid pattern over most of the helmet's surface, and the eyes of whoever had worn it would have been covered.

"I've never seen anything like that," Karil said.

"Neither have I," Qi'ra told him.

"Several religious orders wear helmets," Trinia said.

Qi'ra looked up at her.

"Why would you think of religious orders?" she asked.

"Well, this giant building, beautifully built in the middle of nowhere, almost has to be some kind of temple, wouldn't you think?" Trinia said. "So, religious."

It was a good point. Qi'ra avoided religion as a general rule. Back on Corellia, Tsuulo had been really into something he called the Force. Since Han had to translate everything he said for her, Qi'ra wasn't sure how much of the information she had was accurate, but she knew enough to know she didn't want to mess with any of that.

"Let's get back to the building," Qi'ra said.

By the time they returned, Eleera's party had turned into view. Clearly they hadn't found an entrance, either. Qi'ra studied the damage on the exterior closely, and thought about the body behind her. There had to be a reason that they were in the same area.

"Nothing," Eleera said. "And I gather you didn't have any luck, either?"

"There's this," Qi'ra said. She reached out and touched the blaster damage. "And there's a body in the woods behind us. Trinia thinks he might have been a member of a religious order."

Eleera made a face.

"The blaster scoring I understand," Qi'ra said. She dropped her hand to one of the scratch marks gouged deep in the stone. "But what could cause damage like this?"

"Really unethical archaeology?" Eleera guessed.

She said it as a joke, but Qi'ra didn't laugh it off.

"You didn't find a way in," she said. "And we only found this, and a dead man. What if the entrance is here, and we have to make it reveal itself somehow?"

"Like a code word?" Trinia asked. "Spoken? I don't see any place to type in a digital one."

Qi'ra placed both hands on the stone. It almost seemed to hum under her fingertips, even where she touched the damaged surface. She let the strange hum flow through her, like it was looking for something, and kept her hands on the wall. She breathed like she was getting ready for teräs käsi and felt her heartbeat slow. The temple was stronger than she was. She had to accept that. She couldn't break into it, couldn't force it to do anything. All she could do was admit that she needed a door, and that no matter how hard she fought, she couldn't *make* one appear.

With a click that she felt in her marrow, the stone accepted her and moved backward into the building. Qi'ra almost fell forward but managed to catch herself at the last moment. By the time the noise stopped, a passageway into the building had opened up.

"It really is a temple," Trinia said.

Qi'ra did not disagree with her, even though her blood still chilled at the thought.

"Hilst, you and Drex stay out here," she ordered. "Make sure the comms stay operational. I don't want to lose touch inside."

The pair nodded and moved to flank the doorway. The rest of them followed Qi'ra down the passageway. She waved Trinia up to the front.

"Tell me everything you can about the religion you think this is," she said.

"It's complicated," Trinia said. "And there were a lot of factions."

"Were?" Qi'ra asked.

"Oh, yes," Trinia replied. "They were all wiped out a long time ago. Mostly they fought each other, and eventually they just stopped existing."

In Qi'ra's experience, nothing with that kind of power—the sort it would take to build a temple like this—faded out.

It was wiped out and covered over by other powers. The Empire did it all the time.

"There were light side adherents and dark side," Trinia continued. It was what Qi'ra had suspected. The Force religion that Tsuulo had been obsessed with. "The light side was all about balance, and the dark side was all about anger and destruction."

They made their way down the passage, activating glow rods when the darkness became too much. The walls were covered with letters in a language Qi'ra couldn't read.

"The passageway must have been cut after the temple was built," Karil said. "It was a solid block, and then they came back and carved it out. Look, we can see how the pieces are joined because they were cut after they were put in place."

He was right. Each piece had a series of knobs that protruded from the top of it and locked into place with a corresponding hole above.

"That or they started with the tunnels in mind, made all the modifications to the blocks they'd need, and reverse engineered the building around the empty spaces," Karil continued. He paused, trying to work it out in his head. "No, that's impossible. Not even a master builder could do that."

Qi'ra didn't think it really mattered. Whoever had built this place was long dead, like the body in the forest beyond.

She felt something brush her leg, just above her ankle.

It was like walking through a spiderweb. Minimal resistance but undeniably there. A strange whistling noise was the only other warning she got.

"Down," she said, throwing herself sideways and taking Trinia with her.

A giant blade shot out of a niche in the wall and cut through the air where Qi'ra had just been standing. Everyone else was frozen in place. When her heartbeat had calmed a little, Qi'ra held her glow rod out in front of her and saw at least a dozen other strings threaded across the passageway below knee height. Every breath felt like a fight for a moment while she realized what they had stumbled into.

"It's a trap," Eleera said.

"It's a lot more than one trap," Lopie added. "This is just the first hallway."

No wonder their mysterious overseer didn't want to do this himself. Qi'ra wondered if Vos had known. It wouldn't have made a difference, but she thought he might have told her in advance if he had.

"We'll go carefully," Qi'ra said. "One trap at a time. We can make it through."

Keeping her torch steady, Qi'ra avoided each string in the hallway and didn't activate any of the blades. After her example, the rest of her team made the same careful journey. When they were all through, Qi'ra rummaged through her bag and came up with a folding tin that she could use as a plate or bowl. She expanded it to full size, crouched down, and then threw it down the hallway behind her, as close to the floor as she could.

The strings were cut, and the whooshing noise of a dozen blades filled the air as they swung through. After they returned to their original positions, Qi'ra tossed a second plate. Nothing happened.

"Couldn't you have done that *before* we walked down the hallway of incredibly sharp knives?" Qorsha asked.

"I didn't know how far it was to the end," Qi'ra pointed out. "Now we'll have a clear way out."

She made her way back to the front of the line. Lopie took Trinia's place beside her, his keen eyes scanning for anything that might be the next trap. They walked several steps forward without finding any irregularities, so Qi'ra waved at everyone to follow them. There was a shift in the stone beneath her feet as the group drew close, and the temperature dropped so sharply that goose bumps burst out on her arms.

"Wait!" she and Lopie called out together, but it was too late.

The pressure plate under the block they were standing on was activated, and the block behind them disintegrated to nothing. The creepiest part was that there was no flash or explosion. The rock, which had seemed so solid and real, was just *gone*. Two screams ended very abruptly. Everyone on the block with her and Lopie was fine, but in the dark, with glow rods flashing in every direction, Qi'ra couldn't see who hadn't made it. Eventually she worked her way to the edge and shone her glow rod down.

The new floor was at least three meters below the one they were standing on, a series of razor-sharp metal spikes sticking up from it. They were packed much too tightly together for there to be any hope. The beam from Qi'ra's glow rod illuminated Noyio and Qorsha, skewered and splayed. She heard someone behind her dry-heave. Qi'ra didn't feel sick. She felt determined. She was going to make it out of here and back to the *First Light* with her prize. She would accept nothing else. The temple had let her in because she hadn't fought it, but she was more than willing to fight her way out.

She turned away from the pit, leaving Noyio and Qorsha to rot in the dark, and rejoined Lopie at the front. Shivering, they pressed cautiously on.

CHAPTER TWENTY-NINE

N o one wanted to be in the front, and no one wanted to be in the back. After a sheet of flaming gas descended from the ceiling, reducing Karil and Myem to so much char, no one really wanted to be in the middle, either. At least it wasn't so bitingly cold after that.

"Not that it matters," Cerveteri grumbled. "We're all going to die in here anyway."

Qi'ra didn't entirely disagree with her. Besides them, only Lopie, Trinia, and Eleera remained. Five out of nine—plus Hilst and Drex outside—wasn't a reassuring number of survivors.

At least they were out of the passageway. After escaping the narrow confines, they had found themselves in a wide stone room. The light from their torches bounced off the polished walls, illuminating the area enough that they could move around almost freely.

In the center of the room was a raised stone platform. It was made of the same stone as everything else, and rested seamlessly on the floor, which probably meant it had been carved out of the original solid construction. None of them had worked up the courage to touch the platform yet, but after they cleared the room of any other potential danger, it became inevitable.

Qi'ra joined Lopie at one of the platform's narrow ends. He was studying it as closely as he could without actually touching it.

"I have no idea," he said after a moment. "I can't see anything, but I didn't see the fire switch, either."

They didn't know who had actually triggered the fire trap, only that it must have had a few seconds of delay in releasing, because Myem and Karil had been fourth and fifth in line at the time.

"It wasn't your fault," Qi'ra said. She put a hand on his shoulder. "Everyone is doing their best."

He smiled weakly at her, and she stepped forward. She reached out, pausing a breath away from actually touching the stone. Like the door outside, it seemed to hum. That made Qi'ra feel a little better. The door had let her in. Maybe the platform wouldn't kill her immediately. She took a deep breath and set her palm against the stone. When nothing happened, she blew the breath out and set her other palm beside it. The room was completely silent, watching her.

The platform didn't move, but a blue light began to shine from inside it. They all moved back, but Qi'ra stood her ground with her hands in place. It wasn't hurting her.

The hologram that coalesced on the platform was a figure from a species she didn't recognize. The figure was wrapped in robes and wore a hood. For a moment, it just flickered in place. The tech must be ancient. If it had stopped working Qi'ra wouldn't have been surprised. To her relief, the hologram moved and then began to speak.

"Adventurer." The voice was deep and laced with a sort of pain Qi'ra didn't understand. "You have made it far. I have no reward for you, only the plea of a man who made a terrible mistake."

Trinia came closer, mesmerized by the figure. It must be one of those Force people she and Tsuulo believed in. But dark, or light?

"You have come seeking treasure or a weapon," the man continued. He sounded resigned to all of their fates. "And it is here, for I could not destroy it. I couldn't throw it away or hide it. I had to put it somewhere dangerous, and hope that danger did my work for me, but you are evidence that it has not."

It didn't sound like a compliment.

"My device was built to find darkness in the Force, and eradicate it," he continued. "I saw it so clearly in my mind before I built it. A weapon that would bypass the light and help us weed out corruption. But when I held it in my hands, it burned me beyond measure. I built it to help my fellow Jedi destroy the Sith, and instead it almost destroyed us all."

The hologram was using words Qi'ra didn't know the meaning of, but she could get the gist. Maybe Trinia would be able to fill in some gaps later. Right now, the important thing was to listen. The hum in the stone beneath her hands was starting to make her teeth rattle, and it was very unpleasant.

"It has no pity. No mercy. No compassion," the man continued. "Its judgment is absolute. I beg you, adventurer, do not take it. I can offer you nothing in return but the promise you will live. No Jedi or anyone like them could enter here, so you must be but a messenger. I beg you, again, please do not deliver it."

The blue light faded, and Qi'ra withdrew her hands. She looked down at them and saw they were unharmed. She turned around to face what remained of her team, and a concealed exit door slid open in the back wall, the opposite way from which they'd come.

"I did not come all this way for nothing," Cerveteri said.

"You heard what he said, though," Lopie argued. "If we leave empty-handed, we'll live."

"Do you think Dryden Vos will let you live if you return empty-handed?" Eleera countered.

"Who does Vos want it for?" Trinia asked.

Qi'ra didn't like the answer to that question, and her mind shied away from it, refusing to follow her own train of thought to its inevitable conclusion.

"Find the holoprojector," she said. "Lopie, where do you think it is?"

With obvious reluctance, Lopie helped her deduce where the projector was. It rested in a small carved hollow in the wall behind the platform. Qi'ra pressed against the platform, and it moved. She pushed harder, and the top began to shift. The stone screeched in protest, and all of them put their hands over their ears, but it kept moving. Finally, it reached the point of no return and tipped off the far side. The crash reverberated through the floor, but Qi'ra paid it no mind and walked back toward the platform.

It wasn't a temple. It was a tomb. Whatever safeguard the dead Jedi had set up to protect the device from intruders had killed him, too. In the sealed environment of the stone, his body had petrified, his clothes a memory and his skin stretched tightly across his bones.

"There's nothing in there but him," Lopie said.

Qi'ra looked more closely, searching for anything out of place. She hadn't seen a body in this condition before, but it seemed like it had been preserved pretty well. Bodies in the Corellian sewers bloated and burst, if the scavengers didn't get to them first. In the safety of the stone, even his skin had remained intact.

A second later, she saw it. There was an irregularity in his rib cage, a protrusion where the skin was pulled tight everywhere else. That must be where he had hidden it. In his own chest.

It was like breaking through very tough paper. The Jedi's skin gave way with some resistance, but once she had made a hole, it was easy to make the hole bigger. Lopie turned away in disgust, but Qi'ra had come too far now. She pulled his ancient ribs apart, and there it was.

"Did he swallow it?" Trinia asked.

"I hope not," Eleera said.

Qi'ra couldn't imagine how else he'd gotten the thing inside his chest. She couldn't tell what it was, just that it was cube shaped. She reached down to pick it up, stretching her fingers out all the way to grasp it with one hand. It burned her, and she let out a surprised gasp but didn't drop it. The pain was nothing like what she'd expected, based on what the Jedi's message had said. Nonetheless it was uncomfortable, and it increased the longer she held the strange object.

Trinia held out a box, and Qi'ra dropped the glowing prism into it. The relief she felt was instant. When she checked, her hands were still unmarked.

"Let's get out of here," Qi'ra said as Trinia passed her their prize. She could grip it in one hand, but only just.

No sooner had the words left her mouth than a horrible creaking noise filled the chamber. It was even worse than when the platform lid had moved, and Qi'ra knew that more rock shifting definitely had to be bad.

"The ceiling!" said Eleera.

With alarming progress, the ceiling was lowering, getting closer to the floor. There was no doubt in Qi'ra's mind that it would go all the way.

"Run!" she said.

They took off for the door at the rear of the chamber, because it was closer than the way they'd come in. They had to sacrifice the dubious safety of the tunnel they had cleared and move forward into the unknown. Lopie was closest and made it through without a problem. By the time Eleera crossed the threshold, the ceiling was only two meters or so above the door. Trinia made it through, but before Qi'ra could follow, Cerveteri blocked her way.

"Give it to me!" Cerveteri demanded. "Give me the box and I'll let you out."

Facing death, Qi'ra learned two things. First, Cerveteri was an even worse liar than she'd thought. There was no way she was going to let Qi'ra escape. Second, for all her focus on survival and all her fight to keep going, she would absolutely rather die here than have Cerveteri get to go back to Vos with the device and win Qi'ra's victory. It was a strange realization. She'd always chosen survival before.

The ceiling was level with the top of the door now. Eleera was trying to move Cerveteri, but Cerveteri was locked in position, and Eleera didn't have the leverage. The ceiling was only just above their heads. Qi'ra was shorter, though, so she was able to stand up straight for a fraction of a second longer than Cerveteri could, and a fraction of a second was all she needed.

The moment Cerveteri's knees bent, Qi'ra was in motion. Teräs käsi was about being overmatched and winning anyway. About being dealt the losing hand and playing to victory. Both of Qi'ra's feet slammed into Cerveteri's knees. She heard the unmistakable sound of snapping bone, and the other girl went down. Eleera grabbed Qi'ra's hands, clutched around the box, and dragged her toward the door. Cerveteri couldn't make it to her knees to follow.

"No!" she screamed, pain and panic rising in her voice.

Eleera pulled Qi'ra to relative safety on the other side of the door. She looked back into the chamber where Cerveteri was trying to drag herself to the door on her hands, her lower body dead weight.

"Qi'ra!" she screamed. "Qi'ra, please!"

Even if she had wanted to, there was nothing Qi'ra could do now. Lopie started vomiting before the ceiling even pushed Cerveteri flat to the floor, but the sound of his heaves did nothing to cover the shattering of bone. Qi'ra watched until everything was still again. The tomb had stopped fighting them, for the moment at least. When all was quiet, she closed her eyes and listened to herself breathe in the dark.

Trinia took one of her hands, and Qi'ra held the box in the other. She had survived. She had survived.

When Qi'ra's eyes opened, she made sure that any sign of weakness was gone. She pulled her hand back and tucked the box into a pocket in the lining of her jacket. It was much too large to fit comfortably, but she didn't trust the cargo anywhere other than right against her side. They still had to get out of the tomb and back to the ship.

"Come on," she said. "We're almost done here."

As they walked down the quiet tunnel, Qi'ra realized that her sense of direction had been completely baffled by the tomb. She had no idea where they were going to come out. That was probably intentional. Now that she thought about it, she wondered why it hadn't been more of a maze. Maybe the builder, that Jedi, had been in a hurry and had to settle for just making all the pathways deadly instead of making them confusing on top of it. Lopie wasn't eager to speak with her, but when she asked, he paused for a second to mentally retrace his steps.

"We're heading back to the same side we came in on," he said eventually. "I don't think it'll be the exact spot, but we should be able to see Drex and Hilst when we exit."

As it turned out, they would only see Drex. And it would be very good luck indeed that the door had let them out somewhere he wasn't expecting them.

CHAPTER THIRTY

Qi´ra had never been so happy to see daylight in her life, even if it was the unfamiliar sun of a world she would hopefully never have to return to. It didn't take them very long to find the exit, and there were no additional traps waiting for them. The old Jedi must have expected anyone in the chamber not to have the presence of mind to make it to the door. Their exit was some fifty meters away from the entrance they'd used, and once her eyes readjusted to the outside brightness, Qi'ra turned to look for Drex and Hilst.

She could see Drex, his back to them and his blaster pointed at the other door. She thought it was odd that he'd be more concerned about what would come out of the tomb than what might come out of the trees, but maybe he'd heard the screaming or the rumble of moving stone. Her eyes drifted toward the tree line, and she finally saw where Hilst had gone. The Zabrak was splayed out facedown on the ground with a gaping blaster burn in her back. There was only one possible explanation. Drex had shot her.

Qi'ra started to pull everyone close to hide them from the murderous Rodian, but it was too late.

"Drex!" Lopie said. "Drex, we're over here!"

The Rodian was shooting before he finished turning around. Lopie had a gaping hole in his chest and a confused expression on his face, like he couldn't figure out where he'd gone wrong. The blaster kept firing, and Qi'ra flattened herself against the wall of the tomb. She saw Eleera drop to the ground and crawl toward the trees for cover. Trinia was behind Qi'ra on the wall.

"I was really hoping you'd be Cerveteri," Drex said. He had figured out she understood Huttese, after all. "I had an arrangement with her. But I suppose now I don't have to split the profits."

Trinia had a blaster but couldn't shoot over Qi'ra, so she passed it forward. Eleera preferred close combat, but was never unprepared for something else. Qi'ra heard Eleera's blaster returning fire, and raised Trinia's blaster to join her.

Drex ran toward them, confident in his advantage of having set them on their heels. The sun glinted off the polished rock, making it difficult to see him. Eleera had stopped firing for some reason, but Qi'ra couldn't see her, either. Drex was closing fast, and making so much noise that Qi'ra had plenty of time to pass the blaster back to Trinia and stand up to draw her batons.

Just as Drex realized that close combat with Qi'ra was not something he actually wanted, Eleera came hurtling out of the trees, throwing the full weight of her body into his side. She was tiny, even for a Twi'lek, but her impact was enough to bring him down, and then her knives were ready.

"Do you want him?" she asked, once she had him immobilized.

Qi'ra looked down. She might have cared, once, what Drex's motivations were. Maybe he'd finally bought into Cerveteri's jealousy. Maybe he was just an opportunist. The truth was that it didn't matter. He had lost.

"He's all yours," Qi'ra said.

With a feral yell, Eleera unloaded all of her frustrations on the traitorous Rodian. The tomb had made her angry, and now Drex was going to know about it. Qi'ra didn't stop or look back. She just kept walking toward the ship. Trinia was close behind her and did look back every now and then, but she kept up.

Eleera caught up with them before they reached the clearing. She was still upset, but clearly her physical therapy had made her feel a little bit better.

"Do you think Vos knew?" she asked.

"No," Qi'ra said.

Eleera looked at her with some doubt.

"I don't think he'll mind what happened, or miss any-one in particular," Qi'ra said. "But he wanted this to be a success. If he could have helped us, with a warning or more information, he would have."

"Next time, Vos is going to pay us double," Eleera said.

Qi'ra nodded but didn't really believe what she was agreeing to. It wasn't actually Vos's mission. The more she thought about it, the more it seemed like the person who oversaw the five syndicates wouldn't have been able to enter the tomb. The device was too important to leave to a sub-ordinate without a very good reason. Even teräs käsi was a clue, a fighting style designed to use when you were fighting an opponent who could overpower you.

Crimson Reach was right where they had left it, and Qi'ra felt a surge of relief. She hadn't really expected the ship to disappear or get swallowed by a sinkhole or something, but it would have been just her luck. They ran a quick systems check to make sure Drex hadn't left them any surprises. Hilst had been with him most of the time, and Qi'ra didn't think she was in on whatever vague plan Cerveteri had cooked up, but there was no reason to take chances.

At last, they were as secure as they could make themselves. Qi'ra had never flown a ship before, but she had always been a quick study. Eleera more or less knew what she was doing,

so Qi'ra let her worry about the takeoff and turned her attention to the navicomputer. It was a simple matter of reversing
the calculation, but Qi'ra still double-checked everything
she input, just to be sure. When the course was laid in, she
let Eleera take care of the rest. Qi'ra sent a quick message
to Vos, letting him know they were on their way home, and
went to sit on the pilot's bunk with Trinia.

"Is it bad that I'm not more upset?" Trinia asked.

"Do you think it's bad that I'm not upset?" Qi'ra asked.

"No one expects you to be," Trinia said. "You're . . . well,
you're different from the rest of us, and you always were.
That's why Cerveteri hated you and that's why Vos chose you
to elevate."

"Like it was that easy?" Qi'ra asked.

"More or less," Trinia said. "You're reliable, Qi'ra. You
don't let anything get in the way. You find a way when there
shouldn't be one."

"I didn't always, you know," Qi'ra said. "Once I made a
bad call, and it almost cost me everything."

"You still smile when you think about it," Trinia said. "It
can't have been that bad."

"How are you always so close to what I'm really thinking?" Qi'ra asked. It was as much as she could say without
admitting it was true.

"Oh," said Trinia blithely, "I'm just good with faces."

It was probably a great deal more than that, but she said it so easily that Qi'ra didn't mind accepting her explanation.

◗

Their triumphant return to the *First Light* was a bit sober, due to the fact that only three of them had come back. Vos had to at least pretend that the deaths of his agents mattered to him, and Qi'ra found it easier than usual to play her part since she actually would miss most of them. Aemon met them at the bottom of the ramp when they docked *Crimson Reach* in its slip, and informed them they would be taken straight up to Vos's office.

Like Qi'ra, Eleera and Trinia were covered in grime and pine sap—and in Eleera's case, blood—but there was no argument to be made. They got in the lift with Aemon and another Hylobon. The trip was short, but there was still enough time for the Hylobons to say something in their own language that Qi'ra was sure was a slight against her dead teammates. She let them have their fun. The dead could not hold grudges, and she had to please the living.

The lift doors opened on the most subdued version of Vos's office that Qi'ra had yet seen. There was no music, and everything felt gray. Vos was seated on one sofa, a drink in his hand. The Mizi and a giant with pincers instead of hands, whom Qi'ra didn't recognize, were sitting across from him on the other sofa, clearly talking about something completely unrelated to her mission, something about clearing out a nest.

"Qi'ra, forgive me, my dear," Vos said, getting to his feet. "I know you're exhausted and want to get cleaned up, but I was so worried. I had to see you right away."

"It was certainly a trial," Qi'ra said. "But we three survived, and we were successful."

She went to his side. He set his drink down so that he could hold both of her shoulders and check her over. His concern was casual, a performance, but at least he didn't intentionally go looking for a bruise.

"I bet in your favor," the Mizi said. "It doesn't matter what the mission was. I know a smart pick when I see one."

Vos turned to look at the other two surviving members of Qi'ra's team.

"Trinia, Eleera." He placed a hand above where his heart would be, in theory. "I am so grateful that you escaped the tragedy. I knew it was going to be a complicated mission, but I had no idea it would be so deadly."

"I think Cerveteri was halfway to organizing a hit, but I don't think she would have been successful," Eleera said. She glanced sideways at the Mizi, as if reminding herself not to say too much. "The, uh, circumstances we faced just hurried her demise along."

"All's well that ends well," Vos said. "I think you two should go and turn yourselves over to Margo. She'll make sure you're taken care of, and anything you need repaired or replaced will be done."

"Thank you," Trinia said, because it was good manners.

She and Eleera left, leaving Qi'ra waiting for her next orders.

"Where do you find these girls, Vos?" the giant asked.

"They find their way to me," Vos told him, not looking away from Qi'ra's face. "Talent always rises to the top."

She put a hand on her jacket, showing him that the device was on her and letting him decide what to do next. His lips curled in half a smile, and then he turned back to his guests.

"My friends," he said, his arms thrown wide. "It was lovely to see you as always. Unfortunately, we must be off."

"We look forward to hearing about the operation you have planned," the Mizi said. She led the way to the lift, which had already returned to the deck.

Qi'ra gave Vos a small, tired smile. He was looking at her too closely again.

"I'm always glad to see you smile," Vos said. "Especially on a day like today. Was it truly terrible?"

"It was very unpleasant," Qi'ra said. "It was a tomb. Trinia thinks it was designed by some sort of religious cult who believed in the Force. There were all sorts of traps. That's what killed most of the team. Only Drex and Hilst died because of Cerveteri's coup."

"Come," he said, leading her over to a sofa.

He didn't seem to care that she was filthy and that his suit was as pristine as ever. When she was settled, he brought her a tray of the always available appetizers that seemed to be on hand in his office whenever he wished for them, and a glass with twice as much of the amber liquid as usual. She downed it in one go, and he refilled the glass without a word.

"Now," he said, turning her so that her knees angled into his on the sofa and he could lean toward her. "Tell me everything."

CHAPTER THIRTY-ONE

Vos listened to her report without interruption. Even his facial expressions didn't change much, the red lines not appearing. That made it a bit easier to relive the entire thing in telling it to him. It was like talking to a wall, or a recorder. He did make sympathetic noises when she described the deaths of the others, and something fierce flashed in his eyes when she relayed what had happened to Cerveteri. Then he let her eat in peace for a few minutes while he marshaled his thoughts.

"You mentioned that Trinia said she thought the temple was built by some sort of Force religion," Vos said. His tone was just a bit too casual, his wording too precisely imprecise. "What do you think?"

"At first I wasn't sure what to think," Qi'ra admitted. "I had never seen anything like it. But as we went through the tomb, we learned more about it. Especially from the hologram. It said that no one like a Jedi could come in.

Presumably that would include the dark Force users that Trinia mentioned, as well."

Qi'ra paused for breath before revealing the final piece that she had worked out: "I suppose our mysterious benefactor could be a light side Force person, but it seems unlikely."

"Indeed," said Vos. "I am so glad I found you, Qi'ra. So glad I listened to the Mizi and went all the way out to that wretched jungle world to meet you. Thank goodness Sarkin let you go so easily."

Qi'ra took the opportunity to eat another canapé.

"When I think how close I came to losing you, because we didn't know enough about where you were going." He shook his head. "We must make sure we have more information next time."

"Next time?" Qi'ra asked, swallowing.

"Oh, yes," Vos said. "He's going to be very pleased with you. The syndicate heads are all too busy, and he hasn't found anyone trustworthy enough to fetch him the artifacts he wants. You are perfect. We'll just make sure that next time you have a better crew. Or a more expendable one."

"He can't touch the object," Qi'ra said. "I could barely touch it. It didn't leave a mark, but it burned while I was holding it."

"I don't know why he wants these things," Vos said. "I was a younger man when there were still Jedi roaming around the galaxy. No one really believed everything about them, but you'd hear stories. A friend of a friend, or someone's great-grandmother. I've learned since that a lot of it was true, and that there are many things the Jedi tried to hide."

"That's what he wants found," Qi'ra surmised. "All the hidden things. And some that are just lost."

"Yes, Qi'ra," Vos said. "You always figure it out."

A comm on his desk beeped, and he excused himself to deal with it. Qi'ra kept eating. Years of practice made her able to keep food down even when her stomach was roiling. The Mizi and her strange companion must have disembarked. The *First Light* was cleared to jump wherever Vos wished to go. Qi'ra didn't recognize the coordinates he gave. It wasn't a place she had been before.

"We will be arriving at our destination in a little more than an hour," he said. The *First Light* transitioned into hyperspace so smoothly that Qi'ra usually missed the jump unless she was looking out the viewport. "I imagine you'll want to get cleaned up before we do."

He didn't have to say where they were going, because it didn't matter. What mattered was who they were going to meet.

She reached for the pocket on her jacket, but he stopped her hand.

"He'll want you to give it to him," he said.

Qi'ra didn't waste any time. Trinia wasn't in their room when she returned to it, but she was more than used to taking care of herself. She skipped her preferred bath and steam, and went straight into the shower. Most of the grime had been on her clothing, luckily, so she just sent the whole outfit to the incinerator. It was easy to scrub her skin and hair clean under the endless stream of hot water. She turned it up as hot as she could stand, skin turning pink as the temperature rose. By the time she turned it off, the bathroom was almost a sauna, but she had no time to enjoy it.

Wrapped in a soft robe, she opened her wardrobe. Once the sheer number of options would have overwhelmed her—and that was before she thought about what they cost—but now it was easy to make selections. Black shimmersilk trousers, elegant and simple. A red shirt with a deeply cut neckline that wrapped around her body, tied off with gold tassels. A black bolero that highlighted hips she was finally eating enough to give shape to.

Qi'ra didn't dress this way to be alluring. There was no one she wanted to attract. She did it because it was expected of her. Vos had furnished the clothes for her, and so she wore them. They were similar to the clothing that everyone on board wore, though hers were undeniably fancier. It wasn't a uniform, not quite, but it was an aesthetic without a doubt. Nothing in Dryden Vos's sphere was going to be out of place if he could help it.

She put on the Crimson Dawn necklace, pressing the black leather flat against her collarbones. The overall effect was striking, especially once her hair was up in the swooping ponytail that she had come to rely on. She didn't have time to curl it like she usually did. She liked the look and it gave Vos something to play with, but they would both have to do without.

She picked up her discarded jacket and pulled the box with the device in it out of the pocket, unwilling to open it again. She didn't even want to know what it was, and only had a vague idea what it did. She had paid for it with eight lives—though she was absolutely fine with losing one of them—and she hoped that what it cost her was worth it. She supposed she'd find out soon enough. After a long moment, she took one more thing off of the dressing table, tucking it away before she could second-guess herself.

Her door chime sounded, and Margo entered when Qi'ra called out permission to do so.

"Do you have everything you need?" Margo asked. "I was told you have a very important meeting and I wanted to be sure you were completely prepared."

It was the first time they'd been able to speak privately since Corynna died. Margo was testing her, as always.

"I am fine, thank you," Qi'ra said. "And you? Are you settling in well?"

"Yes," Margo said. "It certainly keeps me on my toes, though. It's amazing Corynna had any time at all for extracurricular activities with everything she had to take care of."

"I am sure your skills at time management will be more than up to the task," Qi'ra told her.

"And you will keep working to make sure that yours improve," Margo said. "Corynna got complacent and used to routine. I don't think you're the type for either."

"Thank you," Qi'ra said, even though it hadn't quite been a compliment. Being polite to Margo cost her nothing, especially now.

"Do you think she thought she'd actually win?" Margo asked, façade dropping for a moment.

"Yes," Qi'ra said. "But I don't think she thought any further than winning. And you have to think very far ahead to beat a man like Dryden Vos."

Margo didn't reply to that. For a moment, Qi'ra was worried that she had given away too much. It wasn't that Corynna's plan hadn't been good; it was just that it hadn't been good enough. After a brief hesitation, Margo nodded, and Qi'ra knew that they understood one another. They might be allies reluctantly, but they would work well together.

Qi'ra finished her preparations after Margo left, and was back in Vos's office well before her hour was up. He smiled when he saw her, touching the Crimson Dawn sun and pressing it into her skin.

"You look lovely," he said. "I always admire your choice of armor."

The stars around them stilled as the *First Light* dropped out of hyperspace. A striking planet—red and black in turns as clouds swirled across its surface, their cover punctured now and then by sharp spires and merciless cliffs—hung below them, and Qi'ra heard the engines fire as they prepared for landing. She expected Vos to go to his desk, or perhaps tidy some of his displays, but he did nothing of the sort.

"He won't come up," he said, when her unspoken question became too loud to ignore. "I'm afraid you must face him alone, on ground of his choosing."

Qi'ra hadn't expected Vos to be her defender during the meeting, but she had thought he would be present.

"Take this lift all the way to the bottom. There is an exit there. He will be on the other side of it," Vos instructed. He opened a panel, revealing the secret turbolift she'd been so sure existed.

She nodded and moved to open the door. He reached out and grabbed her hand, pulling her back to him for a moment.

"It's a vicious fighting style, teräs käsi," he said, his voice low and more genuine than she had ever heard. This wasn't the showman Dryden Vos. This was just him. "It takes no prisoners, exploits every weakness, and plays by rules some might consider uncivilized. But that's because they lose."

It was her final warning, the last bit of preparation he could give her before she went to face her fate. Vos stood up to his full height, the showman back in his shoulders, ooz-ing deadly charm from every pore.

"And I'm afraid that's the only help I can give you, my dear," he told her. "But, as I have said, I have faith in you. And the Mizi is right. I would never bet against you."

Qi'ra went into the lift and pressed the lowest button on the panel. The doors shut on Vos's smile, and he held her gaze until she couldn't see him anymore. As the descent began, Qi'ra's thoughts drifted to Han even has her hands drifted to the dice she'd brought with her at the last moment. Not for the smile that she used as a weapon, but for the warmth his memory conjured in her. Without him, she'd still be on Corellia, either dead or scraping out whatever liv-ing Proxima allowed. For better or for worse, and in many cases both, he had changed her life. He had been foolish and reckless and brave, always dreaming and hoping. She would never be like that. She would never allow herself to be like that. It was too much to even imagine, knowing how tire-lessly she'd worked to become hard and gilded, more like the dice than the boy himself. A symbol of something lost. But remembering that someone *could* be like him, in this dark mess of a galaxy, made her happy.

The descent continued and Qi'ra breathed deeply, con-trolling each rise and fall of her shoulders so that her heart rate would be under control when she reached the bottom. It was the beginning of teräs käsi, and the gentlest part of it. What came after was always quick and violent, fierce and final. It fit her personality. Qi'ra always fought to win.

The lift began to slow. She closed her eyes, giving herself one quiet moment before the storm began again. When the lift came to rest at the very bottom of the *First Light*, she opened her eyes, her face set. She was as ready as she could be.

The doors slid open, the familiar hiss giving way to an unfamiliar corridor. This was Vos's escape route, or one of them anyway, and now she had seen it. Nothing she did was ever singular. She could squeeze usefulness out of stone. She made her way down the hallway. The engines must have been turned off after they docked, because there was no hum running through the bulkheads. Everything was quiet, just as she was. Everything was waiting.

Qi'ra reached the end of the corridor and lifted her hand to the panel. It accepted her palm, and the door opened into a new world. There never had been any going back. The future would happen, and she would overcome it, or be overcome. But she always knew what she was fighting for, which was more than could be said of most.

Qi'ra stepped down into the black, and into the red. The true soul and beating heart of Crimson Dawn.

*F*or ten giddy seconds, she lets herself think about the life she might have had, if only things had gone a little bit differently.

Qi'ra lets herself imagine that everything has worked out. That the balance of power has been restored the way she planned. That she has any part at all in the celebrations that are happening all around her and all around the galaxy. That there is anyone who cares about her enough to fear her, even just a little bit.

It's a nice dream, made ever bitter by the fact that she came so close and failed so utterly. Another almost to haunt her, now that everything is done.

The ice in her drink is melting fast, another race of inevitability that she will lose. She's alone now, more alone than she has ever been. The walls she built in self-defense were unassailable. She forgot to leave any room for friendship, for true respect. At least Vos was put out of his misery quickly after he was beaten. She's not sure he lived long enough even to know he was. But she is going to have to linger on in this world she didn't make, watching as it passes her by. The footage of her failure is being broadcast on loop, and no one even knows that she failed. It's all she can do not to smash the screen.

She's not so out of practice that she doesn't notice when the mood in the bar shifts, ever so slightly. There is still jubilation and relief, but there's an undercurrent of mystery now, as well. Mystery is dangerous, even as the whole of existence celebrates the downfall of a tyrant evil beyond imagining.

When the figure makes its way toward her, she can see every step out of the corner of her eye. It's not who she expected, because she didn't expect anyone.

She is nothing now, just another person left homeless and without roots by the war. She's not worth contacting. Not worth reaching out to. She has nothing left to offer. Nothing to barter. Nothing to trade. Her secrets are bought and sold, and she has nothing new to replace them with. It's like it was before, a bottle of coaxium on one side of the glass and her on the other, meters and parsecs away at the same time. Everyone in her world knows that it all fell apart, and few people outside of her world know that she survived.

She catches the bartender's eye and motions for a refill plus one more. The drinks are set down moments before the figure arrives at her side, ice still crisp against the sides of the glass. It's her favorite of the drinks she's learned to love. Too sweet for how she's feeling, really, but there has to be something about this day, this victory by other people, that isn't entirely sour.

So many new lives. So many new beginnings. So much hope. And all she can see is her end.

"Well," she says, because there isn't much left to say. "I guess I should have known it would be you."

Beside her, she sees a cloak. A sleeve. A hand. Casually reaching for the glass.

ACKNOWLEDGMENTS

I don't know what this says about me, but this one was SO MUCH FUN. There was a moment during the outlining process when I realized I was going to write an Indiana Jones murder temple knockoff, and then ANOTHER moment when I realized I could use LEGO *Star Wars* philosophy in said murder temple, and I have to tell you: I was living my best life. Also it turns out that writing Dryden Vos is an absolute blast.

Jen Heddle, it was a pleasure as always to work with you. Here's to the next one (I hope). Emeli, it's awesome to have you on Team Novel, and I look forward to working with you again. I feel like Mike Siglain and Josh Adams put out more fires than usual, and every one of them was greatly appreciated.

Thank you to Rae Carson and Mur Lafferty, whose excellent characterizations of Qi'ra precede my own. I love it when I get to work with a team on this stuff, and even though mine is a later entry, it was super fun to build off of what they had already laid down. Thank you to the comics creators for *War of the Bounty Hunters* and beyond the ticularly Charles Soule and Greg Pak on the writing side and Luke Ross, David Messina, Ramon Rosanas, Paolo Villanelli, Raffaele Ienco, Neeraj Menon, Guru-eFX, Rachelle Rosenberg, Arif Prianto, and Jesus Aburtov for illustrations, colors, and inks.

As always, I would be absolutely sunk without the Lucasfilm Story Group, though I think I may have scared them a little bit this time. Thank you for correcting every time I mixed up the spelling of ~~Hyloban~~ Hylobon. The Disney Lucasfilm Press production team continues to make magic, and I'm so pleased with all the art (Julian D. Paulsen) and design (Beryl Capahay and Jason Wojtowicz).

To my readers: thank you for following me into another corner of the galaxy far, far away. I'm so glad I get to keep writing these books, and you are the reasons why.

Crimson Climb began in the parking lot of the St. Anthony Foodland and was written entirely in a chair at my own desk, which is kind of a big deal.